BROKEN AS THINGS ARE

BROKEN
AS THINGS ARE

· A Novel ·

Martha Witt

HENRY HOLT AND COMPANY · NEW YORK

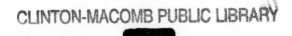

Henry Holt and Company, LLC
Publishers since 1866
115 West 18th Street
New York, New York 10011

Henry Holt ® is a registered trademark
of Henry Holt and Company, LLC.

Library of Congress Cataloging-in-Publication Data
Witt, Martha.
    Broken as things are : a novel / Martha Witt.—1st ed.
        p.   cm.
    ISBN 0-8050-7595-X
    1. Girls—Fiction. 2. Autistic youth—Fiction. 3. Southern States—
Fiction. 4. Problem families—Fiction. 5. Brothers and sisters—
Fiction. I. Title.

PS3623.I877B76   2004
813'.6—dc22

                                        2003057003

Henry Holt books are available for special promotions
and premiums. For details contact: Director, Special Markets.
First Edition 2004
Designed by Victoria Hartman
Printed in the United States of America
1   3   5   7   9   10   8   6   4   2

To my mother, this, my book.

BROKEN AS THINGS ARE

FOR MANY YEARS, our mother laughed in the retelling: a laughter so quiet and seemingly unwarranted that it could easily be mistaken for something else—a slight wheeze, a muffled sigh. "For two straight weeks after you were born, I was laid up with a fever," she would say, unable to remember the roses Aunt Lois claimed filled our hospital room. Instead of flowers, our mother spoke of tiny women in flaming dresses, of closing her eyes on small lit fires, knowing all the while there was a baby in the room. There was danger.

"I really believed we were burning up then, Morgan-Lee," she'd tell me, her fingers flitting to her forehead and down again. "And hard as I tried to save you, I couldn't. I was just too tired. Much too tired."

"She was. She was tired," Aunt Lois would confirm,

patting different powders on the back of her hand to check for color or unpacking boxes of newly arrived creams and lipsticks. When she found the right powder, she'd puff some on her nose and forehead, wave away the extra particles that glistened in the sunlight, and arrange her bottles in ascending order according to height. She'd wait patiently for our mother to finish speaking about the aftermath of my birth.

When it came to her part in the story, Aunt Lois stopped whatever she was doing to tell it. She liked her part. "I brought the two of you home on the hottest June day North Carolina had seen in fifteen years," she'd say, her violet eyes opening wide, pleased at the thought of her own strength. "I literally carried the both of you. *Carried.*"

No one ever asked where our father and Uncle Pete were, because of course they were there. Aunt Lois never had children. She had never really carried anyone in her life.

Our mother would listen without comment as Aunt Lois continued. "Oh! You were such a pale white thing with all those veins glowing blue under your skin. You looked like a little machine, something mechanical out in all that blazing sun. You were just so white," she would conclude, disappointed, her fingers resorting to the smooth glass bottles or plastic makeup kits.

Aunt Lois had always maintained that beauty was a question of shadows, so she took it personally that my face was blank as a stretch of desert. Even as a baby, I had not been beautiful.

"Ginx," she'd begin again, whispering my brother's name, "Ginx's face, though. Even when he was a newborn, you could tell he'd be *extraordinaire*!" She'd pause then to draw in a quick breath, as if preparing to mention the dead. "It's not the first or only time I've witnessed God giving abundantly in one area to make up for another." No one ever asked her to elaborate.

Our mother would interrupt then, the bones in her cheeks so delicate I was surprised they hadn't shattered all those years ago during the fever of my birth. "Ginx thought you belonged to him, Morgan-Lee. He would sit on our big couch right there in his sailor's suit and hold on to you for dear life. We have a picture of it somewhere—Ginxy holding you on that couch like it was a ship about to go under."

When they brought me home from the hospital, Ginx was one and a half years old. Even in the years that followed, he would not speak except in invented words lined one after the other. I was told that he stared hard at the faces of adults who repeated "Mom-ma, Dad-da" to him. Aunt Lois said she'd get worked to tears just trying to teach him those two words.

"He didn't speak normal till he was five," Aunt Lois told me. "Then—*bang*—one day he's just talking away in complete sentences. But he wouldn't say *I*. He said *we,* meaning you and him. 'We're hungry,' he'd say." Aunt Lois shook her head while our mother laughed in her quiet way.

At night, Ginx said his own words. I could not have been

much older than two, but I swear I can still remember my brother's hand when he reached to caress my scalp, a pure ray of moon against the wall. Occasionally, he caught the filaments of my hair in his fist and pulled. *"Aduage,"* he would say, if I started to cry. *Aduage*—a word that contains all words the way white contains all colors. His small arm would point toward the moonlight that parted our curtains: *aduage.*

Ginx did not want our parents to come in, their tired faces breaking the dark. I must not have wanted it either, because our father said I was such a quiet child. No one ever had to sing me a lullaby. Some mornings, Ginx would still be holding to the bars of my crib when our mother came to wake us. "Ginxy," she would say. "Ginx," she'd whisper more loudly, if he was asleep. He might look up, but he rarely moved. Often she was forced to bend down and pry open his fingers as he watched, detached and curious. "Oh, Ginx, you'll be okay." He was a small child, quickly up and against her chest. He did not hold her as she squeezed him, turning away from me. She covered the back of his head with her hand so that his chin rested on her shoulder, his face peeking through her abundant hair. Aunt Lois once told me that when Ginx was around four, he would shrug and wince when our mother tried to hold him. "And to tell the truth," our aunt mused, "after that I never really saw her hold any of you unless she had to."

When Dana was born, our parents put her in the crib,

and I got a narrow bed with bars on the side. Ginx slept in a regular bed with no bars. In the mornings, our mother would open the curtain and stare out our window. "Oh, it's day," she'd finally say, blinking as if the concept were new and difficult. The universe was all one piece then: hair, skin, the coming light.

When he was around five, Ginx started to practice his figure-eight drawings. It was after our father gave him a train set with a track in the shape of a figure eight. We put the train on that track and let it run. Ginx sat in an overstuffed armchair, and I sat on the ground. "Look," he said. *"Pannot."* And the train went round and round in its figure eight, the circles melding into one another. I never spoke about our train, because I soon realized that other kids built towns or made tunnels over their tracks. Other kids had their trains run on bridges or stop to load and unload pretend cargo. Ginx didn't even open the box of toy houses, trees, and tunnels that Aunt Lois had given him for his birthday. We would just sit, watching the train. Sometimes, Ginx would rock, but usually he sat in the armchair, digging at the cloth in the armrest. By the time he was six, the armrest was covered in dug-out circles, and our father gave the chair away.

"There's a figure eight," Ginx would say, pointing at a cloud or a swirl in the river or a patterned rug. "Right there,

Morgan-Lee. Figure eight." I'd turn to where he was pointing; I wanted to see it too. And so I stayed close to my brother, looking where he pointed, listening to what he saw, and feeling protected as long as he was there because other people were as blind as I was and had no clue about what lurked behind even the most normal objects. *The blind leading the blind* was one of Aunt Lois's phrases. I worried for other people who had no one to explain how the world was wired, the sounds and shapes hidden everywhere. Ginx had learned all of it by himself, and slowly he was teaching me.

"Ginx is not my real name," he told me one day in the beginning of my ninth-grade year. We were outside raking leaves.

"Yes, it is." I pulled the rake as quickly as I could, wanting my arms to grow muscular. I knew girls had to work harder at it.

"It's not my name," he said, pulling his own rake over the same grass again and again because he would not stop till it was utterly clean of leaves.

"What's your name, then?" I pinched each of my arms to check out my muscles, but they were still slender and long— no different, really, than bone. Ginx stopped raking. His arms and legs were too long for his torso, so his clothes hung strangely, as if he'd dressed years ago, before his limbs had grown. He was thin and often hunched when he walked. He was wearing a colorful striped shirt, buttoned up to the collar, and brown corduroy pants. Aunt Lois had taken those pants in at the waist and let them out at the hem as much as possible, but they were still an inch too short, and the sleeves of his shirt didn't quite reach his wrists. If our father didn't remind Ginx to change clothes, he would have worn this same outfit every day. It wasn't that the pants and shirt were comfortable—they were not—but he liked the shirt's stripes, which encircled his body, holding certain things in and keeping others out. The brown stripe matched his corduroys.

"You're not born with a name," Ginx said, returning to his patch of almost leafless grass. "You are given a name."

"Like I didn't know that," I huffed, pulling my rake so hard two of the metal teeth bent. I wondered how long it would take me to do the whole yard. Probably I could do it faster than it would take Ginx to finish two patches.

"So 'Ginx' is only the *sound* of the name Momma wanted to give me."

"Why didn't she—" I began, then stopped to rephrase the question. "How come she didn't just give you the actual name then?" If he had to choose someone to look at, Ginx would choose to look at me, but he preferred in general to avoid faces, usually settling for the third button down on an oxford shirt, the nadir of the V in a T-shirt, or the fold line of a turtleneck.

"That way the name is secret."

"What *is* your name, then?" I wanted to know.

Back in fifth grade, the teachers had encouraged me to skip a year, but our father said I wasn't mature enough to advance so quickly. So I didn't. I didn't care about not skipping a grade; what I wanted was for Ginx to consider me smart. I was pretty sure he didn't.

"What is it?" I asked again. His brown hair hung in his face and grew shaggily around his ears.

"Don't know," he said. "If you're lucky, you find out before you die." He wiped his right hand on his pants and resumed his raking.

"Everyone has a different real name?" I asked. My brother shook his head, and I could see he was trying not to laugh, forcing his lips down, as if my question were as ridiculous as asking the color of green grass. He shook the hair from his eyes.

"No. Most people's names are just fine for them," he said. *Dunapull.* "Most people just get their names and that's it." He picked up his rake and began to rake out a new patch. "But other people get a sound, a clue," he told me, "and then they have to look a long time, and sometimes they might get close, but most don't actually find it."

"But Momma knows your real name?" I asked, looking at our small brick house with its black shutters and little stone stoop. Our father painted the shutters every year, so they were always a shiny black, and he had made the stoop himself.

Ginx shrugged. "She knew what it sounded like." He cut me short, quickly adding, "That's all I know." I did not want to ask if I was one of the people with a real name; I wanted him to tell me. And Ginx would have told me without my asking, but he would have told me another day, in the middle of some other conversation, and this, of course, was basic fundamental information, more important than knowing your primary colors or the letters of the alphabet. If I were the kind of person who didn't have a hidden name, I would forget about growing my muscles. I would no longer want to go to the river or study math or tell my brother stories. I'd give up. I could barely ask it.

"Is my name my name?"

Ginx did not even pause in his raking. Again, I saw he was trying not to laugh.

"What's so funny?" I asked, irritated. "Just tell me."

"No." He looked at me now, spearing the rake at the ground as if it were a shovel. "No, Morgan-Lee. No and not. That's not your name. It is the *sound* of your name; you should know that." And then, in a low voice, he added, *"Cantaloupe."*

"I know," I told him, happy now and strong enough to rake our yard and Aunt Lois's and even Old Mrs. Dean's. *"Dalla,"* I added, in refrain.

"Yes." My brother returned to the original patch of grass, which the wind had now scattered in leaves. "Is that Poppa hollering?" he asked.

I didn't answer. Our father was at the supermarket. Our

mother was weeding the garden and spreading a fresh load of rinds and vegetable scrapings on the compost pile. Aunt Lois and Uncle Pete were helping her; after all, they benefited from the garden too. No one was hollering.

So I spent my first year of high school knowing what to listen for. It wasn't so much that I expected after my ninth-grade year to have pieced together the fragments of my real name—that could only be done little by little. It was enough that Ginx believed I had one.

BEAUTY

THE DAY MY ninth-grade year ended, the official beginning of our summer, the first thing I did was go to the tree
house to see Billy. By the time I finally got to Aunt Lois's, she
was already preparing dinner.

"Hello," I called to our aunt, who was sitting in her dining room snooting string beans, pinching each head between
two beautifully manicured nails. The beans dropped once,
once, once, against the bottom of her large aluminum pot.

I hadn't even closed the front door before she sat bolt
upright in her chair to look at me, suddenly aware of the
hour. "You're late," she accused, the red curls sculpted to frame
her face, her lips a trembling heart. She shook her pot of
beans, but she did not ask where I'd been. I kept my visits
with Billy secret, which was why I never met with him more

than once a week, forty minutes each time, but the first day of summer was sacred. "Now, help me get things ready. Go on and set up. We need to straighten," she declared, leaning forward to scrutinize the living room. There had once been walls to separate the dining and living areas, but Aunt Lois had them removed after studying large glossy photographs from one of her magazines that featured an airy and welcoming living-and-dining-room combination. "Get the kits set up. Go on, now. I've got clients coming in a half hour."

I never obeyed Aunt Lois right away. She looked at me as I stood, not budging.

"I'm done. The beans are ready to go," she said, her violet eyes shuttering down to the white leather chair where Ginx sat with his *Time* magazine, humming and turning the pages with a slap. It was a special issue about the threat of nuclear war and what President Reagan was doing to prevent it. Ginx had just finished a report on this issue for school.

"There will be a big explosion," my brother said. "And he's doing nothing and nothing." Ginx read a lot about nuclear war.

"Hi, Ginx," I said. My brother paused, looked around the room as if he had forgotten something, then returned to reading, making it clear that I should not have been late.

"He could sit somewhere else," our aunt grumbled.

Aunt Lois had paid a lot of money for that chair because she loved the thought of her red hair against its cream-white leather. When someone complimented her hair, she'd say, "I use a natural heightener made specifically *for me* by a woman out in Dallas." No one who heard this knew what a "heightener" was, but the way she'd say it, and the way a curl would lie precisely just below each ear, put a stop to any questions.

"Can I watch tonight?" Dana asked, coming out of the kitchen where she'd been stuffing marshmallows into sweet potatoes for a second batch of candied yams. I looked at my sister. A few weeks earlier, she'd moved in with Aunt Lois. "I'm moving in for good," Dana said. "Momma's always tired anyway, and I'll be better off." She was watching our aunt, waiting for permission to help with the makeup session. But Aunt Lois did not answer immediately. Perched on her stool, she wiped her fingers on her apron and swept her gaze over the entire living room in the way she must have learned to appreciate a crowd on her Beauty Queen's float back in high school.

The cooking yams loaded the room with their warm, tender smell. Ginx bent toward his magazine. In her slow, royal gaze, Aunt Lois enjoyed her own plush carpet, the white linen curtains, and the delicacy of the porcelain statuettes on their stands. I went to the dining room and knocked into a chair, which banged against the table but did nothing to interrupt her joy.

"That there really is a beauty," Aunt Lois said in one exhale, as she pointed to the small brass desk lamp she claimed to have bought at an estate sale. One evening during dinner, she'd gone on with some story about how she'd grabbed the lamp out of another woman's hands and slapped down her cash. She had talked about that lamp until Uncle Pete finished gnawing at the bone of his pork chop. "You're a piece of work," he spat out. She stopped to smile at his compliment, which was the only reason she'd told the story in the first place. We all knew there had been no estate sale, no woman, no grabbing. But it didn't matter. Our father declared, "What a find! Of course you had to be insistent." Dana asked our mother why our family never bought nice things. Only Ginx accused Aunt Lois. "Lie," he repeated again and again until Uncle Pete slammed his big hand against the edge of the table, clattering the coffee cups in their pink-and-white-saucers. Ginx knew there were things he was just supposed to let go, but he could not help it. He hated lies of any kind. Lucky for us all, Aunt Lois chose to ignore my brother. Uncle Pete's compliment was still tickling the air, and for the remainder of that dinner our aunt's face glittered, a small, sucking, chewing planet hauled down to sparkle before us.

Aunt Lois picked up her big pot and shook it again, rattling the beans. Her lips pressed to a fine point; then she consented. "Yes, Dana, honey, of course you may watch. You can help me with color."

"Christ," I muttered, bending to open the bottom drawer of the large china cabinet where Aunt Lois kept all her makeup supplies. She did not like the Lord's name taken in vain, but she needed my help too much to criticize. She frowned once and gave a firm twist to each of the pearl earrings Uncle Pete had given her for her forty-third birthday. Ginx looked away from his magazine and up at me, his fingers working against the leather of the armrest. I was forgiven. He enjoyed my small triumphs.

Aunt Lois brought her beans to the kitchen, chin cast over her shoulder. "Two!" she sang out. "We need two cleansing kits and two bowls of water. You can then make coffee, Morgan-Lee."

"I can make that," Dana offered, clanging the yam pan on the counter. "And I'll also get the water." The telephone rang luxuriously, not like ours at home that just sputtered out a series of thin rattles. Dana had begged our father to buy a phone like Aunt Lois's for her bedroom. For years he'd promised Dana that she'd have one as soon as she started eighth grade. If she decided to move back home again, then come September she would cash in. Aunt Lois scurried to answer.

"Yes?" our aunt asked brightly into the receiver. "Oh, sweetie." There was a long pause. I put each pink kit squarely in front of a stool. "Okay, baby. . . . Well, we'll have dinner for you when you get home. That's okay." Stretching the cord, she turned to watch me. "We got the kids tonight. Marion wanted a little break, you know, as usual. Dana's going to help me with a session before dinner. In fact, they'll be here any minute now." She snapped her fingers. I looked up, and she mouthed "two" at me, as if I hadn't understood the first time. She blew a kiss into the receiver. "I know. Bye-bye."

Dana put the water bowls on the table, and I arranged the four long-backed chairs neatly in their places. Those dining room chairs were also a creamy white, supposedly to match the living room chair, but they were made by a different company and their color had disappointed Aunt Lois, who claimed, only after they'd arrived, that the creaminess of the white was not rich enough. "Nuances are everything," she had instructed the two deliverymen, who stood staring at the chairs, muttering in awkward agreement.

Aunt Lois straightened the tablecloth and looked down at Ginx, who immediately shifted his gaze to the bottom of the page, then glanced up, saw she was still watching, and looked down again. He hated to be watched. But she watched. Ginx was fifteen years old, and still our aunt refused to reconcile his beauty with his strangeness. She did not know how to look at him. "Please don't look at me," he finally told her, then stretched his legs, which he could retract so quickly he sometimes looked like a child again.

Aunt Lois sighed in response. "I will most likely have to ask you to move, Ginx." She spoke to my brother as little as possible, but when she did I understood why it was that, when he was little, it had taken her so long to teach him "Momma" and "Dadda."

"Why must I move?" he asked, but she knew better than to answer.

Aunt Lois continued, "We'll have to shut the sliding doors so the clients don't see into the kitchen. Oh, Dana, sweetheart. Those yams're smelling so *fine*." She quickly exchanged her cooking apron for the pink-and-white striped one she wore during makeup sessions. I was standing near the table, arms folded. My sister dried her hands and doused them with lotion. Dana's fingers were chubby, the tips forming five perfect domes, thick as link sausages. She hated her fingers so much that she'd shut them into fists whenever she thought someone was looking. The rest of Dana was full and well proportioned: tender skin, solid arms, arched eyebrows, and dark hair that slipped through fingers as easily as water. She had small brown eyes that skipped casually from place to place, as if in constant search for the prettiest people and brightest objects.

"The yams're almost done," Dana said, flipping back her hair. She had begun to select soaps and shampoos with care and smelled cleanly of spearmint, a smell that promised her commitment to roomfuls of jabbering, laughing, shiny-haired girls.

The doorbell rang, and I leaped through the living room to open it.

"Oh, not yet!" Aunt Lois chirped as she quickly slid the kitchen door closed, shutting Dana in.

"Wait!" Dana complained. But Aunt Lois was already dimming the lights and scooting behind the table to perch her fingers on its lace cloth. I waited by the door until she was completely ready. "Okay, open up. Go on, now."

"Hello! Hello!" I called out ceremoniously into the

muggy pink of the evening. The two women on Aunt Lois's stoop could only have been mother and daughter with their identically startled smiles and vague, moon-wide faces.

"*Tone. Plum. Roll,*" Ginx said, when he saw them.

"Come in," Aunt Lois cooed, promising safe harbor.

"We've come for makeovers. Is this the right house?" the mother asked, her eyes pushing past me to search for Aunt Lois. I figured the daughter was around my age, and I smiled, imagining that the women had journeyed a long way for a rare and forbidden elixir.

"Yes," I answered loftily, stepping aside to let them in. Daughter first, then mother shuffled past, and I thought, You will be given beauty but must leave your souls with me at the door. My brother pulled himself straight and laughed for no apparent reason, a choppy *haw-haw* that Aunt Lois covered by beckoning more loudly. "Come, come."

Still holding the door, I turned to look at our aunt. The cool from the air conditioner mingled with the outside heat as she spread her arms wide, the pointer finger of each hand graciously indicating two chairs. The kitchen door slid open, and Dana appeared in one of Aunt Lois's spare aprons. My sister looked at the women, obviously disappointed. Dana always hoped for beautiful clients. Aunt Lois, on the other hand, tittered; the plain and unassuming were her favorite. "Good." She brought her arms back down, allowing her fingers to flutter through the air. "Good." I looked at my brother, whose eyes retreated, turning slender as arrows. He'd been told that it was not polite to read in front of guests, so he closed the magazine and promptly folded his hands.

"I don't know if you remember us from the church potluck. We only came that once, but we're . . ." the mother began. The daughter studied us somberly.

Our aunt brightened. "Yes, of course. Please sit, Mrs. and Miss Mulvahill." The daughter looked around, tugged at the black velveteen belt holding up her jeans, and refused to be impressed. She was thick-boned and pale, her mousy hair jolting as she aggressively pulled back one of the chairs. Ginx could not help himself; he started to smile and slid a finger over his well-drawn lips: back and forth, back and forth. He looked at me only after both Mulvahills were sitting at Aunt Lois's table.

"Mother and daughter," Aunt Lois confirmed to herself, speaking low through the dimmed light. "Wonderful. How nice you could come together."

The mother nodded in a shy mixture of awe and gratitude, like an overgrown girl. The daughter grumbled as the mother slid her fingertips against each other, positioning them next to the pink kit that I had set for her. "We just wanted to treat ourselves," the woman confessed. Aunt Lois clapped her hands twice.

Had she been twenty years younger, our aunt would have plucked up that girl of a woman and eaten her for lunch. As it was, she just smiled.

"Christ Jesus," the daughter muttered, rolling her eyes at

her mother's smile but not looking at any of us. She was not there to make friends.

Aunt Lois straightened and frowned. "Please," she complained, "no one in this house takes the name of the Lord in vain." But her tone changed as she touched the mother's arm and whispered, "You sure deserve a treat." Bending at the waist, our aunt hovered over the mother to adjust the mirror on her kit. Aunt Lois's hands were slender and efficient as blades, experts on faces, smoothing coolly over eyelids, perfecting skin. Dana sat by the dresser, ready to be of use.

"Circles," Ginx said. I smiled. Normally, Aunt Lois would have ordered us upstairs, but she hadn't even told me to close her front door, so I stood there, enjoying the mingle of hot and cold air.

"Jolie. . . . Très jolie!" our aunt exclaimed, over a variety of color squares she selected, the pink heart of her mouth pulsing around the French she'd learned in high school and perfected by studying Deena Fae makeup labels. Then she began as she always did: "It's nice to be women together for a while. There are so few times in our busy lives for intimacy, but this evening we can just be women together." Her violet eyes slid greedily over the mother's pale lips, which provided a marked contrast to the Belle Rose of her own. Aunt Lois was good at intimacy. "Now, dab your cotton into the cleanser on your left and apply it to your skin in small quick circles." Mother and daughter obediently dabbed their cotton balls, then raised them to circle their cheeks. Ginx nodded.

"Circles! Circles like this," Aunt Lois sang joyously, a finger darting up to cut the air in small circles. I was getting bored, so I pressed my back against the edge of the door and, with one hard push, sent it flying shut, slamming an end to whatever world those women had come from. I'd made it my personal duty to pay homage to the lives women left behind them when they entered the house for Aunt Lois's makeovers. I'd told her this once. She'd laughed in her up-and-down roller-coaster way.

Our aunt looked up. "We *close,* we do not slam, the door," she scolded, as if I were a little girl. "You and Ginx go upstairs now." Dana shrank against the wall so that Aunt Lois wouldn't include her with us.

"I'm being good," Dana whined when Aunt Lois turned in her direction.

"You may stay."

Ginx rolled up his magazine and hit it once against his knee. "Good-bye," he said, senselessly and to no one, as he got up from the big chair.

When I was small, Uncle Pete and Aunt Lois's house next door was exactly like ours in its construction. The upstairs had consisted of four bedrooms, a big bathroom, and a long hallway, but when they redid the house, Aunt Lois had the wall dividing two of the bedrooms knocked out for a Master Suite, as she liked to call it. Whenever we spent the night, I stayed in the Guest Room, Dana in the Baby's Room, which was the room she'd moved into, and Ginx slept in the living room. Throughout seventh grade, Dana had been sleeping at Aunt Lois's more than she slept at home. To encourage her to stay, Aunt Lois had given her exclusive rights to the Baby's Room, with its bright yellow walls, blue wainscoting, and light pink curtains. It had been fixed up many summers back for the baby Aunt Lois had claimed was growing inside her.

"That woman and girl are not attractive," my brother said, as he followed me into the Baby's Room. He thought for a little bit. "That's too bad. It is unfortunate."

"Wish we were going home for supper tonight," I told him. Ginx had slipped to the floor and was leaning against Dana's bed. "Sure wish we didn't have to stay here," I said. But I, too, was getting ready. I had moved to the window, which looked out onto the side of our house. My back was turned to my brother, but I would know. When he was ready, I would begin.

"Momma's tired," Ginx told me. "That's all. She's just too tired." He began his slow rock against the bed frame.

"I know, Ginx," I said, "she's always tired."

I listened to the bed's rhythmic creaking and fixed my stare on the side of our house.

Then I went down.

Past the muffled voices from downstairs, Aunt Lois's laughing, Mrs. Mulvahill's cooing, past our own silent house across the way where our mother slept, past the failing light. Down below lay the Luccas' lush green field, which I watched for a while on my own. Then I took a breath and began the story.

"Momma Lucca does not want to move. She is on her porch swing, her legs crossed. She's got her hat on her knees," I said. It would be a story about what happened once when a boy fell in love with Sister Lucca.

"Oh, hmmmm," Ginx said.

"She takes out the large flowered fan Sister Lucca brought home from church."

It was true that Ginx was too old for stories, but he did not understand what being like other fifteen-year-olds entailed, and his difference shimmered inside him, a black stone in clear water. Although the stone hurt, Ginx insisted on guarding it close, examining it with the force of someone trying to understand light by staring at the sun.

"Rocking back and forth, Momma Lucca raises her hand." I tried not to pause over the scene but couldn't help myself. Down there it was a humid late-August afternoon, all the hazy grief of day collected, stretched and hanging, particularly golden on the narrow ledge joining field and sky. I turned so I could see Ginx, because when Momma Lucca raised her hand to slip his stone away, hiding it in the pocket of her deep fist, Ginx would smile, his lovely face losing its anger, and in those moments our future happiness seemed assured.

~

Right after I'd turned eight, we started sitting in our mother's room on hot summer days. She would close the curtains to shut out the light. Dana started off sitting on the floor, leaning against the bed where my mother rested while I sat on the carpet near the dresser; Ginx sat at our mother's tiny desk. "I want you kids to always be able to tell me everything," she said one day, her face full of enthusiasm over the thought. "Not like I was with my mother. I didn't tell her a thing." As usual, and without our mother's seeming to notice, Dana eventually slid herself onto the bed. "People can become sad from years of not talking to each other. I mean of not really talking," our mother told us. The gray light of the room kept me fastened there. Ginx studied our mother's face as she spoke. By the time he was ten, his stare had turned hard and serious. He'd memorized the area codes for every major city in the United States, including Anchorage, Alaska. I remember Uncle Pete quizzing him and breaking into rough laughter because he never got a single one wrong. Dana was lying on her side, an elbow propped on one of our mother's white pillows. My sister didn't look comfortable, but she could not risk lying down completely or our mother would tell her to go lie down in her own bed.

Ginx watched me while our mother explained to us that time was passing, that we must use time wisely and be efficient in our progress. "That is what you need to learn," she said, glumly capping the palms of her hands over her knees. "I've not been very efficient." I pulled in my legs and sat Indian style.

"How do we learn that?" Ginx asked. He was grateful for

any prescriptions with rules that were easy to follow so he could use his concentration for what actually mattered to him. "How do we do that, Momma?"

"I don't really know," she answered with a laugh, which was even more confusing. "You probably should not be spending a beautiful summer day indoors with your old mother."

"You're not old; you're only thirty-four," Ginx cut in. "Thirty-five is middle age, and seventy is old age, so you still have more than half your life left before you're old, if you think about it. Really." Ginx sat straight, and I hugged my legs closer to my body even though my knees hurt. After these discussions, our mother would sleep, and Dana would allow herself to lie down fully alongside her, but Ginx and I never did. We would wait in our positions, sometimes two hours, sometimes longer.

Before our mother went to sleep, she told us it was healthy to spend some time just sitting and thinking. She was wearing white cotton pants and a white blouse—her yoga outfit. "Few children do that," she explained, "but maybe there would be less violence in the world if they did. In India, everyone meditates." She told us, "Too many kids in this country watch television. Now that is really a waste of time." Then she stretched her arms upward and moved slightly farther away from Dana. My sister immediately sat up in order to use less space on the bed.

"What about the news or nature shows?" Ginx wanted to know. "Are those a waste of time?" Our mother raised one arm at a time toward the ceiling, as she'd been taught to do in her yoga class.

"People have different ways of learning," she said. "I am not necessarily right, but I think people should spend more time learning about one another, figuring out relationships. That might make the world a better place," she said. "Imagine if we didn't have to hide so much, could open up more."

"After I have kids," Dana told our mother, "I plan to have a babysitter at least twice a week so that me and my husband can have a candlelight dinner alone. I'll dress up for it, too."

Our mother paused and then, as part of her stretch, leaned forward and grasped her ankles, dropping her head between her knees. "After you have kids, chances are you won't have energy for candlelight dinners." She raised her head, gave a brief laugh, and turned back to Ginx. "My own parents, your Aunt Lois's parents and mine, well—you know they died before you were born—they had nothing at the end of their lives." She curled her feet and burrowed them down into the folds of the white bedspread. Dana put her hand on the headboard behind where our mother was sitting. If her hand accidentally slipped, it might well have brushed against our mother's hair and down her back. "To hear Lois talk about it, you'd think our parents were these active, creative people, but they were just sitting there, you know, waiting to die."

Ginx started humming and playing with his earlobe. He

wanted words chosen according to their sounds rather than their meanings, and the bulky descriptions of our mother's mother—our grandmother—sitting on the sofa in the dim light, filing her nails while her husband nodded in and out of sleep at an age when other people were still playing golf or even, for God's sake, hiking, aggravated him. It could have all been wrapped into a few words repeated three or four times. Ginx supplied *Rowling* and *Disaster,* the sounds barely distinguishable from his hum.

When she was done with her story, our mother asked him, "What did you say?"

Ginx stopped humming. *"Rowling* and *Disaster,"* he repeated. The sounds included our grandparents' large living room sofa and all their waiting.

"That's right," encouraged our mother, smiling, "that is perfect." She scratched her big toe.

Dana asked, "What's perfect?" but our mother just repeated Ginx's words.

I knew full well that other children were outside playing in the sun. Our mother continued watching Ginx as though waiting for more, as though eventually he might supply a sound to match all the episodes of her life, including the disappointments that would otherwise remain locked inside her. But maybe it wasn't the sounds she cared about; maybe what relieved her was his hard stare and the attention he burned into whatever interested him. Perhaps she thought that, since the three of us were still so young, if we sat with her together in the dark long enough, she could teach us where to turn our focus, and then she'd no longer be alone. "You can't just tell your own parents, 'Get up off the sofa and make something of yourself,' can you?" she asked. "I mean, people end up being who they are at a certain point."

"No," Ginx countered, "people do not usually end up being who they are. Not usually. That is not true."

It was my turn to add something, so I quoted one of our father's favorite lines. *"Life is what you make it."*

"Momma," Dana began, but our mother interrupted her.

"Oh, God, you all spend too much time with Lois." Our mother laughed. I laughed too. Ginx lowered his gaze and joined in, and our mother said, "Isn't this nice, now," which is when I looked back to Dana and no longer felt like laughing. I wished our mother would lean to her right, even if it were just part of her stretch, and caress my sister's cheek. I wished our mother had some leftover need that would drive her to comb our hair before school or ask for a hug sometimes, or occasionally linger when kissing us good night.

These sessions with our mother ended when I was twelve and my brother thirteen. The day was particularly hot, the kind that made the pavement all warbly, so I didn't mind being inside. Dana was ten at that point and was spending most of her summer days at her friend Myra's house. As usual, Ginx sat at the desk and I sat on the floor. Our mother's back curved against the headboard of her bed like the body of a question mark. Ginx had begun to grow what Aunt Lois called peach fuzz on his upper lip, and he was constantly pulling at the hairs.

"You know," our mother said, "I have something to tell you." She pushed herself up and sat Indian style, gently pushing down her inner thighs. Of course, she was looking at my brother. He shrugged up his right shoulder to shield himself. Aunt Lois had taught me that the perfection of a face lay in the symmetry of its proportions. "I once took a ruler to that boy's face," Aunt Lois said. "Did it when he was sleeping. Completely symmetrical. A good many people would give their eyeteeth for such features. God sure does work in mysterious ways."

"It's got nothing to do with God," I snapped back. "Ginx takes after Momma!"

"Oh, now, your momma's attractive, but she's no beauty—not to the trained eye, anyway," our aunt countered. I did not ask Aunt Lois how or when she measured Ginx, because of course she was lying, but I also knew she did not need a ruler to size up a face. He rarely cut his light brown hair, so it was always hanging in his eyes, meaning he was constantly having to split it apart to see anything well. His eyes verged on black. "I'd name that color *après minuit*," Aunt Lois said. His cheekbones were high and finely drawn right down to his jaws, which jutted out for the single purpose of carrying his mouth, as though it were a well-cut ruby carefully placed in the center.

"Oh, Ginx," our mother said, after she had closed the

curtains and we had taken our usual positions. "You are gifted. A gift deserves great respect, a red-carpet treatment, doesn't it, Morgan-Lee?"

I didn't answer. The comment made Ginx shrug his right shoulder up to his ear; our mother closed her eyes. Sitting there with her eyes closed may have made her forget that we were only children, her children at that.

"Sometimes I wake up in the morning and think of how Lois and I used to talk about being married when we were girls. Of course, she was four and a half years older and was always silly about it, but I have to admit I thought . . . I thought, too, that marriage would be different, that—" She stopped here, but she did not open her eyes. She smiled. "Pete tried to get me to go steady with him even after he'd been on a few dates with Lois. 'Oh,' I told him, 'you have no idea who I am!' Of course you can guess what he really wanted . . . but can you imagine?" Our mother opened her eyes, her face enlivened as if, finally, she had rested enough. "He was handsome—I mean, by most people's standards— so I gave it two seconds of thought, but of course I said no. Oh, God, I could hardly keep from laughing! I told Lois about it a few years later. She didn't take it too well."

I waited, twisting my hair and sucking on the ends, which were dry and limp. Aunt Lois wanted to trim and feather my hair along the sides so that I'd wear it the way other girls my age did. I looked away from our mother and concentrated on finding Sister Lucca, who was resting on her birch ready to pounce. I did not want to know about marriage, not how she was telling it anyway, so I focused on Sister, the long stretch of her body in the warm sunlight and the simple heat of her white birch branch. Ginx was covering his ears and humming more loudly than usual because he'd been caught off guard.

"That's enough, Ginx," our mother reprimanded, when he began to rock. "Bring it to an end." But she seemed to be speaking more to herself. She was angry. "If we can't talk openly we should just forget it!"

Ginx kept humming and rocking, not looking at either of us. He put both hands behind his head.

"Okay, that's it," our mother declared. "It's over. No more." She shot herself off the bed and onto the floor. She walked right past us and out her bedroom door, leaving us there. On that day in our mother's dark room, I told Ginx about Sister and B.J.'s pact, how they would always be together, how they would never leave each other. No matter what happened, Sister and B.J. would always love each other more than anyone else.

⌐

I could hear the women downstairs moving into the living room for their Polaroid pictures, which meant the makeup session had ended. It was time to conclude my story. "Momma Lucca is on the porch smiling, all those freckles dancing in her face like the Fourth of July. She slaps her old hat on her head and puts both hands on her hips as B.J. and Sister approach. They are dragging Adam, who had stupidly fallen in love with Sister so she was forced to pounce and smother him in the tall grass. Momma touches the brim of her hat the way men used to do when they wore hats and tells them to wash up for supper. Sister Lucca looks from Adam's carcass to Momma, carcass to Momma, wishing that love were a whole lot easier and didn't include all the kicking and wriggling and fighting. In the morning, Sister will hammer down Adam's bones till they are smooth, flat, and clear. Smooth, flat, and clear so she can cut them in patterns and hang them with the other leaves on the money trees."

I looked at my reflection in the window. Every morning, I rigidly pulled a comb through my hair, parting it exactly in the middle, so two dark-blond flanks dropped evenly to my shoulders.

"*Portent. Bilous. Mustard. Enough,*" Ginx muttered.

I smiled. They were soft words with sounds that absorbed and comforted.

"*Plop. Comma. Through,*" he added.

"Soft," I qualified, as the dining room light in our house went off again. I wondered if our mother was going back to bed or had just decided to sit awhile in the dark.

"*Wonder. Marvelous. Redolent.*" He held his knees and looked up at the ceiling. I closed my eyes as he went on. I thought about Billy, about the letters I had to write and take to him before Thursday. I no longer looked forward to Ginx's chatter as I once had.

"Push. Plunder. Carnival. Roar."

Our mother knew about the Luccas. She had walked in on us more than once over the years, catching enough snippets of stories to piece together some idea of what I told Ginx, why he occasionally burst into a flood of his words. "Morgan-Lee and Ginx," she had reprimanded, leaning her thin hip against the doorframe. "Stop with that. It's time you grew up."

"We're not growing up," I had shot back.

"Rhombah. Pollo. Prawn." Now Ginx was rubbing the side of his face with the entire palm of his hand.

"Enough!" I admonished, still not moving from the window. But he was not finished.

"Oohlahoolahoolahooo!" he howled, in imitation of Sister's scream.

I wondered if the women downstairs could hear the noise. Ginx slowly drew his imitation of Sister's yodel to an end, and for a little while there was silence.

"Kids! Kids! Come down and see what we've done here." Aunt Lois was calling us.

"Come on, Ginx," I said, turning to him, though I knew he wasn't finished. He spread his long fingers over his knees. In almost every way, Ginx was the opposite of Uncle Pete, whom Aunt Lois called "a man's man."

"Let's go downstairs," I said, but my brother didn't move,

absorbed once again in his chatter. I walked right past him and out of the room, letting the door close quietly. Ginx's words became harder as I started down the stairs without him.

"*Tuck. Crack. Ribbit,*" he said.

I wanted to hear anything but his chatter: the women talking about their new colors, the way Aunt Lois had chosen exactly the right ones, Dana's giggle, the TV news. I got to the bottom of the staircase and paused. Mother and daughter were sitting next to each other, their chairs now in the living room. They were facing me. Aunt Lois was kneeling before those two, her Polaroid camera to her face as she hurled the question at me over her shoulder: "Aren't they just beautiful?" Only I knew that, on the floor above us, Ginx's eyes were shut, his lips moving quickly over his words but never stumbling.

"Hi," the mother said, her blinking eyelashes freighted with mascara. Her eyelids were shadowed a combination of Vert sur Vert and Extase Jaune. Rose du Jardin blossomed generously on her cheeks. Aunt Lois's camera clicked. "Your aunt has just fixed us up so nice, now," the lady gloated, with a skittish glance at her daughter. "Hasn't she, honey?"

"Yeah, Momma, fine," the daughter snarled. I was sure the daughter had chosen the gray eye shadow herself, because our aunt only gravitated toward pastels for the unattractive. Both mother and daughter had selected Très Rouge for their lips, a red much too bright.

"Here we are," Aunt Lois said, pulling out the picture

and waving it back and forth to dry. "The two of you are absolute naturals before the camera. Plain naturals!" Aunt Lois handed the mother their snapshot. I moved next to the door so I could let them out when they were ready. Ginx was now standing on the landing upstairs. I could see his fingers gripping the banister. He was perfectly still. I looked at the big girl in front of me and thought of the beginning to a love letter that some boy might order for her: "Your moon face shines tonight. . . ."

"Dana has wrapped and bagged your purchases all nicely," Aunt Lois declared, as my sister came into the living room, offering two pink-and-white bags. "Now, promise you'll come back and see me," Aunt Lois chirped out as she skirted the women toward the door. "You promise?"

The mother nodded and promised they would; then she turned just enough to look imploringly at the daughter, as if wishing that she could for once draw words of gratitude up from the girl's heart and out her throat. Maybe then, she wouldn't have to work so hard at her own politeness. "We certainly will."

"Y'all come back in at least a month for a checkup so we can be sure you're following the correct cleansing procedure," Dana instructed loudly. I hopped to open the door as wide as it would go. Both daughter and mother scuttled past without looking at me. The mother focused on the back of her daughter's head as they stepped over the threshold. I didn't shut the door right away because I imagined announcing, "Your first breath in this new womanhood." The daughter walked quickly down the two stairs and through the yard, but the mother stayed rooted to the stoop a few seconds longer.

"Well, it's gonna be just all right," I heard her mutter. "We'll be okay," she said more clearly as she stepped down and into the yard to join her daughter. I stood there, planning to note down later this small insight into how other lives went on—the kind of yearning involved.

"Good-bye!" I said to the woman and the girl as they stood blankly on the curve of the cul de sac for a few seconds before unlocking a white Chevrolet. I waved in the sad, exaggerated way of a movie mother watching her sons go off to war. "Good-bye!" I called again, after the women were already in the car. The mother sheepishly returned my wave. Then I shut the door and leaned against it, the palms of my hands flat on the wood. I looked hard at Aunt Lois and waited there only a second before whispering, "How much?"

"Sixty-four dollars and twenty-eight cents in cash," Aunt Lois announced, fanning out those bills in her smooth white fingers. She winked at me. When it came to money, we understood each other perfectly. "Set the table, my babies, it's suppertime!"

I obeyed, skipping to clear the cleansing kits. There was something beautiful about money, even when it wasn't mine. My brother was coming down the stairs, counting each one as he stepped.

"Thirteen, same as always!" Dana told him, as if he were

actually looking for an answer, as if he had forgotten the number of stairs since the last time he counted.

"That's correct," he said. "Thirteen."

I took extra care while placing the silverware on the mats: knives on the right, forks on the left. The tiny dessert spoon lay perpendicular to the wineglasses, which Aunt Lois insisted upon setting out, though she never filled them with anything other than Welch's grape juice. But when Dana looked at the table and smiled, I regretted having done such a good job. I knew my sister was comparing it to home, where the knives and forks lay dully side by side on their paper napkins.

Uncle Pete did not return when he said he would, and he did not call again. "Let's go ahead and eat," Aunt Lois suggested, an hour and a half later, trying to sound cheerful. She lit the candles and dimmed the lights.

"It's beef stew," Ginx confirmed, once Aunt Lois pulled back the aluminum foil. Dinner had gotten cold, so Aunt Lois heated it up.

"Stewed beef!" I announced. My brother circled his fingers around the bottom of a glass vase, the opposite forefingers and thumbs almost touching.

"Don't get the roses too close to the flame there," Aunt Lois warned.

He looked up. "No," he said, shaking his head, "I sure won't."

"When will Uncle Pete be home?" Dana wanted to know.

"Okay," Ginx was whispering, as he pushed his fingers more snugly around the vase.

"Later," Aunt Lois cut in. "He's got houses to show. People aren't always on time, you know. It's impossible to have a schedule when you're in business." Our aunt looked at me, and I nodded. It was my job to remind her of how deeply she was loved and, of course, that a man would not be late for her unless it was beyond his control.

Aunt Lois had taught me about love. When I was ten years old, she'd begun bringing down her collection of love letters, graciously untying the satin bow and picking out a letter. She would read to me from across the dining room table. Later, I would scrawl certain words into a journal to create love letters of my own: *Want, Blush, Roses, Lips, Charm.* I sounded them out till one day I came to realize that they were dull words, which is when I began to combine them: *The Bloses of your Charmlips.* I'd even written a love letter from a pretend girl to a pretend boy. One day, I showed it to Billy, who said it was okay but that I needed practice.

I stopped writing after that, but I still listened to what our aunt told me about her past loves. I'd close my eyes and try to picture younger versions of Johnny Johnson, the mechanic, or Burt Hope, who sold hardware downtown. I'd think of Newton George, who had no job at all but to sit in the tiny station near the railway tracks in West Hillsborough and watch the trains pass by, freighted with old car parts or bales of raw cotton. Head in my hands, I'd try to refigure those men smart and handsome, the way Aunt Lois described, not at all how I knew them. I imagined them, years back, in the candlelight of romance, pen in hand as the thought of our aunt cracked open their hearts, love words spilling recklessly over the pages.

"I can do nothing but think of you" or "Your kiss last night left me staggering all the way home," our aunt would read with a trembling voice, her eyes moistening as she swallowed down the sob that threatened somewhere deep in her throat. During these readings she was always on the verge of emotion. "I am on the brink of just breaking down and weeping!" she'd exclaim or "I'm on the brink of laughing myself silly over how foolish I was back then." Although Aunt Lois complained that I was neither sentimental nor sympathetic, she never spoke of what I *was,* the kind who could carry a secret to the grave, who did not need instruction on what needed to be kept unspoken.

Our aunt taught me that Hillsborough was not at all what it seemed. It was a town full of apparently ordinary men capable of harboring extraordinary feelings. Trip Wallace, the postman who was always on time every morning, who, if it was raining, carried the mail to our front door; Jay Bridgett at the drugstore; even Paul O'Keefe, who sold used cars near the town dump—all of them had once taken part in the collective passion for our aunt. In those years before my existence, there had been so much raging, pillow kissing, screaming, ecstasy, threats, and jealousies over her that any other town would have combusted, gone up in smoke, ripped toward heaven like a shooting star. But Hillsborough remained quiet, smoldering love, turning its young men old and simple, giving them families and routines. "Oh," Aunt Lois would sigh, "Morgan-Lee, you should have heard all the hearts breaking when I married your uncle Pete. I can't even tell you—it was one large crack. The composite grief of those poor men!"

There was always a pause that followed a reading, our aunt's face silently confronting the shadows in the room while I remained perfectly still so as not to remind her of my existence, of how much time had robbed, how things had changed. "That's how it was," she sometimes stated. "That's what things were like back then, Morgan-Lee."

"Yeah," I'd say. "Different."

"Different, I'm telling you."

I never read the letters myself, and she never offered to show me one. I was her listener, and in exchange she appreciated my stillness and discretion, which I believed to be my only true talents.

"Those women were fat," Dana said, referring to the mother and daughter.

"Oh, now," Aunt Lois instructed, resisting a smile, "they were pleasantly plump."

"Not so pleasant," Ginx stated. "The young Mulvahill was not pleasant at all," he added upon reflection.

"That's not what matters," I said. Aunt Lois swallowed a forkful of candy yam. She licked the fork clean, her indication that she'd eat no more. "What matters is that they paid."

"Well, tomorrow I'm going shopping so I can bake some pies for the fellowship supper. The church elders asked me if I'd do my special lemon meringue," Aunt Lois said, then paused, tracing the rim of her plate. "With extra meringue." I looked at my brother, who had caught the exact note of the air conditioner and had begun to hum. Ginx was so good at humming to machinery that, unless he slipped from the one long flat note he was practiced at attaining, only I could hear him. He hummed without swerving throughout Aunt Lois's chatter and Dana's questions.

Under that steady, familiar sound, I went down: beyond the breathing and Dana's giggles, under the switching clink of Aunt Lois's wedding ring against the wineglass as she swallowed her grape juice. I passed through various afternoons: slight rain, blazing sun, pockets of cloud, lingering light in bare winter, the horizon etched with tree branches, a dark that falls too early. Finally, I arrived at a warm, still day, a thick arm of light stretched around the edge of the deep green field in front of the small house. And there was Momma Lucca leaning a large shoulder against her half-cocked screen door, smelling the heavy air, thinking it was surely going to rain. She peered out into the field a long time, until night settled in, and there was Sister Lucca, raising her skirt and peeing straight as a moon ray.

"Supper!" Momma called, walking onto her porch. Sister Lucca jumped up almost as high as her birch branch. She was long-legged and fast as she bounded home toward Momma, who stood there waiting, arms spread. Sister laughed to see those arms, yelped and laughed and jumped up into them, her legs wrapping around Momma Lucca's waist, head against her shoulder. Night fell in one thick curtain.

"Look at this night sky, Sister," Momma Lucca said quietly, holding her daughter as if she were just a baby girl again. But Sister did not look up. She was young, and to her the sky without sun was no more interesting than a steel-black shade that other people could go on and on about. Besides a few bright points, the night sky was just plain sad.

"It's sad," Sister announced, so Momma burst into a private laughter over that still uncrossed boundary between childhood and its end, which has everything to do with learning the romance of the stars and darkness. So Momma swayed on her porch while a breeze picked up, the moths swirling around that single bulb, the whole of Sister's talk rising up warmly against her chest, riddled with misunderstanding, maybe, but true nonetheless. Momma could listen to Sister for hours.

I had glimpses of the Luccas that Ginx would never know about. Mornings, evenings, afternoons, times I went down for myself alone: quiet moments on the porch, lonely instances watching Sister by herself in the field, whole hours in which Sister lay stretched on her birch branch, just thinking. There were parts of the Luccas' lives that were all mine.

"Come fall, you'll be an eighth-grader." Aunt Lois smiled at Dana, then threatened, "You're nearly a woman. Maybe you'll be just like your mother." Dana winced, and Aunt Lois patted her wrist.

"And come September I will be a junior, and Morgan-Lee will be a sophomore," Ginx said. "A wise fool, wise, wise fool."

"Maybe when I grow up I'll be like you, Aunt Lois," Dana suggested.

Our aunt considered the possibility. "Well, then, you'll certainly get less sleep," she said. "I suppose I could just run off to bed anytime I felt like it, but somebody's got to watch after you kids." Aunt Lois sighed. "Anyway, a body gets accustomed to shouldering the burden." I coughed, plopped another candy yam onto my plate, and passed them on, fat, orange, and glistening.

I once asked our mother why she was so tired. "It happens as you age," she said. "You lose something," she tried to explain. At her best, our mother was able to defrock the world of its mystery. She could make Ginx happy. When our mother used to push me on my swing and sing, it was clear she knew things that other people did not, and I trusted that she would protect me, that I'd be okay. But as I grew, she got into the habit of rising early, squinting out the window, and then heading back to bed. She quit her teaching job and asked fewer questions. Even making dinner or eating it could sometimes be too much. It seemed that whatever mystery had once kept her intrigued had changed shape and eluded her. And because I still believed that she understood what other people could not, I dreaded growing older.

TRUTH

Besides a few bright points, the night sky is sad, I wrote late one night, allowing myself only that sentence. The rest was normal, perfect, just the way everyone expected a love letter to be. Ginx and our parents had been asleep for hours. Dana was at Aunt Lois's. I recapped my pen and went to bed. Only I would ever know that this letter was about lost love. Otherwise, Billy would not have been able to sell my letters. Kids wanted letters for crushes and going steady, so I had to carefully disguise what they were actually about, sneaking the entire meaning of a letter into just one sentence, one sentence that was all mine. Our mother had told me that an Irishwoman will knit an irregular stitch into every sweater she makes in order to mark it as her own. This single sentence was my private marker. It was the last of the three letters I needed to finish that week.

When Thursday came, I skipped through our side yard, between the boxwood trees, and into Billy's yard. Way down on the border, between Billy's grandmother's yard and the woods that led to the Eno River, was our tree house. I ran toward it as if I were eleven again instead of almost fourteen, as if I were meeting him for a play date instead of a business transaction. I stopped before the rope ladder and then climbed up. The ladder shook with my weight, the wooden rungs creaking. I climbed through the opening to pop into the small room, where I landed with my knees squarely, expertly, on the cushion placed there for this purpose.

"Hi," Billy whispered, from where he sat against the wall, his arm resting on the rolled-up sleeping bag he kept there for nights he couldn't sleep in his own bed. "I hear them in there making it sometimes, Morgan-Lee, you know. It's so awful I can't sleep," he'd told me once, referring to his mother and Amos. Billy's face was jagged and angular as if constructed from pieces of different puzzles, his bad eye staring over my shoulder.

Billy hadn't been born with a wandering eye. It got that way in a car accident when he was seven, out in Nevada. His father was killed in the fire caused by the crash. I imagined how, on that day, Billy's eye had chased after his father, followed him into a place beyond, and then just flat-out refused to leave. Nothing the doctors did could tempt it back.

Right after the accident, Billy and his mother left Nevada and moved in with Billy's grandmother, Old Mrs. Dean. Two days after they moved to Hillsborough, I saw him naked in a tree down by our river. It must have been a cool day, because I was wearing a jacket, and the clouds were swirly. "Clues," Ginx used to call them. "Look at the clues!" As if the clouds pointed toward some answer.

I had taken the shortcut down to the river and was sitting behind a bush and looking at the clouds, perhaps inspecting them for signs. It was so quiet that the sudden splash from the river fractured both water and air. "Whooo!" It was a call of affirmation, and I hugged my knees to my chest and watched. The water was still for a few seconds, and then the new neighbor boy sprang up from the river, naked. I dug my fingernails into my kneecaps so hard they actually scarred. There was an old rope that some teenage boys had attached to a tree on the riverbank. Billy gripped it, pulling himself up a few inches at a time, feet curled against the knots in the rope. He emerged, white as a cloud on a clear day, his bare body a pure fact: skinny, with sinewy muscles. I didn't want to care about his penis, but I saw its raw skin and thought it must hurt to have such a thing hanging from your middle all the time.

Billy kept focused on the branch above. He was intent and climbing, ignoring the cold. When he got to the branch, he held to it, stretching over the river, which belonged to Ginx and me. He so obviously wanted it for himself. His nakedness seemed attached to faraway Nevada, and when I saw he wanted to be king of our river, I closed one eye, fit his body between my two fingers, and crushed his small wriggling self. He didn't care that he was a newcomer, that he had nothing to do with us, that he had left a desert and a dead father and a childhood of his own far away. He had come to steal. The starkness of his body stood out against the trees, the brown water, and the rock where I always sat. He'd left his clothes strewn on the bank, not the way someone afraid of being discovered would have left clothing. Billy had climbed that rope and sat up on the branch above the water, looking over a world—my brother's world and mine—that he knew nothing about.

It was Old Mrs. Dean's idea that Billy and I become friends. Old Mrs. Dean had always been nice to me; she'd even made my costume for the elementary school play. Occasionally, she came over to Aunt Lois's, but never for a makeover. "Oh, now, Lois, what would I possibly do with a makeover at my age?" She laughed differently from the other women who visited. After Young Mrs. Dean and Billy moved in with her, she invited me and Dana and Ginx over, but our mother waited four days and then sent only me.

"I don't know if we are staying here or moving somewhere else," was the first thing Billy said to me. I just shrugged. "So it's probably not worth becoming friends," he clarified, all the while assembling a model airplane.

I watched him glue a piece of the wing onto the body of the plane. I said, "That's why my brother and sister didn't bother coming. My mom sent me to check out the situation so we don't waste time. Just in case you're not staying."

When Billy didn't answer or look at me, I added, "We're both seven years old. My aunt said your birthday is September eighteenth. That's exactly three months after mine." When he continued focusing on his plane's wing without talking, I went on to tell him, "People here don't climb trees naked, for your information."

"People shouldn't watch people climbing trees naked," Billy said, not surprised, still not looking up. I was about to leave when he said, "If you want, I'll show you where they put my daddy's ashes. The *remains*." He blew on the wing of the plane and set it on his bookshelf. Finally, he looked at me, his bad eye scrambling away.

"My aunt says you were in the car with your daddy when it wrecked, but you got out alive."

He sucked in his bottom lip. "Just don't let them know I'm showing you the urn when we go into the living room, or it'll make my mom cry. They were really in love," he went on.

Ginx had taught me all about seeing what needed to be seen without letting anyone know. "Let's go," I told Billy. He'd understand soon enough what an expert I was. "Just show me."

After that, for three summers in a row, we'd meet once a week after dinner and go to the river. I'd sneak down with Billy, and we'd catch fireflies. He'd whisper excitedly, "Let's hunt!" We'd walk together without speaking, our breath tugged deep, released only at the clap of our hands around a bug. We poked holes in the lids of our Mason jars to give the bugs air, then screwed the lids on tight when we were done. Two jars full of lightning bugs. They were our own private moons. I placed mine on the windowsill of my bedroom, where its light failed to a deep green as the bugs died throughout the night. The real moon left no traces of its burning, but my jar by morning held black carcasses, to be scattered out the window like ash.

"How come I have to save my dead ones?" Billy used to ask. "Why not you?" But I never answered that. It was my rule, and he knew how things worked.

Billy and I kept up these hunts until a few days after my tenth birthday, when Ginx found out what we'd been doing and pushed me down so hard in the Deans' driveway that I passed out. "No more fireflies with Billy!" he'd shouted. "No more!" He'd figured out that I'd been secretly scattering their carcasses. Ginx knew how ritual worked, how it sealed love. So the day he found my jar, he ran through our yard, arms outstretched. I saw him coming but merely turned my back so he could shove, breaking me of any interest that did not involve him.

"I saw it from the window: Your son ran right at Morgan-Lee. Just pushed her to the pavement," Old Mrs. Dean told our mother. "Your little girl didn't even put out her hands to break her fall." When our mother later recounted the event to the doctor and the child psychologist, she emphasized what Mrs. Dean had said about how I hadn't tried to save myself, speaking as if this fact were the strangest of all.

When the psychologist and I were alone, he said, "You've had a concussion." His name was Dr. Sampson, and his white mustache spread like a seagull's wings. When he spoke, I watched his mouth and thought of Aunt Lois carefully twisting the ends of that mustache with her red fingernails; blood on snow.

It had been our father's idea to have me "talk to someone." He'd wanted Ginx to go as well, but our mother had flat-out refused. "Ginx is not going to any doctor, not that kind anyway," she'd insisted, folding her arms tightly against her chest. Our parents were standing on opposite sides of my hospital bed. "Just let my son be. Please. Let him be."

"Some children are afraid after a concussion," Dr. Sampson went on to tell me.

"Why?" I asked, flattening my hands against a cushion, the green cover as shiny as a cough drop. The little man nodded. My own blood on the asphalt had smelled familiar, like fresh paint or the pages of a new schoolbook, but I had no reason to speak about it. He waited, both his name and his face as shiny and lickable as his furniture.

"Some children are perhaps afraid that their thoughts or dreams have been lost," he said. "Are you afraid?"

I looked around the office: wooden toy box, board games like Candyland and Clue, orange dump truck, two big dolls and a smaller one. I wondered if dreams had been lost in that very room, and then I remembered an evening down by the river when Ginx had found a beautiful bottle made of blue glass. He'd picked it up, then tossed it into the water. "Look," he said, pointing to where hundreds of white maggots squirmed in the soft clay through the fragile remains of a dead squirrel. I thought of other children's losses, their loneliness, their tiny dreams squirming behind the toy box or under the dump truck. Surely the insides of those dolls were most unsafe. Dreams had been left there, and the children had grown up. I folded my arms and stared in silence.

"Nothing makes me afraid," I finally said, narrowing my eyes, "and I don't need to play with toys or dolls." Ginx would have refused to speak without needing to explain. Dr. Sampson's face darkened as his fingers went up in a triangle, each one leaning against its opposite, the apex lightly touching his lips. I imagined all the other kids this man had tricked into kneeling on the carpet and playing games. I knew how vulnerable other kids were, not like Ginx and me. They would have been immediately duped to the floor, spilling their secrets over Mastermind or Monopoly. There were plenty of places to hide and hatch unfettered dreams, and the doctor obviously counted on this, greedy as he was to incubate as many as possible. Ginx would have shaken his head at talking to strangers. He might have recited the alphabet or counted to ten over and over. I stared at my feet, sitting in that office feeling sorry for other children, understanding for the first time how frail other lives must be.

For many nights afterward, I thought of how our mother

had emphasized the fact that I had not put my hands out to protect myself when I'd fallen. My hands, instead, had immediately covered my ears. I was clutching my head, holding it even as I hit the ground, allowing my skull to crack. Of course, this is what occasioned my trip to the doctor, and our mother was angry, as though I had blabbed a secret to the world that I should have kept to myself. "I'm sorry," I whispered to her the day she drove me home. The doctor had given me a yellow construction hat to wear.

"For what?" she asked, without taking her eyes off the road.

Our mother explained to Ginx that for his punishment she and our father had decided to ground him. She pulled her bathrobe tightly around her waist, looking resigned and exhausted, all except her hair, which remained defiantly abundant. In fact, I'd drawn a picture of her hair when Dr. Sampson had asked me to draw the ocean.

"Go outside today, Ginx," she'd told him quietly, with a wave of her hand. "It'll be your last time for a while. Let Morgan-Lee sleep." Ginx had complied, and a few minutes later I put my firefly jar in a small satchel and sneaked out to meet my brother under our favorite tree. I was wearing the construction hat, so I couldn't lie down beside him but sat instead, knees gripped to my chest, which, as I remember, also hurt. It was Ginx's last day of freedom, so I told him to follow me; it was time for us to go to the west side.

"West Hillsborough?" he'd asked.

"To find those people with missing limbs that Uncle Pete warned us about," I explained, my hands in fists.

He pursed his lips and thought.

"Ginx, it's your last day. Poppa said," I reminded him.

After a few seconds, he crawled out from beneath our tree, stood and looked at my yellow hat, rubbed his hands together, and offered, "*Cock. Clue. Klutz.*" He followed behind me, and we walked to the cul de sac and then down Margaret Lane. We turned west, crossed in front of Mr. Shepard's house, and walked till we got to the train tracks, which we followed, straight through to the heart of West Hillsborough.

Our father had grown up outside Burlington in a place a lot like West Hillsborough. His parents had lived in their small house till they died only a few years after I was born. Our father had had the house demolished and had sold the lot. That was how he said it too: *demolished,* a word Ginx could not help including in his chatter, a word that encompassed both destruction as well as the sweetness of the crumble. I wondered if Ginx felt that same pang of joy when I let him hit me, *pow, pow, pow,* on my chest and upper arms. It didn't happen often, but I wondered if he had something like the taste of *demolish* in his mouth.

"My family was working-class. Your grandparents worked

in the mill," our father had told us. They died when I was only four.

"You were a self-made man?" I asked, because I'd just learned the term.

"Well"—he sighed—"I wanted something different when I grew up. I didn't know then that I'd actually become a vice principal, but I knew I wanted to work in the schools and make a difference in kids' lives." Our father liked routine. He enjoyed waking up in the morning, making his coffee, reading the paper, collecting his things, and getting to school at least an hour before he had to. In the evening, he came home at dinnertime, and after dinner he went for a walk and then to the bedroom to read and organize his papers. He had once explained to me that it was his job to make the family run smoothly, to bring home the money, to get us all through school, to protect us. "It's my job," he said. "Ginx will probably always be my job," he explained. I didn't say anything. My brother was the one who had delivered *demolish* to our father with all its parts revealed, but far from being grateful our father hadn't even seemed to notice.

"Ginx will always live with you?" I asked.

"Probably, Morgan-Lee. Probably he will," our father explained. "Probably, your mother and I will always have to care for him."

Uncle Pete had told us stories about people on the west side of town who worked in cotton mills where their arms and hands got crushed by dye pressers and other machinery.

Ginx worried that maybe we'd get lost, trip over human stumps, be unable to find our way home again. "We'll dodge them," I assured him, but my brother rubbed and worried. I promised that if we kept to the train tracks we'd be fine.

"I'm eleven years old," he said, then added, *"Polish. Roller. Poppa. Trowel."* They were soft, pleasing words, which he was not just wasting; he was apologizing to me. But I kept quiet; it was not yet time to forgive. He was staring again at my construction hat.

"You see, everything's different here," I explained loudly, stepping along a single metal track, making myself concentrate, foot over foot.

In East Hillsborough, there were gardens and tended lawns; driveways were paved or neatly filled with small gravel. The sun rose promptly there, spent the day shining, preparing to roll toward the other side, where it could set in a wild abandon of oranges and reds. Ginx and I walked west together that evening, watching as the sun sank, breaking over the trailers and the small houses, their weather-beaten porches scattered with children's clothing and parts of dolls and trucks. There was a yard with plastic statues of Snow White and the Seven Dwarfs; a small Bambi grazed at the feet of one of the dwarfs. We passed behind Cone Mill, where I thought we would see what Uncle Pete had spoken of. But all we saw was a group of men there, some desperately still and others who laughed loudly enough for everyone. No one, though, was missing limbs as far as I could tell, and Ginx was searching hard as we passed.

We crossed over a bridge above a dirt path, which may have been, in cooler weather, a small stream.

"Stop," I ordered my brother. Just on the other side of that bridge, a small lush green field began. It could have been tobacco that was growing, or maybe corn. I only know that it was the deepest, wildest green of any field I'd ever seen.

"Look there," Ginx said, pointing to a white tree near the middle of the field. "That must be a birch tree." I didn't care what he called it or how that tree had come to grow alone in the field. It was the combination of colors, the way the white and green met, colliding with the reds of the setting sun, that told me we were far, far from home. I swallowed hard and nodded toward a rickety white house. "Morgan-Lee, there's a woman on the porch," Ginx said. He looked at me, gulped, and shifted his weight.

Without hesitation, I told him, "That's Momma Lucca, Ginx. That's who I came to show you." In the silence that followed, I leaned back, careful not to show my own surprise.

"Who?" he finally asked, but he did not ask again. The woman stood up from her porch swing, as if to be more visible. She held a man's hat in her right hand and moved the short sleeve of her flowered housecoat as far up as it would go on her abundant, sunburned shoulder. She shielded her eyes. Her face was so wide I could see all its features. She winced, the skin of her large cheeks pulling up and waggling back down again, slow as honey. She'd risen to search the field, and her gaze scanned right over us. In her determined search for someone else, our unimportance there became clear. I am not sure why her indifference to us provoked me, or why it was I so badly wanted to be a part of whatever she was trying to find, but Ginx must have felt it too. He leaned over and whispered, "We should give her something, a souvenir." I opened my small satchel, took out the empty firefly jar, and tossed it into the field. Ginx nodded. By the time my brother and I turned to walk home again, the story had begun. He didn't care that he would spend the rest of the summer grounded. Together, we had discovered the Luccas.

BIGNESS

~

I SPENT THE DAYS of Ginx's punishment at Billy's house. My true clumsiness was apparent only there. Anywhere else, I was quiet, rigid, and careful. Every day, Billy was witness to my falls and scrapes. He saw me break things. Inside his house, it was easy to break things. Old Mrs. Dean collected porcelain statuettes and crystal bowls. Even the candy in those bowls seemed precarious, and there were times when I'd reach in for gumdrops and come up with a fistful of glass marbles instead. Billy's mother loved colored marbles. I knew this. All the same, it was spooky to be suddenly grasping glass instead of candy. It was like a nightmare in which you're one second holding a doll and in a flash it becomes a live screaming baby. My handful would slip, scattering out over the floor. I became known for breaking things; I'd broken plates, glasses, statuettes, and the handles off of teacups. Old Mrs. Dean used to joke that the cups and saucers trembled as I breathed.

Billy, though, could handle stacks of fine china; he easily negotiated the skirts of porcelain statuettes protruding over corners of bureaus and small tables. Perhaps it was partly this talent, his ability to move through a world of fragile objects without even provoking a tremor, that made me want to be near him. It wasn't long before Billy's mother suggested we go outside and build a tree house. She squinted at the yellow hard hat the doctor had given me to protect my healing skull and told us it would be better if we took our playing outdoors.

"Wouldn't a tree house be nice?" she suggested. "Amos could help y'all build it."

"Will do," Amos cheerfully agreed. He had just begun dating Young Mrs. Dean and was trying to be good, trying to make things okay for everyone, especially for Billy. It was Amos who bought the wood and nails and drew the design according to Billy's instruction. There is nothing I remember from that particular summer as precisely as the details of the tree house's construction, which are still so clear in my head that I can recall the sizes of the various boards used for the roof and walls. Billy stipulated that he wanted no windows in his tree house so we could have good candlelight at any time of day. Amos shook his head at this, but he designed a windowless tree house just as Billy had asked.

I began sleeping till late in the morning, and in the evening I told Ginx Lucca stories. When I left the house to go to Billy's, I made ridiculous, elaborate plans for sneaking out without seeing our mother. If she happened to walk into the living room just as I was going out the door, my heart would grab and my palms would sweat. Our mother didn't ask me where I was going, and she no longer asked me to come home at any particular time. She would sit on the couch reading her old books or practicing her yoga on the living room floor. Nonetheless, I would rush away as if she might find out and call me back, as if she could not bear to have me gone. I spent my time in Billy's yard watching the building of the tree house.

As I ran toward them, Amos would look up, nudge Billy, and swipe a rag from his back pocket to wipe off his sweat. "Here she comes," he'd say, and stand straight, so large it seemed to me that he blocked out the sun. I didn't even need to shield my eyes. I escaped from our house every day that August just to sit on a cinder-block pile while Amos and Billy worked. Perhaps it was the construction hat that convinced them of the seriousness of my condition, or maybe it was my ability to be still for long periods of time. Whatever it was, they treated me with extreme care—Billy running in for a pitcher of Kool-Aid as soon as I got thirsty and, when lunchtime came, making my favorite kind of sandwich, full of tomato and extra mayonnaise. Amos built a roof over the stacked cinder blocks where I sat, two half walls for armrests, and a backrest behind it all. We called it my throne, and from there I watched Amos lift and saw, the muscles in his chest and arms moving beneath his skin like rippling water in a large clear lake. Billy scrambled around, moving things into different piles. It was the first stretch of time I'd spent with anyone other than Ginx, so it took me a while to figure out how to act. I'd lean back and hold my knees, the yellow hat setting me apart as if it were a halo. I could spend hours switching my gaze from the trees, bending in the wind, to the reverberations of Amos's hammering through his chest and arms. Sitting high on that throne, I watched as Billy scurried and sweated, his head darting up every once in a while to check that I was okay. When he asked me how things were going, I'd just nod, not wanting to speak, happy for the ax, the wood, Billy's anxiety over my well-being, and Amos's muscles with their rhythmic fall and rise. Even my head stopped hurting.

I soon began asking Amos questions, well aware that he couldn't answer them. On the last day of Ginx's confinement, I was over at Billy's asking about saints, wondering what they thought, if they really liked following Jesus or if they only did it to feel singled out from the crowd. You know, different. And what about martyrs?

Amos blinked up and smiled, not knowing how to respond but compensating for his silence by nailing together a footrest for me and finishing up a box for storing my hard hat at night. He attached a rope handle to the box, so it was portable.

Slowly, slowly, I leaned forward, took off my construction hat, and asked things like, "Why would it matter if a halo were made of gold or just plain yellow plastic? Why would it matter to a saint who's not supposed to care about objects?"

Billy occasionally stopped work to explain my questions to Amos. He'd either explain or he'd flat-out answer me himself. One afternoon, Billy got so frustrated with having to interpret my talk that he slammed his foot down on a wooden plank Amos was about to pick up and hissed out, "Why are you such a dumbhead?" Instead of responding, Amos stood straight; perhaps he hoped his sheer bigness could absorb the swirling anger of the funny-eyed boy in front of him. Both Amos and Billy turned to me, looking so lost that I could afford to enjoy the good long time it took to put a foot up on my little footrest and clear my throat the way Uncle Pete did before beginning one of his rambling dinner-table speeches.

"Billy," I said, squinting my eyes, zeroing in on him, "I come here to watch Amos work. He's so big, and I like his muscles. That's the reason I come." Billy shivered, his small angular body a sharp contrast to the large dull one beside him.

Amos just stared at me. "You're the strangest little thing I ever met." He chuckled, shaking his head. Billy turned on him.

"Can't you even tell that she's lying?" he shouted at Amos, his anger raw and quick. He grabbed his fingers into fists, his torso jolting. I could see the jealousy working down through him as clear as though his skin were glass. "You're too stupid for her and too stupid for my mother too," he insisted. It was as though I had been waiting all my life to witness precisely this; his jealousy rode a track of exhilaration straight from the outside world through my chest, ushering a strange new happiness down into my heart. Billy declared straight into Amos's face, "We're only ten, and we're smarter than you."

"Don't you sass me now, boy," Amos managed slowly, giving Billy a sharp flick on the cheek so he staggered backward, palms upturned, bereft.

That was justice, I thought: Billy was being punished for loving me. Ginx also loved me, and he had been punished. What I came to understand that day made up for a whole host of unanswered questions. I leaned back under my roof, both feet up on my footstool, and took it as fact that a construction hat can be made of gold or a halo of plastic: I could be a holy saint or merely trying to piece back a cracked skull. It was the feeling I could command in other people that counted. I was startled by the surprising fact of being only ten years old and having already inherited the Kingdom of the Earth.

Then Billy turned on me. "I don't even want this stupid tree house," he yelled, from where he stood on a fat board. I remained unmoved. "It was going to be my birthday present for you, but you can forget it now." Then, dragging the question from depths where questions should be left untouched, he blurted out, "How come you break everything, anyway?"

Rather than answer, I slipped off my throne and ran home.

Toward the end of summer, when the tree house was completed, Billy said he forgave me, and he asked me to marry him. He charged me a dollar twenty-eight, half the cost of the engagement ring. I paid but never wore it. The ring had a gray stone in the center that I didn't even allow myself to kiss, though I'd often heard Aunt Lois talk about how fiancées were supposed to carry on. I locked that ring in a tiny blue box and put it on the top shelf of my closet, where I could look at it whenever I wanted. It was the evidence Ginx was searching for a few nights later when he raided my closet. My brother took that ring, whispering, "No, no, no," as any big brother might do, but with Ginx it was way up close and in the dark, the stolen ring snug on the knuckle of his pointer finger so he could jab its stone into the top of my arm. Tiny bruises sprung up later, sure tellings of the pain love brings, the kind of hurt Aunt Lois could go on and on about. "You'll understand when you're older," our aunt used to tell me with a sigh. "Love hurts." The next morning, I broke off the engagement and informed Billy that I could no longer play with him. Billy told me I could go on and die for all he cared. That is when we stopped being friends.

It wasn't until March of my eighth-grade year that Billy and I started speaking to each other again. He came up to me in the field behind our school. "Morgan-Lee," he said. I looked around, hardly believing that he was addressing me. "Listen," he went on, as if conversation between us were nothing out of the ordinary. "I'm changing schools." I folded my arms and said nothing, but I couldn't look at him. "Amos and Momma are getting married, and we're moving into the Pritchards' house on West Crest Street. I'm going to go to Cresset Christian. Amos says he'll pay to send me there."

"You're joking." It was one of the last schools I could imagine Billy attending, and he didn't even seem to be upset. But I could tell by his eyes that he hadn't been sleeping; he'd dreaded that marriage. Aunt Lois said Young Mrs. Dean had put it off so many years because of Billy, but I supposed she ultimately caved in. I hadn't really looked at him for a long time, but I realized he hadn't changed much. He was skinny and restless as always, his bad eye still bent on escape.

"You're moving?" I asked.

"Yeah, into the Pritchards' old house, like I said," he told me. West Crest Street was only two blocks away. "The Pritchards moved to Atlanta."

I turned toward the woods, where Ginx spent most of his lunch hours.

Once, I'd found him there, sitting against the thick

stump of a tree. Ginx hadn't realized I was there, that we were together. I knew I should have turned around and walked back to school, but I stayed, recognizing the story Ginx was telling himself as one of my own. The truth is there was nowhere else I wanted to be. I had gone to my brother's woods, and I'd found him. So I stood quietly by as he looked up, speaking to the branches, the sleek white skin of his neck tender as the bellies of the wriggling fish Uncle Pete reeled out of the Eno to slit open lengthwise. Ginx was at the end of the story, saying, "Sister Lucca would die without B.J. and Momma." It was an old story, made up quickly one afternoon when Ginx was particularly restless. But there it was, having been shut away, carefully tended, too necessary. Rubbing his forehead with the heel of his hand, my brother continued, "Sister Lucca tried to jump from the branch of her birch tree, but she slipped." He breathed. "B.J. caught her," he said. "B.J. caught her in his own two arms." Ginx wrapped his arms around his chest, cradling himself and repeating these words until I was crying, muffling my sobs as he furiously insisted, "He loves her!" I scuffed at the dirt and leaves, but my brother did not turn around.

Instead of listening to Billy, who was actually speaking directly to me for the first time in almost three years, I was thinking how, if Ginx had turned then, if he had asked me to tell that story again, I would have stayed out in those woods. I would have tried to tell the story the way he wanted it told.

"I want you to write love letters," Billy abruptly informed me. "I'll sell them at Cresset Christian. You know, Morgan-Lee, a business. Nothing complicated. I'll run over to my grandma's, and we can meet in the tree house once a week." He spoke quickly.

"Oh," I said, not understanding. His one good eye stared at my mouth. I told him that Dana had shown me how to write secret messages using lemon juice. "The paper looks totally blank until you bring it near fire," I explained. "That's when the lemon juice turns brown so you can read whatever's written there, like—"

Billy cut me off. "These letters aren't secret that way." He took in a sharp breath. We were no longer playmates; time had passed. He was making this perfectly clear.

I clenched my jaw. "How do you know I can write love letters?"

Instead of answering, Billy just nodded and cleared his throat. "I'll take notes from the clients. All you have to do is include the information I get for you. You know, if the girl or boy likes particular things or, if they're already together, the special moments they've spent. Not hard. We'll split the profits." I looked at him then, longer than I wanted to. His left eye lingered just enough for me to see how cold and gray it was, the knowledge it carried. If we'd been standing very close, in a way I never stood with anyone, I would have confessed that I was the fire over which Ginx's soul became less blank, more legible.

"Let me clarify," Billy stated, still speaking like a small adult. "I'm not asking you to be friends. I'm talking here about a business."

I shrugged. "Whatever," I said.

So when Billy and his mother moved out of Old Mrs. Dean's house and went to live with Amos in the small green house where Louis Pritchard and his sister used to live, Billy transferred to Cresset Christian Academy. He began by targeting a few influential kids in the school. He told me he'd explained to them that he'd met an old woman living down by the river, that she was still grieving over her husband who had died in World War II. The man had been her only lover before or since that war because it was impossible for her to love another. Billy would go on to explain that perfect love does not die, it keeps flowing. There was nothing else to do with all her leftover love but write letters for other people, love letters. She sold them to support herself. This last part, he explained, would appeal to a Christian sense of charity.

I laughed during our first business session in the tree house when Billy told me all this, and I said he made his old woman sound like a milk cow that would keep producing milk for years and years just as long as someone kept tugging at her teats. I imagined the old lady writing letter after letter, the wound of her love constantly pouring forth, unable to scab or scar. "Nobody can believe that," I said.

"Christian kids are a lot more gullible," was all Billy replied. He handed me notes on a boy named Marvin who was in love with a girl, Julie. A few days later, he read the letter I handed him. "This is perfect," he said. I couldn't help smiling.

So we had a business. Mostly, boys bought letters to send to girls they had crushes on or wanted to keep loving: Valentine's Day stuff, birthdays, one-month or one-year "going out" anniversaries, Christmas letters.

"Love letters," Billy said. "That's what makes money." I remembered one afternoon in the girls' bathroom at school. I opened the door and saw a group of giggling girls crowded around Carole Waits. As I walked past them, I saw Carole was pulling open the collar of her shirt to expose a bruise, round and precise as the kind of mark Ginx would leave on me. I quickly shut the door to my stall and overheard the whole thing as I peed. "Jimmy just sucked and sucked!" she said gleefully. "Did it for near a half hour." Jimmy Riggs was tall and squawked when he spoke. I thought of Carole's ugly purple insides squirming and slipping toward his wriggling lips. I couldn't understand why she would ever want to show such a thing to anyone.

No boy at school had ever loved me, so I wondered what could excite a girl over the kind of letters I wrote. Maybe it was the thought of the old woman near the river, the boyfriend carefully detailing his love as Billy took notes, or maybe it had to do with the contrast between the transaction of money and a grief that occurred long before any of us were born. I laughed at how other kids would picture it: Billy running to the old woman's house through the night, undetected, bearing information he'd pick up later as a fully composed letter. Pretty soon, we started getting one or two requests a week. Over the summer between eighth and ninth grades, I wrote three a week so we'd have a stockpile to draw from come fall. That way, the majority of the work was already done and we just had to doctor the letters according to the needs of particular clients. So, throughout ninth grade, Billy and I worked together, barely friends, more business associates.

The summer between our ninth and tenth grades, we organized it so that every Thursday I'd continue bringing him his three letters. He appreciated how smoothly I landed, the letters in my hand, the light between us. For Billy, the whole picture counted. He wanted our setting to be perfect, the alternate hot and cool in the air, the creaking of the boards, my movements. He was aware, alert to any skewed detail that might threaten our ritual. He liked precision, so I made a point of landing as well as possible, my legs folding under me like large wings. I waited for him to smile, which he didn't do until he was holding all three letters.

"Here's to a new summer," Billy said, arching his back to slide a hand into his front pocket and pull out the money. Tugging each bill smooth, he counted out loud, as if he did not know that he had exactly three dollars, as if I'd ever brought him anything but three letters.

I looked at him, his wandering eye by the light of our

candle managing for a few seconds to look straight as a normal eye, then slipping off again toward the dark. His face was haggard from lack of sleep. Ever since his mother's marriage, Billy rarely slept more than four or five hours a night.

I studied his face, his worries so unforgiving they shot him out of bed and into the stingy first light of morning. I pressed my hands against the plywood floor of the tree house. The wood felt good: warm and human. He passed a finger through the candle's flame. Outside in the long grass, crickets were sawing their legs together. Lightning bugs lit up in flashes.

"This will be our second summer in business. We've got it down to a science now," Billy said, stretching his legs out and shaking open one of the letters I'd just handed him. "Let's check the merchandise." He held it near the candlelight. *"Among the mountains there is you,"* he read out loud. Billy always did me the courtesy of reading the first line aloud so I'd know to which letter he would be referring when he began his critique. I sat back on my heels and watched him as he read, his bad eye traveling inward for the task. *I could find you anywhere,* was my second line. During a reading, Billy would not be interrupted. He read the way a hungry person might eat, unable to judge the meal until it was over. *I swallow my sobs,* was the secret line of that letter, a line beautifully woven within a paragraph crafted for sentimentality. Billy cleared his throat and went on to the second letter. *"The fragrance of your neck when you are near,"* he read. When he was done, he folded that letter as well.

"How does a summer end without you?" he read. I exhaled with relief when he put the first two on the TO SELL pile. His good eye remained focused.

Billy's face was cavernous: the sockets too deep, the cheeks sunken, and the nose slightly curved. *"When my sister turned twelve, she cut the summer out of her hair and told me not to enter her room without knocking."* I'd taken that line directly from a poem I'd read in one of our mother's books. The second line began, *I think of you.* Billy's roaming eye was the only one of his features moving away from the candle, the cushion, the letters.

"This one won't work," he said, in reference to the third letter. "You can't sell love letters with no love in them, Morgan-Lee."

I held my ankles. The remark was unfair.

"No love?" I asked. "What do you want me to do, spell it out?" I felt anger coming on, especially as Billy remained unwavering. Ever since our business picked up, Billy had become harder, more driven. "You want flower crap and happy faces?" I asked, clutching my ankles so tightly that it hurt.

"Other kids like flower crap," he informed me, his smile gentle only for an instant—a *nanosecond,* as Ginx would say, meaning one billionth of a second, or a dwarfed second, a fragment of time. I bit my lip, snatched back my letter, folded it, and slipped it into my pocket. I had to concede that he was right. Other kids did like flower crap, and business is business.

Billy pulled at the collar of his T-shirt; then he took the two salable letters, folded them neatly, and put them in his shirt pocket. I wondered how it was that other girls my age made sense of the rich smell of summer grass, the bluing of the light, a sister blundering into womanhood, a mother who could never get enough sleep. How did they explain the connection between these things? How did their lives go on?

"I guess I should go," I finally said. Billy didn't answer. He just leaned to the side and reached behind the rolled-up sleeping bag. He then did what I had never expected to see again. My face went hot. Billy slid a small white plate close up to the candle so I could see the smattering of firefly carcasses he had collected just for me.

"I saved mine," he whispered as he picked up the candle and moved its flame over the bodies. He was careful not to look at me; he knew how I was. The wings crackled under the fire and hot wax drippings till our candle died. My breath stuttered over my ribs. "To the beginning of summer," he said, through the warm dark. I touched the rim of the plate as he held it. There are so few times when someone does exactly the right thing.

"To summer," I repeated. We sat quietly for a little bit; then I told him it was time for me to go.

"All right," he said.

"All right," I said, wondering what it would be like to remain sitting across from Billy and put business aside. But it was time to go. Without another word, I squirmed toward the hole and onto the ladder, wondering if a day might come when we would meet and I could tell him about my private sentences. I began down the ladder, foot over foot. Or maybe I'd write a letter filled only with my sentences, a letter just for Billy. Once at the bottom of the ladder, I felt light, the way I sometimes felt after first waking up, before remembering the things to be done or all the things I'd left undone. *Aduage,* I whispered, using the word as my own.

TIME

OUR MOTHER WAS sitting on the terrace the morning of my fourteenth birthday, sipping at a tall glass of iced chamomile tea and reading a hardcover library book, her hair pulled into a heavy bun. I stood in front of her.

"Thank you for the journal and the stationery," I said. That morning, she'd left a pale blue *Anything Book* and a packet of pink stationery on my desk.

"Happy birthday!" She raised her mug and toasted. "To June eighteenth!" She had arranged the chairs so she could rest her legs. We both studied her slender feet, pale and as thickly veined as two expensive slices of blue cheese.

"Not till eight-seventeen this evening," I reminded her; Ginx and I were particular about time.

"I should know," she snapped. "I was there, wasn't I?" Our

mother didn't see me nod. She sipped more at her chamomile, the ice cubes jingling like wind chimes. She breathed deeply, the way she'd learned to do. I knew she was making an effort not to let the morning get twisted and go enormously wrong, that she wanted my fourteenth birthday to be a success. I waited. "I thought maybe we'd go on a picnic," she offered, remembering to smile. "Oh, you're growing up."

"Sure." I wondered if she'd forgotten that her student from Durham Community College was supposed to come over. Our mother had recently put up advertisements for students needing private tutorials in English. I decided not to remind her that her lesson was supposed to be that evening. Our mother did not like to be reminded of her responsibilities.

"I have that Italian woman coming to the house at seven-thirty for tutoring," she said triumphantly, "so we'll go at two-thirty. That way we can have lunch and supper all in one this afternoon and you-all can just have a snack this evening, nothing that needs much preparation on my part." She took the rest of her tea down in gulps and then patted the chair's metal armrest. "But it does mean that I have to prepare both the food and the lesson before we go out."

"Okay, Momma," I said. She picked up her book again, slicing it open to the right page. Our mother's books had worn corners and pages underlined by some previous reader. Besides some poetry now and then, the books were rarely of use to me. Ever since I'd begun doing business, I studied

Aunt Lois's romance novels to see how men loved women and vice versa, the language involved. I read her religious self-help books on relationships and marriage. Sometimes I stole a sentence or two for my letters: research material.

"At two-thirty, then," our mother confirmed.

I saw our father come out of the house. He sneaked across the terrace, signaling me to be quiet. I smiled. Our mother did not know he was there till he reached forward and cupped a hand over her right earlobe.

"Ouch!" she said, continuing to read.

"Well, hello to you too," our father exclaimed, winking at me. Aunt Lois had once told me, "When they first met, he couldn't see the sun for loving her." I tried to imagine our father, his face turned toward a bright sky, love filling his eyes rather than sunlight, but it was impossible. When he looked at our mother, our father's face was nothing but smiling and patient. "Your father is a patient man," our mother would exclaim, but the way she said it took patience down a notch below other virtues. "So *patient*," she would repeat. He kissed her cheek, and it was clear how completely they misunderstood each other.

Just as I was wondering if I should tell him about the picnic or let our mother do so, she looked up and announced, "At two-thirty, Carl, I thought we'd go to the Eno for a picnic. We'll sing 'Happy Birthday.'"

"That's a good idea." His hand was resting on the back of her chair. He had given me my birthday present a few days earlier, a blue canvas school bag, which would wait out the summer in my closet. "Okay," our father said more quietly, removing his hand. "We will celebrate by the Eno."

At two-thirty, the family was headed down toward the river, our mother tromping ahead of us, our father and Ginx following behind, and Dana walking beside me. "You know there's a new boy working at Johnny Johnson's?" my sister asked. "Did you know that, Morgan-Lee?"

"Yeah," Ginx shouted. "Yeah, Aunt Lois said a new boy's working there."

"Oh," I said. "I think his sister's maybe in my class."

Dana didn't seem to have heard. "His name's Jacob, and I met him the other day at Myra's house. He works with Myra's big brother—been working there since April."

Our mother's steps slowed; then she halted, letting us pass as she looked up at a bird squawking overhead. Our father was telling Ginx about how the cardinal, the North Carolina state bird, got its name.

"So," I said to my sister. "So what about him?"

Dana shook her sleek head. "He's like about sixteen. He doesn't go to school. Just works up there, and Myra told me he saved a man. A car fell down on one of the garage men, and Jacob picked it up! He picked up the whole side of the car so the man could get out."

"No one has to go to school at sixteen," Ginx shouted to Dana, over our father's talk. "No one."

"That's not what I'm talking about, Ginx," Dana complained.

"Look, there's a cardinal right there!" Our father pointed to the sky. Ginx looked up.

"He is a good man; that is what can be said about your daddy," our aunt once told me about our father. It was true. He was slow to anger and made a real effort to think about an argument from all points of view. In winter, he was the one who went outside to scrape the car clean and spread salt on the driveway. Without complaint, he cooked and cleaned when our mother was too tired. He was the one who helped Dana with her math homework and primed her for her spelling bees. Our father had worked his way through a doctoral degree in education and spent his free time reading; this, I knew, was to be admired.

"Jacob picked up a whole car, and Johnny Johnson said he's gonna be Mechanic of the Month. Can you imagine?" she asked. I kicked a stone. The brambles on the side of the trail were already turning brown and dry, but in the early summer they produced dew berries as big as a hand, so big our father would joke that it'd only take three or four to make a pie.

"Morgan-Lee," our mother called out. I watched her back. She'd changed into our father's blue painting shirt, and it hung below her hips. She was wearing jeans, but even dressed like that she was beautiful. "Morgan-Lee, you couldn't possibly remember when you were a tiny baby and I'd bring you and Ginx down to the river behind our house and how wonderful that was."

"Oh, no, Momma, no," I said, as softly as possible, so as not to disappoint or interrupt this good memory of hers. She pulled the band out of her ponytail so her hair fell dark and loose, and I felt a note of happiness reverberate in my chest, flat and steady as Ginx's hum. It had been a long time since we'd been all together heading toward the river.

"It was after the fever," our mother said. "All I wanted to do was to get to the cool water. That fever left me tired; God, I was tired! It got so bad I could barely remember my own name."

"She did," our father recalled. "She used to take you-all to the river—you and Ginx."

"You'd been sick, Momma," Ginx piped up, as if she'd forgotten the right word.

My sister kicked a stone, and I was thankful when our mother included her, which she often forgot to do. "By the time Dana came along," she said, "we'd stopped going to the Eno, really. The few times we did go, I'd wrap Dana up in a beautiful white blanket Aunt Lois had given me when Ginx was born." As she spoke, I felt the swelling distance of the past. "There was," our mother began, then repeated, "there was Ginx's beautiful baby skin. I let him run around naked because he had this gorgeous abdomen with fresh white skin. Sometimes I'd tell people that he wasn't born at all, but dug up from way down under the compost, his skin was that fresh and white and new." Ginx sped up, humming his note, and I realized for the first time that even our mother had felt compelled to explain his beauty. I looked at the ground. The forest thickened as we walked, the underbrush still green, the long stems of wild onions visible now through the brambles. I wondered what it was like to be beautiful. Billy had once said I was beautiful. For a whole week, I repeated the word to myself, and it felt good, though I knew it was stolen and not true.

"I let Ginx run naked," our mother mused again, more to herself.

"Eww!" Dana exclaimed.

Ginx walked fast, but nevertheless one hand went up to cover his ear against the intimacy of the conversation.

"That seems very long ago," our father remarked. He had found a good walking stick and was whacking at the grass and bushes to scare any snakes away.

"There's a good spot!" I exclaimed, pointing aimlessly. The past was becoming difficult. I cut in front of our mother, ran to a place, and knelt there, looking down the bank to my favorite rock by the water.

"Fine," our mother breathed as she approached. She set the basket in the tall grass and rubbed her hands. "It is beautiful here."

Ginx spread the blue blanket before me.

"Morgan-Lee's fourteen today," our father said. Then, unable to leave the past alone, he added, "I'll never forget the day you were born, the hottest June day in my memory. Hotter even than the worst of August." He did not sit down with the rest of us but crouched over the blanket. "So hot your mother was melting, and I had to bring a bunch of wet rags for our drive to the hospital, even with the air conditioner up full blast." Ginx started humming purposefully off key.

"Let's eat," our mother suggested. Our father looked at her, blinking.

"I'm starving," Dana announced, leaning hungrily toward the covered basket. Our mother hesitated. Dana opened the basket and found cheese and lettuce sandwiches.

"Oh, Dana, I'm sorry, I forgot you don't like cheese sandwiches," she quickly confessed.

"All there is for me is fruit?" Dana asked, dismayed, as she sat back on her heels, dutifully emptying the basket anyway. She loved picnics when our aunt packed them: fried chicken and lemon pies and potato salad. Nonetheless, my sister carefully placed each fruit in the middle of the blanket. Ginx grabbed a peach and bit into it so deeply that the juice flooded down his chin. I took a bunch of purple grapes and broke the vine to share them with our father. Our mother picked up a dark red apple, and Dana took a banana. We didn't speak. There was a breeze by the river, so the leaves shivered, making the sunlight dance. Ginx threw his pit into the water. He immediately grabbed a green pear, looked at me, and gnawed. Our mother studied the sky. Our father methodically spit the small grape seeds into the palm of his hand. I didn't know it then, but one day holding a handful of plump purple grapes would remind me of my fourteenth birthday picnic by the river, and that fruit would never simply be itself again. But at the time, the grapes were sweet and cold, tasting only good, reminding me of nothing, so I popped them in my mouth and chewed, bitter seeds and all.

"Myra told me that her brother told her that Jacob is the best mechanic he'd seen in a long while, and definitely the best for his age," Dana went on, unwilling to let her topic go.

"Dana," our mother said, taking in a breath, signifying that she had reached her limit, "that's really enough."

My sister looked at her banana. Myra had recently instructed Dana to break off pieces of a banana rather than eat it head-on. "Otherwise, it can make people think you are doing something nasty."

We chewed for a while in silence till Ginx announced, "Time for frog hunting." He crouched to throw the pear core into the water.

"You have always been a good hunter, Ginxy," our mother told him, her smile including only the two of them.

"You should try out for a sport in school," our father proposed. "There are plenty of things you might like."

"Some fathers say, 'You *must* try out'!" Dana added.

"Must," I whispered. *"Must, must, must,"* I repeated. It was a word I could say again and again in front of the mirror, the kind of word that lost all meaning in its repetition.

"Crust," Ginx rhymed, mid-chew.

Ginx and I had always gone to the Eno to frog hunt, build rafts, and then lie on the bank. My brother could lie still for hours, humming the same flat note, me beside him. Sometimes I'd order him to cut it out, and he'd be silent for a while, but pretty soon he'd begin his litany of soft or hard words, depending on how he felt. I, too, could hold perfectly still for hours, could stretch my arms out like a scarecrow and lie back listening to Ginx pulling out the long blades of grass, one, two, three, regular as rain. I could go down to the river and watch without blinking as he strangled frogs or pulled on worms till they popped apart. I would say a word, and Ginx would find its rhyme.

But other days he was quiet. "Kids at school don't like me," he told me once, on a day in January when school was canceled due to an ice storm. We were sitting on our living room couch drinking hot chocolate that Dana had prepared and looking out the window at cars, grass, and tree branches, all encased in ice. No one could go anywhere, and I thought about our mother's advice regarding efficiency and progress and how our chances for success were better if we strove for both. I wondered if this applied to a day in which everything was frozen. I decided it didn't, and I would therefore not care that she'd consider it a waste of time to read Aunt Lois's relationship books and look for sentences around which to build my letters.

"It's true, you don't have any friends at school," I confirmed, watching as he picked at a black spot on the window. "People think you are strange, Ginx." He nodded. In eighth grade, a boy had peed in Ginx's lunchbox, and a group of kids had watched as Ginx methodically emptied that lunchbox of its contents and proceeded to eat whatever had been wrapped in plastic and not gotten wet. Adam Greene threw a wad of gum at the back of my brother's head, but he'd kept on eating. I know all this because I was sitting at a table in the far back corner of the cafeteria, losing my faith in the Lord. I thought that if God really was like Aunt Lois said, He would lift Ginx up, float him to the ceiling, and when the kids looked up they would see clear through his skin and bones to the places within him where he stored the logic behind what he would touch and what he would not. They would know that he, more than anyone, was aware of where germs were, what should be listened to, what looked at. A God would never have been surveying His earth from above and overlooked that crowded cafeteria with the large table empty of anyone except Ginx, who sat there inspecting his food for pee. A God would not have folded His hands and watched my brother chew and shrug, trying to avoid the staring. God would have seen the gum wad stick for a few seconds to the back of Ginx's head and then drop off onto the floor while the group of kids behind him giggled and shrieked and the girls made vomiting noises and began throwing away their own lunches. The only kindness God showed us was letting all this happen before Dana reached junior high.

"Yeah, it's true," Ginx said. "Maybe you could just tell me a few things so that other people wouldn't be able to tell that I'm strange." He was sitting cross-legged on one side of the couch, and I was on the other. The black spot was gone from the window, but he continued to rub there nonetheless. Although he often forgot to wash himself, he was good at cleaning objects. His clothes were put away in labeled drawers, and he made his bed in the morning with hospital corners.

"People will always be able to tell you're strange," I said. "There's no way to hide it."

"But you hide it, Morgan-Lee. How do you hide it?" Ginx wasn't being cruel, which made the question worse. "We're both strange," he said, more quietly.

I looked away, but I decided to tell him the truth. "I listen to how people say stuff and try to imitate it. Listen to Aunt Lois or Myra or whatever and try making sentences the way they do when I am around other people. But it takes practice."

He rested his mug of hot chocolate on his knee, so he vaguely resembled one of those reporters from the evening news shows that Aunt Lois and Uncle Pete watched, the kind that sat in comfortable chairs near fireplaces and interviewed child geniuses or people dying of rare diseases. I wondered what Ginx would do when he grew up. I wondered what I would do. But I didn't want to think about growing up.

"Let's play Crazy Eights," I suggested, slipping from the couch to the floor and opening the small drawer in the coffee table where we kept our cards.

"Sure." Ginx pulled over a square coaster and placed his cup in the exact middle. "That's great," he said, as any brother might have said on a day home from school. "Then we can play poker."

⌒

When the fruit was finished, our father packed away all the stems and cores and told us that we had close to an hour to frog hunt before we'd be heading back to the house. "Go on now, kids," he told us.

Our mother used to love Ginx's happiness when we came back from hunting, his lovely face giddy as he watched me spin around like a helicopter till I eventually wobbled and fell to the ground in dizziness. She would sit on our terrace and laugh, and I hoped that the sunlight funneled into those moments, somehow capturing them in her mind so she would remember everything clearly, perhaps even the fact that I had been there too.

Most often, though, Ginx and I sat alone on the riverbank after a hunt. "Morgan-Lee," he used to say, "you are my best friend."

"Yes," I would answer, without doubt, "I know." Ginx would take my hand, his wiry, unsure fingers clinging too tightly. My brother would not hold anyone's hand but mine. I knew how much it cost him to be touched, so even though my hand hurt, I never let on. We'd walk down Margaret

Lane and back again. "Aren't they sweet?" Aunt Lois used to exclaim when she deemed us still young enough for holding hands. Then one day she shook her head, scowling at our joined fingers, the single fist between us. "Missy," she once warned our mother, "careful how you raise these children. They're growing up."

"Up, up, and away," was our mother's answer, as if reciting from a nursery rhyme we all knew by heart. "Up, up, up, and away!"

"So, there we are." Our mother sighed as the light through the trees fingered her hair. "You get the frogs. I'm going to nap." She leaned first on one elbow, then slowly stretched to lie on her back, the sleeve of her shirt pulled up to expose a long forearm, which she crossed over her face to shield her eyes.

"It's nice out here," our father said. "A good place for a birthday party."

"We have to go where the water is still," Ginx whispered, as if our mother had fallen instantly asleep. Dana looked from me to Ginx. It had been a long time since my sister had gone frog hunting.

"Come with us, Dana," I said. "Your present to me."

"Oh," our father said, "don't go yet, we haven't sung 'Happy Birthday.'"

"That's okay, Poppa," I said, gently as I could.

"But I got you a gift, Morgan-Lee. It's at the house, cross my heart," Dana protested. It wasn't true. My sister did not like to waste her allowance money on Ginx and me.

"Come on," Ginx encouraged. "Please." Dana looked away without answering, which I took as a yes.

"Great," I said.

"All right, have fun, but don't be too long," our father told us, sitting on the grass beside our mother's blanket.

We walked down the riverbank in the direction of the frogs. "You'll get a big one, Ginx," Dana piped up from behind, so that I knew she was with us, that we were all three together.

"There, down there," he told us, pointing. We crawled down the bank.

"Here," Ginx said, as we reached the stagnant pool that had been left after the river flooded in early April. By now it was stinking, but Dana did not comment. "Be very quiet," Ginx warned us, finger to his mouth like a kindergarten teacher. My brother hunched over the shallow pool and then stepped out onto a stone. Dana and I did not move. I was relieved, believing as I always had that the three of us would be safe from any harm if we stayed together in a place where the woods and the water and the *wickety-wicks* of the birds did not fade. As long as we could stay far away from parking lots of teenage boys with smooth hair and girls with kissable mouths. Dana shrugged but kept her eyes on Ginx, who had stepped out to stand rigidly above that mossy water like a boy about to risk everything. I clasped my hands behind my back.

We waited that way for a long time. Then Ginx stood suddenly straight, lurched forward, and plunged his hands into the water. He slipped, stepped back quickly, and called out, "Heey!" his arms shooting straight up.

"Eww!" Dana cried, as the water splashed over us.

The frog, squeezed between Ginx's bony fingers, let out a wretched plea.

"I got him!" Ginx's stare upward did not waver, his eyes narrowing against the sunlight, his mouth blissful as if the frog had just fallen from the sky and he had caught it.

"Let it go!" Dana pleaded miserably.

"You haven't been frog hunting for a long time," I reminded her.

"Let it go, Ginx," she said again, as if she had never known how it worked. I felt sorry for Dana, but she had known once. She had allowed herself to forget.

"I caught him!" Ginx said with tenderness, his face turned upward, arms toward the sky, the cords of his neck strung so tightly that their music would have echoed long into sunset had I been able to reach out and strum.

The frog kicked against Ginx's wrists, cascading water over his hands, which dribbled onto his mouth and down his chin. The frog would hold very still and then kick again, hard. Soon, Dana was absolutely silent beside me. I wished she could remember how things worked instead of having to relearn these lessons all at once, but then again, I figured, perhaps it was for the best. Maybe some people just cannot see the world until it is kicking and wriggling and dying in their faces. They become sick. It was better for Dana to learn about cruelty earlier rather than later. I had tried to teach her years ago, but she must not have understood. She would have to take her horror however it came. There was little I could do.

The kicking became so weak that Ginx must have felt only soft pulses against his wrists.

"Throw it back, Ginx," Dana begged again, as if it weren't already too late.

Ginx looked at Dana. He had the cartoon face of a happy boy. The caption would have read, *This is a happy boy.*

"Throw it back," Dana begged again, hand cupped over her mouth to keep from vomiting, the light catching her hair just right.

"*Him,* Dana," Ginx corrected, because we were in his domain now. "I will throw *him* back," Ginx promised, quiet as a mother mending a small child's scrape. "I will throw him back."

"Don't worry, Dana," I said. Ginx would have wanted to bury the frog, but he could be generous in a way that Dana and I were not and gave up certain pleasures.

"Okay," Ginx said, holding the body in only one hand and then tossing the frog behind him so it splatted against the muddy bank, then slipped into the pool. "It's okay, Dana. Don't worry," my brother said, looking only at her.

"He'll save himself," I said. But even the simplest lie was too difficult for my brother.

"Not always," Ginx cut in. "But I hope this one will. Okay, Dana? Please?"

She nodded and wiped her eyes with the hem of her shirt.

"Go to the rock and talk to each other," Ginx suggested brightly, pointing. "The water's low. Go on, now," he said.

"Okay," Dana responded, relieved. I put my arm over her shoulder in order to turn her, because dead bodies sink into water at first but then they pop to the surface and float. I pulled her to me the way girls at school did when another girl was upset. Dana sniffled and looked at me with surprise. I did not avoid other people the way Ginx did, but it was still rare that I ever touched anyone on purpose.

I guided Dana away from Ginx. Then we slipped apart, she following behind me. A wind picked up, so the air was perfect, a little cool, full of decay. There were butterflies at the Eno, butterflies that were big and unafraid. When I was younger, I'd actually been frightened of these butterflies because it didn't seem natural for anything that beautiful and fragile to fly so close to my face or land on the backs of my hands. I knew that boys would net them just to pin their colored wings to the thick pages of a scrapbook.

Dana and I walked to where the river bent. A tree had fallen so that it bridged the water to my rock. We wouldn't even have to get wet. I'd only ever sat there alone, so for a second I hesitated, but then I said, "Come on, Dana." I took the lead, balancing foot over foot across the tree like a tightrope walker. "Let's sit on the rock." Dana followed, crawling, as I hopped onto the rock and sat to dangle my feet, skimming the water with the soles of my tennis shoes. She carefully lowered herself to sit beside me, dry-eyed and thoughtful. We were silent for a while, then she turned to me.

"Do you think we'll ever get married?" she asked.

"I guess," I said, then spoke more loudly. "I mean, you will. I could never live with someone like that." I did not know how to make the answer simple, one that she would understand.

I decided to try. If we had been anywhere else—Aunt Lois's house, our yard, anywhere—I would have just told her, "I won't marry." But I wanted to explain what I thought because it seemed there was hope that Dana would not give up on Ginx and me so easily if she understood. But I was not sure how to begin.

"Dana, I only know Ginx. I don't know any of the boys at church or at school. You say something like *frog* or *water* to them, and they don't know that you also mean skin about to burst, and that ripping sound in the frog's croak because there is no more air for him." I went on to explain to her about Ginx. "See, Ginx knows it's terrible to hurt live beings. He cannot help it if sometimes he has to hurt something. There are times he has to, and that's how it is. He's not as weird as you think. You have to understand his system, the way he does stuff. You can't love someone unless you understand that." I stopped myself for a second, avoiding Dana's face so as not to see her confusion. I knew I was telling it wrong but insisted on going on. "Dana, it's just an example, but let's say the man I marry doesn't know what *river* or *frog* mean to me—and if I don't know what *river* or *frog* mean to him, how're we supposed to love each other if we don't even know each other?"

Dana sucked in her lip, and I was sorry I'd tried to explain what I thought about love. We sat silent a few minutes studying the river, how the lines of current intersected, what the water carried. Then she looked at me, brightening.

"Well, maybe you can find someone like that one day."

"No, Dana," I said, a tiny pang in my chest. "I'm not gonna get married."

"Well, I am," she asserted, "and I hope he's never caught a frog before in all his life. I hope he's never played in or even seen this nasty, icky river." She splashed up water with the toe of her shoe. A big yellow butterfly landed in the space between our hands.

"Oh," I responded, keeping careful watch over the butterfly. "Anyone in particular?" She looked at me.

"Okay," she said, "but you gotta promise not to tell."

Her dark eyes invested themselves in my face, her breath working in and out, as if carefully marking off the time we had left till our ways would inevitably part. I wasn't sure I wanted to promise anything.

She studied my face. "I actually saw Jacob again. Yesterday. I went with Myra over to Johnny Johnson's. Jacob was working with Eric in back, and Myra and I saw him."

"Is that it?" I asked.

"No," she said, hurt. "I have a crush on him. He started working when he was eleven years old back in Asheville. He quit school early. That's why I said before that he was sixteen; I didn't want Poppa to get him in trouble or anything about school. He's really fifteen, and he isn't gonna go back. He's older than me, but not by that much. I mean, three years isn't that much older, and girls mature faster anyway."

"Fine," I said. "That's good." I was trying to be gentle, but her face darkened.

"Gawd! I'm sorry I even told you." Dana looked away from me and up the river. She banged her shoe against our rock, but the butterfly between us still did not move, so I finally had to shoo it away with a small stick.

"I told you, Dana, I've seen his sister. She's in my grade. She started coming to school back in April." I bit my lip and then added, "I mean, she couldn't have come to school more than four or five times. The first day, Mrs. McKee told the class to welcome her; then, when a few weeks went by without her showing up, Mrs. McKee started just skipping right over her name at roll call." I remembered that she had a long black braid and never said much. "Weird-looking," I told Dana.

"What's her name?" Dana asked.

"Sweety-Boy," I said.

She brightened. "Maybe you could get to be friends with her. You know, it's not like you have a lot of friends to hang out with or anything, Morgan-Lee." I let the comment go. I had friends. Not really anyone I spoke to or spent time with, but surely I had friends. The sun retracted.

"Dana, Morgan-Lee, Ginxy!" It was our father's voice, but it seemed to come from a place far in the distance toward which I was not eager to return. We sat quietly a few minutes longer, until he called again.

"What is it, Dana?" I asked her, because her expression had grown strange.

"Morgan-Lee," she said, sitting very still and speaking firmly, "you know what I think about you and Ginx and me? This's what I really think," she began, looking straight at me. For Dana to speak that way was as rare as my slipping an arm around someone's shoulder. She wanted to tell me something. But I messed it up, missed it.

"Come on, let's get out of here," I said, quickly hopping up. I didn't realize it then, but her words had startled me, making me scared the way I'd get as a little kid when those butterflies came unnaturally close, when they'd brush my face or land too freely on the backs of my hands. I walked across the tree again and let her follow behind. I scrambled up the bank, Dana still following me. "Come on, Dana," I said, but I did not slow down.

When we reached our picnic spot, Ginx was already there.

"Here you are," our father said.

"Morgan-Lee," my brother piped up. He was sitting next to our mother, who had awakened. I shrugged. "It's time to go," Ginx said. I knew that my brother had a birthday present in store for me. We no longer mentioned presents to each other in front of our parents so that we could give them in private.

Our father packed the picnic basket, and we set off toward home.

"Did you have a good birthday?" our mother asked.

"Yes," I told her, "thank you."

"Oh," she said, "I'm glad. I'm glad. We'll go to Lois and Pete's this evening for cake, but it's good we had some family time, isn't it?"

"Yes," I agreed.

⌇

When we got back from the river, Ginx sat in the living room and read. I went to my room. At seven-thirty, he knocked on my door and told me to follow him. "I don't know if I want to," I said, teasing him.

My brother smiled. "Out to the tree, just to see something. Don't you want to see something, Morgan-Lee? Discover something by accident?" he asked. Our pine tree was on the otherwise empty property facing Aunt Lois and Uncle Pete's house. Uncle Pete had somehow gotten ahold of that property, and then he bought a boat that he'd spent his weekends refurbishing. In order to have enough space, he'd taken down the trees growing on that little plot of land, all except the big pine tree. After Uncle Pete sold the boat and no longer used the land, Ginx and I claimed it as our own. "I started digging out near the pine," he told me when we got outside.

I nodded.

"By accident," he said.

"It's not by accident if you started digging there," I instructed. But I knew what he meant. Accidents were good; after all, I'd found the Luccas by accident.

My brother winced and smiled. "Come on." I followed him to the property on the other side of the cul de sac; it was overgrown with wild onions and flowers. I noticed that our tree looked dry and bent, and as we approached I saw that Uncle Pete's shovel lay in the grass. I looked from the large hole to my brother. Ginx's body was supple as a girl's, his chest and hands pale, his face a little pinkish from the sun. I stopped beside him as he leaned against the tree, his slender shadow on the grass almost matching the tree's shadow. He pointed, so I looked back at the hole.

"Nothing should happen to the world," he informed me, stroking his chin, "but just in case it does, Morgan-Lee, I have decided to build a bomb shelter for us. A pit." I looked at the pit. He had marked out the complete square of space that he planned on digging up, just as our father and Uncle Pete had done when they'd built our terrace. He saw that I was staring. "It's for your birthday." He tried again. "It won't be all that big, even when I'm finished," he conceded, "but it'll do for two." I exhaled. "I still have lots of work left, I know. But I do not foresee a nuclear war anytime soon." He began tracing small squares with the tip of his left shoe.

"What about Dana?" I asked quickly. "What about Momma and Poppa?"

Ginx continued to stroke his chin, and his breathing roughened. He was not looking directly at anything. "There most likely will not be a war," he told me, "but I will stock up with cans of food just in case."

"But what if there is?" I pressed on, feeling panicked.

My brother watched me. He dropped the hand from his face and clenched his jaw like a brave sergeant in the midst of an untenable situation. "There is only room for two," he repeated loudly, sticking to the facts, watching as I considered how Dana, our mother, our father, Uncle Pete, and Aunt Lois would die, choking and screaming in poisonous gases while Ginx and I huddled underground against our cans of stewed tomatoes, peaches, and ravioli. "I will put in a carpet," he added brightly. "We will have one chair and will take turns sitting in it; I really think it is necessary to have a chair, but the space won't fit more than one. More than one chair won't work. I thought about it, Morgan-Lee. Just too small." He looked angrily at the pit, and I knew that he, too, was thinking about our family's death, but he had to contend with the reality of the shelter's dimensions as well as his own digging capabilities. "There's only so much one person can do," he told me quietly. *"Shoot."*

"What about light?" I asked. He nodded, his face not complying with the evening light; it demanded shadows in certain places, pooled the sunlight at the tips of his cheekbones and along the generous, pale curve of his forehead. He pushed back a dark tuft of hair. I swallowed.

"Candles," he answered. "Mostly candles. I'll have a bookshelf, you know. And we can stack the candles like logs: candles and candles and candles. White, probably. The light from them is really pretty good, and anyway we'll be sleeping, too. We should sleep about nine hours, anyway, but with nothing to do it might be more like ten or twelve or even thirteen." He paused and fretted. "Then I'll have a flashlight too, for when the candles become boring or burn too fast." My brother took a step backward. He was rubbing his right thigh: up, down, up, down. He shifted his weight. "But it takes a long time to get bored of candles. Candles burn all different." He rocked gently forward and back again. "Listen." He whispered even though no one was in sight. "I stocked an Emergency Kit and hid it under the television stand in the living room: a hairbrush, clean underwear, and two T-shirts. Just in case there's no warning. In case the missiles are close to hitting and no one knows till the very last seconds. There is a leather case with stuff. Just to make the first few nights a little more comfortable." He was becoming nervous. His eyes were shifting from me to the pit, from the pit back to me.

I began firmly, as if I knew the story by heart, the only

real way to begin. "When the world was born, before the first Lucca, God had a candle so big and long that He tied the sun to it."

"Oh, of course." Ginx breathed out in relief.

"The melting candle created oceans, and fields formed around these oceans. The world was thick with white. It was difficult to walk or breathe, with all that thickness, and difficult to wake up in the morning with no color. The creatures and all the monkeys except one pair soon died from the boredom of it. That one pair were so in love they never missed color."

"In love," Ginx muttered, looking into the distance.

"Momma Lucca's primate ancestors," I told him. "The only survivors."

Ginx slipped away from the tree and knelt beside a patch of torn-up turf. He pulled at the pieces of grass sticking out from the dry dirt. He moved to sit Indian style, his knees practically touching the ground.

"That is how the world began," I informed him gently. Then I knelt beside him, also pulling grass from the dug-up mounds of dirt. "One couple so in love they weren't even bored without color."

"Follow. Plow. Jasmine," Ginx continued, closing his eyes.

When he was done, we remained kneeling in front of the tree where we had spent hours and hours of our childhood, and before us was the pit where it was possible we would spend the tail ends of our lives. The sun was sinking, breaking apart, etching the sky with its pinks and reds, and Ginx was happy.

He checked his watch. "It's exactly eight-seventeen," he whispered, without looking at me. "Exactly your birthday." He was looking toward the edge of the overgrown field. I could not deny my happiness. Behind the trees was Queen Street, then Ewing Road, our church, the old Presbyterian cemetery where Dana and I used to do grave rubbings, Mayor Kates's house, the Baptists with their huge cross out front, and the Daniel Boone complex. There was a braiding of dirt roads that intertwined with paved roads, and then eventually there were highways that led to Durham, Raleigh, Chapel Hill, Greensboro, Winston-Salem, and Burlington.

I was exactly fourteen, and the horizon where the sun lingered away served as a constant reminder that the earth was unfathomably large and there were towns in faraway places containing lives we could not possibly imagine. My brother's hand was rubbing the ground, inching toward mine, but he would not touch me. He looked up at the silvery clouds lined with pink, took in a breath, and let it out with a vague laugh. Living my whole life over again, I thought, I'd only be twenty-eight. Ginx's age doubled was thirty. Many years were left for hacking out a path, for learning what to hide and how to be less afraid, for flirting and earning a living. Stacks of yet unused life lay before us; there would be time to straighten things out and to become a good person. I wanted to take everything about myself that needed changing, ball it all up, and toss it far away, out toward fate or destiny or any of those other places that grown-ups often went on about. I wanted to keep only what was good about myself. At least for an evening, I wanted simply to be okay. I looked at my brother. "The first Lucca," he said. We laughed. Ginx took up a stone and held it, cocked his head, and smiled at me. It was clear that, in a primitive world of wax, he would have been part of the monkey couple that did not need color to be happy, so in love it wouldn't matter how dull the world surrounding him had become.

"We should go home, Ginx," I said. He tossed the stone into the pit.

"A little longer?" he asked. "The birthday picnic's over. There's nothing else." I shrugged and stretched out my legs. "Just a little bit," he reassured.

"Okay, Ginx," I told him, but dread began creeping through me, a spreading fear that one day I might disregard or muddle where adulthood began and childhood ended. I felt unprepared and wondered how I would know what to do when it was time to move on. When nothing was left of the sun, I quickly stood and informed my brother it was time to go home.

"Where do you want to be so badly?" he asked. "Why don't we just stay here? I mean, stay."

"No," I answered, and tried to explain. "It's not that I want to *be* anywhere."

He got up and shoved his hands deeply into his pockets. He scuffed at the ground and cleared his throat the way our father did when he had something important to tell us. "Morgan-Lee, if you ever hear an alarm on the radio or in the mall on the PA system or something, you just rush right out here, you know? Or if Russia ever gets so provoked that you think they might press the button over there." He looked toward Aunt Lois's house. "Even if you don't know where I am, or I'm standing in the wrong place when the bomb hits, and I am most certainly going to die." He winced and bowed a little. "You run right here and stay. You know?"

"Yeah," I said, turning to take the first step toward home.

"I'll try to be careful, though, and make it here too," he promised, not moving. "But you come here no matter what, Morgan-Lee," he said.

I nodded as I walked. He caught up with me. Together, we walked back through that evening, which, it suddenly occurred to me, on the exact opposite side of the world, was someone else's daybreak.

JOURNAL

AFTER DINNER, I went straight up to my room and took out the journal our mother had given me. I transferred sentences and words from scraps of paper onto the first few pages. I wrote, *Foot over foot.* It was a sentence about things being easy, being clear. I looked at it for a while, wondering what to add, and reread the sentence on the night sky, reread earlier ones on shapes of light against a wall, the swollen river after too much rain. I understood the link between them, yet saw where one idea ended and the other began. *Dear* _____, I wrote, intending to begin a love letter. But my hand was trembling, and I shut my eyes.

I had to be careful not to let the boundaries between categories begin to blur. I could too easily become like Ginx, allowing feelings and thoughts to melt together, the dangerous connection of things that should be kept separate, edges that I knew should never touch. My brother squeezed frogs with a desperation that was considered legitimate only for a boy in love grabbing hold of a girl's hand. Ginx, who could separate a sharp word from a pudgy, soft one, could not distinguish between the kind of flesh he should cling to and the kind he should reject.

Our father had once sat me down to explain that Ginx lost sight of the boundaries between people and objects. There were times for Ginx when a person might as well be a stone, or a stone could just as well be a person. "I'm not saying anything bad here," our father had quickly clarified, "I mean nothing against Ginx. He is my son—and, of course, your mother's. I'm only trying to explain his *condition*."

When I didn't speak, our father had filled the silence by telling me that Ginx's inability to separate fantasy and reality, his anxiety and—at times—even violence, were the sign of a certain kind of unwell-being. Dr. Sampson all those years ago had told me I was living with someone who had a sickness like permanent flu or a bad leg, only different. I did not care about his opinion, but his definition of sickness had weaseled itself into me, making me feel weak even on that day in his office when I'd been resolved to remain unafraid.

I passed my hand over the smooth pages of my journal and swallowed hard. Foot over foot and the sad night sky, the patterns of light on a wall, the swallowing I'd done a few days before in Billy's tree house, the bluing of the light, Momma Lucca's big hands, and Dana's blundering into love: All of it became one, each thought dependent upon the others.

I sat there stunned, unable to imagine squelching fear without also recalling how I'd messed things up with my sister. Mess, my sister, the fear were then intertwined with the blue of a warm June evening. It became all too apparent that a tree-house floor could easily slip to feeling like human skin and that the quick pass of a finger through a flame, a damaged eye, and the bones of an angular face could be dismantled and neatly stacked on shelves in a bomb shelter to await a nuclear war. One thing melted hopelessly into the next; one thought sprouted thousands of others. I was afraid the sickness might be waiting inside me.

The door to my room opened, and our mother quietly entered. "I've come to say good night."

I quickly shut my journal. "Good night then," I said, actually hoping that she had recognized the signs of my impending illness and had come to rescue me. I was not even surprised when she walked fully into my bedroom and let the door close behind her. Stopping at the window, she reached out to finger the delicate white lace of the curtains, which Aunt Lois had bought for half price during a bargain basement sale. "Well, then, good night," I tried again, hoping she'd turn to touch my forehead. Against the wall there was a fuzzy stool in the shape of a mushroom. Our father had brought home twin footstools for Dana and me after a trip he took when I was in the seventh grade. Our mother turned around. In one awkward gesture, she picked up the red mushroom stool and brought it near my chair. I closed my eyes and reopened them. There were certain moments in which I so deeply wanted to be beautiful.

"Morgan-Lee," she said, suddenly dwarfed, the height of her cheekbones out of place. I winced. "I am glad you and Billy have become friends again. It is good for you to have a friend like Billy." She did not touch me. My fists tightened as I leveled my eyes to stare, resolved not to understand her. I asked her to clarify; I had been careful about sneaking out to meet him and didn't know how she'd found out.

"What do you mean?"

"I am glad that you and Billy are friends is all." Her face softened; she looked hurt.

"You're making no sense." I pressed on in my deliberate noncomprehension, feeling light, unburdened by my usual need to search for the deeper meaning of her words. It was a relief not to understand our mother. "Don't you realize how unclear you are being? What do you want to tell me?" I asked, genuinely delighting in this new way of addressing her. Maybe, I thought, Dana was smarter than I was; maybe she'd discovered this trick of pretend confusion long ago and used it on us all.

"Spend time with Billy and stop spending so much time with Ginx," our mother said. But I was not finished.

"No point in talking unless I can understand what you are trying to say," I forged on as our mother tilted her face to the side, the edge of her chin sharp as a blade.

"I won't take that from you," she scolded, in the way that

Myra's mother would have spoken. "Don't sass me." But our mother was not used to scolding.

"No one," I said, calm and level, "no one would call this sassing. If you were speaking clearly, then we could have a conversation. It's not sassing when the other person simply doesn't understand what's being said."

Our mother's eyes rested on mine, and she wheezed out a sigh as if being forced to take measures she would have preferred to avoid. Raising her right hand, she cut the air in the way Aunt Lois did when directing a client to a chair. Like Aunt Lois, she had an acquired tenderness in her face, as if assuring that she knew exactly what the trouble was, understood it wholly, and would address it for me and me alone. I knew this ruse of our aunt's so well I could anticipate just how many steps a client had to walk into a room before the directing hand went up, the smile bloomed, and the silent promise was given that everything—everything—was solvable in exchange for money and a good two hours. But in our mother, this skill caught me off guard. I felt small, no more self-controlled than a child.

"Baby, you're growing up, and it's time to let go of those childish stories," she said, addressing me in a way she never did. "Ginx doesn't need anyone else convincing him that he's not like other kids. He's got enough of that, believe me."

"Momma," I whined, interrupting her and stretching my arm along my desk, "Momma, I'm tired. Really, I'm tired." I wanted to fall against her, but instead asked, "Could I be sick? Could you touch my forehead and see?" Our mother's fingers went to my forehead, where they rested in a touch that I knew could vanish at any second but into which I leaned nonetheless.

"No," she declared, "you're fine."

I breathed out. "You know," I continued, talking fast, wanting to tell her things, "I meet with Billy every Thursday in his tree house." Her hand, to my surprise, stayed where it was, and I did not even worry that I should pull my head away before she got too tired to support me. "I write love letters for him, see, so he can sell them. All last year and the year before he brought me notes from kids—clients—but over the summer I am just writing generic letters that we can tailor for kids during the school year. That way it's more efficient. They're kids I don't know anyway, kids from Cresset Christian." I looked down, appreciating our mother's silence, how expert she was at it. It was a stillness that preceded mine and was so obviously more practiced.

After I talked awhile, she interrupted to say, "Morgan-Lee, just leave Ginx alone. I don't want you telling him those stories anymore, you hear?" She paused, then stroked my cheek with her thumb pad. I tried to convince myself later that she touched me so gently in order to soften the blow of what she was preparing to say next. I even believed that the stroking was her version of a reward for the way I'd opened up to her.

But then she spoke, terse words that left no room for

confusion. "Let my boy be. You go on and on, like he needs it, like you've got lessons to teach, but he is all right. He just needs to be let alone. You don't see that all those stories are nothing but selfishness."

At the time, I understood only enough to pull away from her hand and sit up straight. She didn't care about the business, about my letters, my fear of illness. She had come to protect Ginx from me. From *me*.

Her hand slapped her knee. "I hope we're clear, Morgan-Lee. "

My chin trembled as I tried to tell her to get out, but she had left no space for me to speak.

"Get Billy to listen to you, just not my son, not my son." She ended in a whisper, as if offering an intimacy, a good motherly piece of advice, something I could return to later on in life if I married a man who left me or a loving boyfriend who drank too much.

"Thanks," I managed, even with sarcasm. "This has been a big help."

"I know you understand what I'm telling you." She got up from the mushroom stool, her white cotton blouse clinging to her small breasts. I sat back. I was trying to go down, to see the Luccas' field, but the way was blocked, without even a crack to slip through. "We need to help each other," she stated firmly. "We need to get along, all of us. I once was—" She stopped. Rather than speak about her past, she went on to spout off a few platitudes about mothers and daughters and sisters and brothers. Whatever message she was trying to deliver about growing up got smothered under useless piles of sentences and arrived stilted, changed, broken. All I understood was "Good night."

"Knock next time," I instructed curtly, as she opened the door to leave.

"That would be appropriate," she agreed, the way a mother might speak. "Now, go to bed. Sleep." After the door shut behind her, I waited a few minutes. *Foot over foot like a tightrope walker,* I finally wrote, as a first line for my new love letter, and put the journal away. I lay down in my bed fully dressed, thankful at least that I wouldn't have to get changed in the morning. But I could not sleep for a long while. I knew that, had our mother returned to my room, had she knelt by my bed and put her hand back on my forehead to stroke shut each eye with the soft pad of her thumb, I would have begun all over again, telling her things that no one could possibly find interesting. I wanted her to listen to me; my desire for this was undeniable.

I finally managed to push away these thoughts and to begin a rigid sleep from which I awoke at precisely 7:23 A.M. I sprang out of bed and ran to the bathroom before anyone else got up. I brushed my teeth and hair, glanced only once at the mirror, then covered it with a towel. I realized how sick I actually was. It may be forgivable to fall innocently and blindly into someone's trap because the territory you've stumbled upon is unfamiliar to you, but it is quite another matter to know that you almost fell and to be willing—no, wanting—to fall again. Our mother had come to save Ginx from me, and I was ready to tell her all my secrets. I was worse than one of those moon-faced women who blindly returned twice a month for fresh supplies of Aunt Lois's Je T'en Prie Noir or Mais Oui Bleu. I was worse than those soul-dropping clients who closed their eyes when Aunt Lois applied their mask, who listened intently each time to all steps of the cleansing process despite the fact that they had heard and heard and heard the instructions before. My needs were sadder, more pathetic even than theirs.

KNOWLEDGE

TOWARD THE END OF June, our mother sat in the dining room saying, "I have. You have. He, she, it has. We have. You have. They have." Valeria was not a fast learner. "Now, please repeat it, Val," our mother said distinctly, emphasizing the good American nickname she had given her.

"I haaave," she began, her *a*'s overextended.

"Math work?" Ginx asked me. I grunted, continuing to stare at the word *hypotenuse*. Since I'd gotten a *C–* in math, our father insisted that I study over the summer. "You always get *A*s," he pointed out. I was two years ahead of my grade level in math, which I pointed out, but he just replied that I needed to get back to work.

"You're going to study over the summer," was the remedy he offered, and I accepted it without argument.

"We encourage," Valeria blurted.

"Good, now make a sentence," our mother said. There was silence.

"We encourage you to shut up," Ginx rasped, flipping another page of his magazine with shiny pictures of gas masks and other paraphernalia.

"Not too loud, Ginx," I said. "They'll hear you."

"We encourage you always to eat your meat," Valeria said.

"Good," our mother exclaimed. "Now the present. The immaculate present."

"What is she saying?" Ginx asked. "What?" He was frustrated and kicked at the base of his chair. He did not want our mother to teach in the house. It enraged him.

I turned the page of my geometry book. Again the word *hypotenuse*. I needed to get my studying done because I had to deliver another installment of letters to Billy that evening.

"Go on now, Val," our mother said. "Tomorrow, yesterday, the day before yesterday." Then she annulled it all with a quick, "No, no, no. Let's stick to verbs instead."

"Okay, yes," Valeria agreed. She sounded both eager and bored. I forced myself to memorize the definition of *hypotenuse* and wrote it down in my notebook. Our father tiptoed down the stairs. "Your mother's tutoring?" he asked me, pointing in the direction of the dining room. He was glad she was working again. "Don't make noise in here," he told us.

"Okay."

Ginx began a monotonous hum that was loud enough to be noticeable. Our father looked at him, a frown cut into his brow.

"Ginx, your mother is working."

"I know," Ginx said, "I know, I know, I know, *hi-ho*!"

"Just came down to get this." Our father picked up his briefcase. "If there's something you don't understand, I can help you tonight, Morgan-Lee." Both of us watched him retreat back up the stairs, then Ginx got up and went over to the television.

"Look here, Morgan-Lee," he told me, "just so you know." He bent down, slipped his hand under the television stand, and pulled out a slender leather briefcase that had once belonged to our father. "If there should ever be a war and I am not around," he began, "this is the Emergency Kit. Just to make the first few days more comfortable."

"I know, Ginx. Put it back," I said.

"How would you conjugate the verb *to encourage* in the past tense?" our mother asked.

"I encouraged, you encouraged, he encouraged—" Valeria interrupted the litany to remark, "It is not good that English hardly has a subjunctive."

"Oh, yes!" our mother rejoined, as if Valeria had made a happy discovery. "Our subjunctive is very insubstantial— very little, that is—compared to yours in Italian. We have *if I were* and *I wish I were*—" she began, but Valeria cut her off.

"Your subjunctive is so un-sexy," she announced, in such a decided way that I was forced to cover my mouth while Ginx hunched down, shrugging up his shoulders as he slipped the Emergency Kit back under the television stand. I had not quite finished with *hypotenuse* and went back to staring at its place in the triangle.

"Interesting choice of adjectives," our mother commented.

"The subjunctive is so good," Valeria insisted. A silence followed. Any other teacher would have kept up the conversation or resumed the grammar lesson or offered to teach Valeria new phrases in English, but our mother was silent, most probably contemplating the meagerness of the subjunctive in our language.

"Sounds like a funeral in there," I said to Ginx, in a voice loud enough for them to hear.

"You encouraged," our mother immediately resumed.

"They encouraged," Valeria concluded.

"Good," she said. "Now use the verb in a sentence in the past perfect tense."

"They have to stop," Ginx said, his head springing back against the chair, eyes snapping shut and open, quick as a lizard's. "They just must stop." Of course we could have gone somewhere else in the house or even outside, but that was not a possibility we would consider. If our mother was teaching, we wanted to hear her.

"We had encouraged the girl to walk on a Tuesday in

June" was the phrase Valeria created. "We encouraged his rancor." Despite her fading and unmemorable face, Valeria's inclusion of certain words and exclusion of others was odd enough that her sentences hopped through the room, forcing Ginx and me to pay attention.

Radius, I read, skipping to circles. *Radius*, I wrote down. *Diameter*, I wrote.

"Wonderful," our mother cooed.

"She had encouraged us to seek," Valeria went on, pronouncing each word distinctly.

"Yes," our mother praised. "Now, the future perfect."

"D=2r," I wrote.

"By the time she's thirty, he will have already asked her to marry him," Valeria said faultlessly.

"The perfect future," Ginx said. I looked at my brother. He rubbed his wrist and watched the door, then stretched his legs, kicking his left heel against the carpet. He went back to rubbing at the circle he'd worn into the armrest. I was trained to my brother's moods the way farmers are trained to the weather. I crossed my legs, my palms already sweating.

"He's got the face a girl should've been born with," our aunt at times declared, "but no one in this town will ever appreciate him. Ever. He'll have to go up north for that. Or go to Europe. People in Europe can appreciate his look."

I had to do something.

"As long as Dana and Poppa are away," I told Ginx, who was pulling at threads. I kept my eyes on his face. The ridiculous conversation in the other room would continue for another fifteen minutes, so there was time. Ever since our mother had warned me to stop telling Ginx stories, I'd been more careful to do it in secret. I shut my book, which fell, opening up again on the floor. My brother drew in a breath.

"There is," I began, "a dangerous god." I studied Ginx's eyes, his nose, his mouth. "He is fourteen, and is naked and damaged, and has climbed way above the field, the house, Sister's long white birch branch. He is watching."

"Oh, oh," my brother softly gasped, immediately relieved, relaxing back into his chair.

"The present continuing," I heard our mother say, "the impeccable present." I wondered if what I was doing was, in fact, wrong, if telling Ginx stories was keeping him sick. What if we ended up in his bomb shelter for the rest of our lives, hauling out the alphabet over and over or forcing together words that had lost all definition, and I never kissed any boy ever?

"Then, not a god," Ginx said, "then it happens, when the neighbor boy," he declares, considering for a moment, "tries to take over."

"Another present continuing," Valeria continued from the other room. "I am bending Marion's book." Our mother giggled.

"It's late afternoon. The neighbor boy is in Sister's tree. He climbed up there while Sister and B.J. were asleep in the grass."

"They were in the grass," Ginx said, nodding, passing his index finger back and forth over his upper lip. I was about to continue when he asked, "Say what they were doing in the grass."

I saw the long grass, thick and cool as a good head of hair, and there was a bird in the distance squawking and circling, and the tiredness came from having eaten so much, and having laughed—and the sun, of course. They were naked; I knew my brother could see it too. They were next to each other and naked, and Ginx wanted to hear about the wind on their skin and the in-and-out of Sister's breath against B.J.'s shoulder. And her small breasts with their dark circles, and B.J.'s arm snaking around her waist. He slipped to the edge of his chair and looked at me.

"They are naked," I confessed.

"That's right," he told me, anxious, smiling. But I didn't go on.

"Listen, Ginx," I said, folding my arms and looking down, which I never did when telling a story, "we're too old for this. I mean, in the fall you're gonna be in eleventh grade. We're not little kids anymore." I wiped the palms of my hands against the armrests of my chair.

"They are naked," he repeated, trying not to lose focus. "Go on."

I rubbed my forehead and realized I was sweating there too; my hair was wet with sweat. I spoke.

"Sister loves B.J."

"What is happening? Tell me what B.J. and Sister are doing," Ginx insisted. He spoke slowly and firmly. He was tapping his right foot to a beat that must have been somewhere in the story but that I could not hear.

"The neighbor boy comes down from the tree to talk to them."

"Shut up," Ginx rasped, throwing himself against the back of the chair, pressing hard against it, fighting his urge to turn to one side or another. I was the one who could not look at him. "Tell the truth," he reminded me.

He sounded as scary as the boys at school who threatened to raid your locker, the kind who wanted passion in their letters, who groped their girlfriends when their parents were away or met in empty parking lots to drink beer and smoke. Ginx was watching with that same intensity, that same need to ward off emptiness, the boyish lust that is really more a life-preserving instinct than a desire for any person. He was pressing his entire pointer finger against his nose and mouth as if warning me to shut up before the danger hit.

"Why is it so difficult?" he asked. *Difficult*. The word fit the moment perfectly, its outstanding consonants structured to accommodate the fine bones of his face. *"Catapult,"* he added.

"No," I said. "It's not." I refused to repeat his word, *diffi-*

cult: to offer the refrain he wanted. "What about when you're forty and married? What about when you've got two kids and are living in Arizona with a car and everything? You want me to call you up and tell you about the Luccas? That's what?"

Ginx's foot stopped tapping; the story was gone. "Forty," he repeated. "I won't be forty and married. And neither will you."

As if he actually could promise we would always be together, as if he could swear this to me and I, in turn, could tell our mother that she was wrong about progress, and that efficiency is good for taking apart and pounding out syllable by syllable, for making the wind chime on a money tree.

Ginx moved from the chair; he even took the time to stand straight before semicircling the coffee table to get to me. "That's not how it goes," he instructed, as if I'd been repeating a familiar fairy tale and had gotten the end wrong, as if I'd skipped his favorite passage. "That's not it." He bent two fingers in a miniature fist and pounded again and again and again into my upper arm. I sat there, tensed but still. He hit twice on my chest, just under my neck bones, and then he was satisfied. While hitting, he was able to look at me without difficulty, without a single word, no match for the dull, small thuds that later on sprang up as violets. I allowed each jab to have its way, to demolish the fragments of me that he did not want. *A Unique Educational Experience. A Special Someone. A Relationship to Cherish.*

"All to yourself," I heard our mother instruct from the

other room. She was trying to teach Valeria a few American expressions, perhaps thinking it would help her integrate more easily into our culture. "An example of its usage would be," she went on, then cleared her throat and began more simply. "An example would be, 'Some things must be kept all to yourself.'"

"What does it mean?" Valeria asked.

But our mother didn't answer. Ginx paused, coughing. Nobody in the world could have held as still as I did. "You are okay," he told me, merely retracting his hand and backing away. I could have invented something entirely new, a new game. But I sat as always, breaking no codes or rules, maintaining the established Give and Take that Aunt Lois's relationship books so highly recommended.

Our mother said, "Repeat after me: Keep what I tell you all to yourself." My heart contracted over her sentence. It expanded too far; it contracted too much.

"She could stop for once," Ginx said, "just once, for once."

Our mother went on and on. I closed my eyes so that her voice became waves beneath me, for which Ginx's *once* was a tiny boat bobbing in the distance. Without Momma Lucca, I would be alone on the flat, real surface of the earth. I held my knees and understood why other girls tried to cover themselves by smelling of spearmint, laughing like the tinkling of coins, and buying things. I was far from knowing how to be like girls my age. There was so much to learn.

Ginx was heading toward the stairs. "You're not a genius, Morgan-Lee," he said. "Momma's not a genius either." I continued staring straight ahead. He went through the whole family. "Aunt Lois is no genius." By the time he got to our grandmother, our mother's mother, he was already on his way up. *Genius* you could chew for a while and not get bored. There were others, like *Jelly Bean, Jewel,* and *Jews,* but *Genius* was his favorite. *"Hopscotch. Piggy. Roo-roo. Poopy-hole,"* he called out to me.

They were childish, unworthy words. I just picked up my book and returned to *hypotenuse.*

"Well, that's good," I heard Valeria say, with an almost perfect American accent.

"Okay."

"I will have run, you will have run, he will have run, she will have run, it will have run, we will have run, you will have run, they will have run," Valeria conjugated. Our mother should have seen that it was time for her student to do more complicated exercises. The backs of my jaws stung.

"She is a terrible teacher," I whispered to myself, wiping the spit from the side of my mouth.

"We've done enough for today," I heard our mother tell her student. They finished their lesson. I heard the books close and Valeria packing her satchel. The living room door finally opened, and Valeria spoke to me in a painstakingly constructed sentence. "Hello, Morgan-Lee, I did not know you were still here."

"Hey," I said, my arms, legs, and face slowly piecing themselves together again.

"Speak to Val in clear, full sentences, if you will, Morgan-Lee," our mother asked of me.

"Yes, Valeria, I am still here, where I was before. I am here doing my math work," I told her absurdly. I would not use that stupid nickname.

"Are you doing your work?" our mother asked, looking at Valeria and pointing to my math book.

"Yes," I affirmed again. "I am doing my work."

Valeria opened the door. "Good-bye," the roly-poly woman said, smiling at our mother and me with no acknowledgment of our efforts on her behalf. "Good-bye, and I see you next week."

"Yes," our mother responded as Valeria left us. We watched out the window as she walked from our house to her car. Our mother and I then watched her get into the car, a white Mazda. She pulled out of the cul de sac. Our mother stood by my chair. We continued staring out the window together in silence.

"Well now, I did well today. It takes a lot of effort," our mother told me. She turned and smiled, hugging her arms together to stretch her back. I looked away, and she said it again, as if trying to get me to agree that we had both walked long miles over the same rugged terrain and had finally arrived, intact and together, at some resting place. She waited almost a full minute. Apparently her sparse words and breath were supposed to be enough for me, but I wanted her to know that our ending in that same spot was purely accidental. In no way had we made the same journey.

"Valeria needs to be given more complicated exercises," I finally said. "Don't you see that?" Her smile disappeared.

"So that's all you have to tell me," she said, stopping mid-stretch. "I raised a spoiled girl. That's the problem, and there's no turning it around now." She refueled her energy with a long inhale. "There can't ever be a word of praise. That is too much for you?" Her complaint was ancient, far older than I was, but at the time I did not understand this. I held up my book and slammed it shut.

"Don't ask me that," I said. "I don't care. That's what's wrong!" I breathed, exasperated.

"What?" she asked, making things worse because it was a genuine question; she raised her eyebrows as if I were, in fact, capable of telling her how to go about making things better.

"Jesus God," I said, clasping my shut book like some Bible-belter about to launch into a sermon. "You don't see it, do you? You have no idea what to say or when to say it or even who you are saying it to!"

Our mother's lips drew thin as a hyphen. She corrected me in one spooky syllable. "Whom," she said. "And don't end with a preposition. What you should say is '*to whom* you are saying it.'" She turned triumphantly and walked back into the dining room, leaving me alone.

Outside, the afternoon was crumbling into dusk. I

rubbed my arm and then my neck. "What a crazy day," I muttered, because this is what people say in order to lay one day to rest and prepare to pick up another. It was a good, useful phrase, one that I thought Valeria most certainly needed to learn. I continued to look out the window, wondering if all the languages in the world had a sentence for cutting things loose, for dropping a day into its category, for clearing the decks.

BUSINESS

NEITHER BILLY NOR I talked about the fact that our letter stockpile was already too big. The truth is, we'd begun the year by selling one or two letters a week, but by the time school had let out we were down to one or two a month. Since I gave him three letters a week, we stockpiled whatever we didn't sell, but these extras plus what I'd taken him so far that summer were enough that I could have vacationed for a good year and not frustrated a single client. I tried writing on various colors of stationery and with different-colored pens. But I knew it was time to change my style or else stop writing and wait till the school year, when the stockpile would, we hoped, dwindle. I doubted that it ever would. Aunt Lois had ordered a new shipment of religious self-help books, which I decided to read thoroughly. My ninth-grade

English teacher had stressed the importance of "knowing your audience."

"Anything about the Lord you want to know, you can just ask me," our aunt said when she came into the Baby's Room and found me on Dana's chair reading one of the newly arrived books. "I would be happy to tell you."

"No, it's for Billy," I blurted out, not able to come up with a better answer and wanting to avoid any discussion of God with my aunt. "Billy was just wondering something," I added.

"Oh, that boy has really changed for the better since Cresset Christian!" Aunt Lois declared, pulling Dana's sheets off her bed and tucking in a fresh new set. "It's a wonder your parents don't invest a little in your education and send you there too."

"I wouldn't go if they paid me," I retorted. "Besides, Poppa knows what a good education is." I pretended to go back to reading the book, but I knew Aunt Lois was not finished.

"That boy's got a certain je ne sais quoi," she mused. Now she was fluffing the pillows and arranging Dana's stuffed animals. My cheeks went hot; I kept reading the same sentence over again: *"Eve was made from Adam, and thus the natural love between man and woman was born."*

Our aunt continued. "He's no beauty, now, don't get me wrong. He's what they call *a type*, you know, the kind they appreciate in New York City or somewhere like that. He's got that intellectual look. But he's not bad, Morgan-Lee, and a northern girl could easily snatch him right up from under you."

"Billy and I are friends. We were neighbors," I said, but I couldn't look at her. The conversation had somehow ridden onto her turf, and of course she had the upper hand.

"Weren't you engaged once?" she asked.

"That was first grade!" I said, angry at my shrill voice.

"Well." She went on with a sigh, as if I were trying her patience, as if I had asked for advice and then refused to take it. "It's high time you found a boy that interests you." She was arranging Dana's bureau, lining up her hairbrush and comb, setting the knickknacks straight. "Besides Ginx," she said.

I looked at her before realizing the trap. "What is that supposed to mean?" I demanded.

Our aunt stopped what she was doing. She smiled at me in a mix of pity and understanding, obliging, as though I had barged in on her but she would forgive me. "Time you worked on getting a boy," she said. "Picked one and got him interested. Do it first just for practice if you have to, Morgan-Lee. Don't wait any longer. If you don't start now, by age nineteen or twenty you'll end up with scum or no one at all. It's not like you have all the time in the world. And the pretty girls are going to choose first, so pickings are even slimmer than they seem because the first tier of boys is wiped out from the get-go." She slid the closet door shut.

"I'm not like you!" I shouted. "Okay? Do we have that straight?"

"Oh, my!" Aunt Lois exclaimed, pressing three fingers against her mouth as if to squelch the laugh that nonetheless escaped in small puffs. "Oh, sweetie, not at all! Couldn't be more different." She tsked as she looked around the room; then she brushed her hands together and told me to get back to my reading. "Anything you want to know about Jesus and relationships," she reiterated, "don't hesitate to ask!"

I turned back to the same sentence, the third sentence in the second chapter, and stared hard at it before I was able to pull myself back on track and understand what it was I was reading. After I finished the second chapter, I skimmed the third and fourth. The book was about allowing the Lord to guide love and not despairing if sexual attraction dies because, like all things, it can be born again in a new and perhaps more inspired way. There were steps that could be followed if a wife wanted to remind her husband of their conjugal love.

I copied out *The Lord calls us to love one another.* I tried to think of a line to follow this, but I kept thinking about sitting in the tree house and watching Billy read, how I would miss that when our business ended. "Write about what you know," my English teacher had also told the class. If it weren't for the fact I had to write a love letter for someone else, I would have written that I wanted the Luccas out in the world. I wanted them independent. Then they could howl and tip hats and love each other without my always having to monitor them. I would write that I never wanted to live in the pit, and I didn't mind time's being kept by a regular clock, and I didn't want to hold still so often or be hit or be the only one responsible for Dana's learning how to grow up.

BROKEN AS THINGS ARE

Early on in our business, Billy told me that a girl had framed one of the letters I'd written. "Janie framed the letter you wrote for Peter to send her. It wasn't even one of your best," he said. "She told him she knew he meant it because it was all thoughtful and filled with personal stuff, not just one of those Hallmark things. She said the old lady really did know about love, that she could tell by the way it was written 'cause it was strange and all but it was really true." Billy that day was leaning away from the candle, his back against the wall of the tree house. His chin was raised, so his good eye was looking down at me, and he was smiling, which he didn't do a lot. He looked different.

"The only thing I like about Cresset Christian is our business," he said. "Otherwise I hate that place."

"I know," I said, happy over the fact that a girl I'd never seen had my letter framed on her wall and that the woven-in line was there as well, like a secret whispered way up close from me to her. I wanted more letters framed; I wanted them hanging in every household, solemnly centered above the fireplace or over the bed, the same words read again and again, their meaning changing each time.

"You look happy," I said. Billy shifted position, stretching his legs to either side of the candle.

"So do you," he said quietly, his thin hands covering his kneecaps. I studied his wrists, then looked up his bony arms to where they disappeared into the sleeves of his T-shirt. Once he'd told Ginx, "You're lucky." My brother had covered both ears, so Billy had turned to me and explained. "I don't know what it's like to have a brother or a sister."

"It's whatever," I'd told him with a shrug.

But sitting there in the tree house, I wanted to give him a gift to keep for the days when he felt alone: I wanted to quote Jesus. I wanted to say, *Lift up your cross and follow me.* No words could ever be that relaxing, ever, ever. *Lift up your cross and follow me.* And you will have no responsibility, no rules to create, you can kick over the whole bucket, and He will make a stream, and all you have to do is follow that path down through the mountains and into the valleys. I wanted to touch Billy, to press both hands on his cheeks and feel the way he talked, the bones moving beneath the skin and muscle.

"Why are you happy?" I asked.

Billy smiled and shook his head. "Just am."

It was late, and I had no more time to waste. *Through the Lord, we can love each other,* I wrote as a second line. It was time to go, so I folded the letter, put it in an envelope, and went downstairs.

Ginx was sitting in Aunt Lois's white chair, holding the remote and watching President Reagan talk with the volume turned so far down it was barely audible. "Here he is. Here's the man who will end the world," my brother said, as though someone were sitting beside him and watching as intensely as he was. I rushed past him and out the door.

"Good-bye, Morgan-Lee," I heard him say as the screen door swung shut behind me.

"I'm going to end business with Billy," I said, but not loud enough for Ginx to hear.

When I got to the tree house, Billy was in his usual spot. He had with him my entire stockpile of letters. I didn't even bother to land on the cushions or fold my legs in the way that I usually did. We did not greet each other. "How many do we have now?" I asked. Billy was sitting Indian style on his cushion. As usual, the candle was between us, but its flame looked pitiful, tacky even, the remainder from an old illusion about what a romance-letter-writing business should be. I blew it out.

"What did you do that for?" Billy put his hand on my stockpile.

"It's still sunny out, Billy, if you haven't noticed. Enough light gets in here through the boards; there's no need for a candle." I moved the spent candle to the side. Billy put my stockpile behind him, as if I'd just dismantled the protective wall and now threatened to destroy the letters. He was wearing a black T-shirt tucked into jeans, and I thought about what my aunt had said about people appreciating his looks more up north. I wondered what would happen when Billy went to college. He could easily go up north where some girl would appreciate him. She would accompany him on his visits home and lord over him like she had been the one on the throne watching while he built the tree house, like she had seen him naked over the river when he thought no one was looking, like she had made a point of coming every Thursday without ever missing one, like she had any talent for holding excruciatingly still and being able to see a thing while pretending not to be seeing it at all.

Billy straightened and rested the pile of letters on his lap. "I don't want to end business," he said, just like that. I watched his Adam's apple bob in his throat, which I would have killed a northern girl for getting too near.

"Read that," I said, flinging the Lord's letter I'd written onto his lap. "You'll change your mind." He looked at me with his good eye while the other stared over my shoulder, as if I had a second head there that was proposing something entirely different. Who knows, maybe that second head was blowing kisses and winking, in which case Billy's confused look would have made sense.

"I don't need to read it," Billy said. He was stroking the edge of the pile with his thumb. "What if you just come here on Thursdays, and we forget business?" he asked. He put my pile on the blanket beside him, and with his right foot pushed the candle over. "Remember that time we were down by the river?" he asked me. "That time last summer, Morgan-Lee? You were down by the river and you saw me there, and I was talking to myself and you came up behind and heard me and you got all red because you thought I was talking to my dead father." He paused. He was leaning toward me now, so I wished the northern girl were watching. I stared at his complicated face and remembered that day I'd sneaked up on him and then felt ashamed. "Then I told you I was talking to *you*."

"Yeah," I said, "but you never told me what you were saying."

"I was saying," he began, but rather than finish he placed his hand on my cheek and drew nearer.

"Billy!" I cautioned, pulling away. "You don't know me. Not really." It was the first thing I could think to say.

"That's not true," he countered quietly, his hand still cupped in the air as if my cheek might return to it.

"You don't," I insisted, swallowing hard. "Just leave me be. I'm here to end our business. That's all, nothing else," I said, though I would have given a great deal right then to let my other head speak, the one his damaged eye was appraising, the one that had for so long, I knew, wanted to kiss him. He pulled back, but slowly, not as if he were trying to escape anything.

"Go on then," he said quietly. "Go home."

"I can't write anymore," I told him, as if in explanation. "It's over," I said, moving toward the hole to leave.

"Over for you," he corrected, looking back at the spent candle.

I searched out his other eye, but it too had changed focus, so I slid through the hole, down the ladder, and ran.

"Tomorrow's July Fourth," Ginx said, as we headed down to the river later that evening. "It's the Fourth of July!"

"What about when you fall in love with someone or I do

and then we have to go to the river with those people instead?" I asked. My brother kicked a rock in the path; two fireflies lit up right near his face.

"I used to want to be like Momma," he told me. "It used to be that I wished to be exactly like Momma. She's tired now because of all the dullness. She's tired 'cause everyone speaks the same and there's no sense listening to everything the same. I don't want to be like her now because I don't want to be tired. But it used to be that I wanted to be like her." Then, without looking at me, Ginx grabbed my hand, clutching it the way he used to do when we were little. His left shoulder shrugged up, but he managed to keep hold. The evening was warm, so I closed my eyes for a few seconds and let him lead me. Down below, Sister was sitting against her birch, and B.J. was whittling a wooden whistle. The summer grass had turned brown at the tips.

"Poppa says if I can't control myself around you he will take me to the hospital, to Dr. Sampson, and Dr. Sampson will have me stay in the hospital, the teenage ward." I opened my eyes. "Poppa says I need to stop hitting you. I need to make friends and control myself. I should be the first one to realize when I am out of control."

"You hit me only sometimes."

"Yes. Sometimes, Morgan-Lee," Ginx confirmed, eyebrows forced down so he could look at me. "But I don't want to. We know that, and I told Poppa that we know that." His grip tightened, so my fingertips were almost numb. "*Sequence.*

Teleological," Ginx said, trying to get us out of the place in which we had found ourselves and offer a bridge over which to cross toward the sounds of the river.

"They are sitting in the grass. Sister is against the birch; B.J. is whittling a whistle," I began.

SWEETS

‿

CLOSE TO SUPPERTIME on Independence Day, Uncle Pete snatched open the door but then surprisingly cleared his throat and spoke with unusual hesitation. "We don't need anything," he said. It was as though he were speaking directly into the muggy air, but then he stepped aside to expose a tall girl, whom I recognized. It was Sweety-Boy, the girl from my class who hardly ever showed up—Jacob's sister. Her black hair was brushed back into a single loose braid. Ginx looked up from where he was sitting at the dining room table reading and said, "Good morning." The girl nodded at him. Dana came out of the kitchen.

"Good morning," she replied, loudly enough for us all. She dropped something, which was when I saw a red metal wagon behind her filled with cardboard boxes. Its long handle clanked against the stoop, sending Aunt Lois's hands to her hips. I folded my arms, each palm cupping an elbow.

"May I?" the girl began, so obviously not asking permission that it was hardly surprising when she walked straight past Uncle Pete to stand in the middle of the living room. Not even Aunt Lois had time to stop her. Really looking at her, I could see that her face was pockmarked and ragged, her forehead shiny with perspiration. She cleared her throat, rubbed her chest with the flat of her hand, and tugged at the faded black stretch pants she was wearing. "Hello," she announced. "My name is Sweety-Boy, and I work for the Smoky Mountain Secrets Company. We make the finest jams and jellies you can buy." As she hiked up a thumb to indicate her wagon outside, her pink tank top slid so the skin of her stomach glimpsed through in the same onion color as her arms and face.

"Now, in stores they'll charge you two twenty-five a jar. Even more, most times. I'm selling for one-fifty and the quality's top."

"We don't need jellies, thank you," Aunt Lois said with polished sternness, but the girl did not move. She scanned the room, raising her chin and blinking her narrow eyes at the landscape painting on the wall.

"Are they good?" Dana asked, genuinely curious, which was when I noticed that the girl was not standing at all still, she was swaying side to side in a pair of black high-top sneakers. Dana didn't realize yet that this was Jacob's sister, the one I'd mentioned down by the river. "Can we have a free sample?" my sister wanted to know.

"It's cheap, but it ain't free," Sweety-Boy snapped. Then, with a gracious nod, she turned to indicate Uncle Pete, still holding the door. "That's something you should know," she informed our uncle, who shifted impatiently but said nothing. Sweety-Boy was in no way done talking to us. She cleared her throat.

"First of all," Ginx said, "what is your name? First things first."

"My name is Sweety-Boy, and I'm from the Smoky Mountain Secrets Company," she began again, as if rehearsing for some later, more important performance.

"Oh!" Dana gasped, startled. "You're Jacob's sister!"

"You know Jacob?" Sweety-Boy asked.

Dana was about to answer, but Aunt Lois cut her off. "As I said, we do not need any jellies, but thank you just the same. Now, good-bye."

"Yes. Thank you," Uncle Pete hastened to add.

"My, my, my." Sweety-Boy sucked in her bottom lip. She looked hurt for a second; her swaying slowed, and her face wrinkled up like a snake about to strike. Then something in her gave, and the movement resumed. She pulled her braid undone and flipped her hair free in one singular girlish gesture.

"You can buy jellies and jams from the store, but they aren't half as good or near as cheap as they are through me." She smiled, and I was certain that Aunt Lois, like me, was immediately drawn to those teeth, which appeared straight as sun rays, so perfect I would have believed they were stolen from another face if it weren't for the fact that the awkwardness of her other features so obviously relied on that straightness. Without those teeth, the girl's face would have had no center, no organizing principle, nothing to help navigate the ragged skin, slender eyes, crooked jawline.

"Now, listen," Aunt Lois said, in an effort to regain control over the situation. "July Fourth is a family day, not a day for you to be knocking on people's doors selling things. It is time for supper, time for you to go home."

"I heard about your makeovers at church." Sweety-Boy gave a closed-mouth smile.

"Church!" Aunt Lois exclaimed.

"Yeah, me and Jacob attend the same Sunday services as you. Sometimes," Sweety-Boy said proudly, her eyes moving to pin Aunt Lois's face in the air for her inspection, only to drop it again, disappointed.

"I've never seen you there," our aunt said.

"Oh, he goes to our church?" Dana asked.

"Pete," Aunt Lois complained.

"Yes, I know," he sympathized, but remained put.

Ginx's fingertips fluttered against the vase. "Where are you from?" he asked the girl, loudly enough that she could've still been outside on the stoop. She looked at him and cleared her throat again.

"Originally Asheville, up in the mountains, you know.

Now I'm living over there in West Hillsborough near Dead Man's Field." Ginx's interest deepened. Dead Man's Field marked the borderline between east and west.

"How old are you?" he asked.

"Fourteen. I'm in Morgan-Lee's class at school." Sweety-Boy indicated me with a nod, and I blushed a little. I hadn't suspected that the girl had noticed me. My brother looked from her to me and then back again.

"Sure is hot, isn't it?" Ginx asked, in one of the few attempts I'd ever heard him make at polite conversation.

"Real summer weather we're having," Sweety-Boy qualified, her eyes gone black as compost after a burning. I suspected we were all involved in some complicated joke to be recapped one evening for other long-legged girls amid cigarette butts and Coke cans on a porch overlooking Dead Man's Field.

"Our neighbors, who now live in the Pritchards' old house, are from Nevada," Ginx offered, as easily as if they were conversing at a church potluck. "More and more people are moving here from all over the country. Our neighbors have been in Hillsborough now for seven years," he added thoughtfully. "Since Billy was seven."

"Oh," Sweety-Boy said. "Well, I moved here last year 'cause my granddaddy lives here. Then my half brother moved in because his momma died." She looked at us before adding an explanation that she seemed tired of having to offer. "*His* momma, 'cause we got the same daddy but different mommas. He works over there at Johnny Johnson's, which you should know if you don't already, because he's the best mechanic they've got." I looked at Dana, but she was wordless, just staring at Sweety-Boy.

"Enough!" Aunt Lois clapped twice for attention. "This isn't social hour. Pete, make her leave this instant."

"You. Girl," Uncle Pete began. He finally let go of the doorknob, so the door creaked toward closing. Sweety-Boy did not turn to face him, but her smile disappeared and Aunt Lois's tone softened.

"Tell him hello for me!" Dana finally burst out, clasping her hands together, "Tell your brother that—"

"Half brother," Sweety-Boy interjected, amused. "Tell me your name, and I'll tell him you send your regards."

"Dana." She beamed. "He might have seen me with my friend Myra."

"We do not want any jams," our aunt interrupted, trying to set things straight. "We do not want jellies. I just want you out." But the girl stayed put. "Jacob or no Jacob," Aunt Lois added.

Dana went on. "Oh, it's just such a coincidence."

"Listen," our aunt cried. "You'd better take heed! I know Jacob Little, up at Johnny Johnson's. He's fixed my car on more than one occasion, and I will tell him about your behavior here today."

"Well, now, I'll be," Sweety-Boy said, "y'all *do* know him." I laughed a little, thinking that perhaps Dana should marry Jacob just so Aunt Lois would be forced to attend the same wedding as this girl.

Aunt Lois glared at my sister, then looked back at Sweety-Boy. "I want you out of my house now," she stated.

"I'm the only one who doesn't know Jacob," Ginx said. "Maybe I should meet him."

Sweety-Boy nodded. "That's a good idea. Yeah, y'all should come to the party. I'm having a surprise birthday party for him at four o'clock next Friday. Y'all come."

Uncle Pete cleared his throat. "Five bucks says you turn around and start walking," he blurted, but the girl showed no sign of hearing him. She looked set to stay.

"Ten'll say I'm out the door," she finally retorted.

Uncle Pete opened his wallet and took out the bill. Even as Aunt Lois's face went ashen, Uncle Pete did not rescind his offer.

"Terribly sorry," Sweety-Boy apologized to my brother, as if she were an adult burdened with a demanding child, "we'll just have to get acquainted next week. Come to the little white house way down Margaret Lane right across from Dead Man's Field. Y'all can remember, right?"

"Okay, we'll be there," my brother replied calmly, the only one of us who wasn't confused. The world was lying belly up, so it made perfect sense when Sweety-Boy spoke to Aunt Lois slowly and deliberately, as if she very much risked not being understood. "I know that you do not want my jams." She shrugged. "Not everyone does. You and me're both businesswomen. We know what it's like."

"Tell Jacob that Eric's sister's friend says hello," Dana chimed in. "We'll be at his party, but I know you can't tell him that because it's a surprise. Just tell him I said hey."

"Will do," the girl promised, turning and walking as if relieved to be moving again, her long strides bounding her toward the door, which Uncle Pete immediately opened as wide as it would go. "Okay, now: out," he said, suddenly bold, holding forth the ten-dollar bill as tentatively as he might have offered a sugar cube to a wild horse.

"Are you crazy?" Aunt Lois yelled at him.

With two graceful fingers, Sweety-Boy plucked that money from his hand and stepped over the threshold and back onto the stoop. I watched where her thick hair swung just below her waist as she tucked Uncle Pete's bill into the elastic band of her pants. She then picked up her wagon's long handle from the cement steps and, without turning to smile or tell us good-bye, she was gone. Uncle Pete quickly slammed the door and bolted it shut.

"How dare you give that white trash thief our money!" Aunt Lois demanded through the prickly quiet of the living room.

Uncle Pete looked sheepish. "I just wanted to settle it and have my dinner, Lois. I've had a hard day."

"Hard day nothing!" Aunt Lois turned and went to the display cabinet. She clanked together four of the crystal glasses and arranged them on the table. Dana sat and looked at our aunt, who hissed, "Ten dollars!" Uncle Pete walked past us and into the kitchen. He returned with a beer. When it came to money, no one argued with Aunt Lois. Our uncle glared at me and Ginx, but he found no way to shift the blame. I'd read in one of Aunt Lois's books that the eyes are the windows to the soul. I actually used this sentence in a letter Billy ended up rejecting. The way I saw it, though, Uncle Pete's soul had windows so tiny that little light seeped into it.

"'Course Dana didn't help out by carrying on a conversation like that girl was our dinner guest or something," Uncle Pete tried.

Dana began to protest, but Aunt Lois raised one hand, hushing her and saying, "Don't be pitiful, Pete." To the rest of us, she said, "Sit down so we can have our supper." I dimmed the lights.

"She's in my class," I told them. "I mean, she never shows up much, but she's supposed to be in my class."

"Well, I'll be," Uncle Pete muttered under his breath.

"The only thing a little tramp like that does at school is take the boys out in the woods and settle a few *itches*," Aunt Lois exclaimed. Then she looked at our uncle. "*Ten dollars!* You are going to church with me every Sunday till I forgive you, is that clear?" our aunt demanded. "Every Sunday." Ginx kept his rolled-up magazine by his plate.

"Jeez," Uncle Pete said, "are you gonna go on like this all night, or can we have some dinner now?" He sucked at his beer, holding the bottle by the neck. Even I couldn't understand why Aunt Lois was making such a fuss. She reached up to the third shelf of her display cabinet, where she kept the less valuable crystal, took down a glass, turned around, and slammed it in front of him.

"Any man with money to throw around should at least have the decency to drink his beer from a glass," she said. "*We're* not white trash."

"Jeez," Uncle Pete muttered again, touching his hair as if its shine might save him. He poured his beer into the glass. Ginx was fidgeting with the tablecloth.

"Stop that, boy," Uncle Pete ordered. "See if you can help your auntie bring me something to eat."

"Leave him alone," Aunt Lois said. "Just leave him be for once."

"We got pumpkin pie left from yesterday for dessert," Dana quietly offered.

"Plop the pumpkin portion on the plate perching in perfect proximity to Uncle Pete," I said as I sat down, taking advantage of the fact that our uncle was undefended. My brother snorted a laugh.

"Shut up!" Uncle Pete insisted, looking at our aunt. "Lois, what's for supper?" he asked. But our uncle had lost all power for pulling the conversation back on track.

"Possibly petrified poopy Pete," Ginx sang.

"Serves you right, Pete," Aunt Lois barked.

PARTY

～

"THERE'S SWEETY-BOY," Ginx said, as we approached Dead Man's Field. He pointed up. I looked at the dusty yard, where the sun was beating down. The yards in West Hillsborough lost their sparse grass in the summertime and turned to dust. I saw the little white house and the girl in front of it. She was dressed in a wedding gown, holding a can of Pepsi in one hand.

"Jesus almighty!" I laughed out loud. I was glad to have something else to focus on, because all morning I'd been thinking about how the business was over and it would be more difficult to see Billy. I didn't mind going to a party, the first real party to which Ginx and I had ever been invited.

"Yoo-hoo!" the girl called, waving at us with her free hand as we started up the dusty little hill of her yard.

"Well, you made it," she said, when Ginx and I stopped in front of her. I got a better look at that puffy white dress, obviously manufactured for a bride on a tight budget. It came complete with a veil, which Sweety-Boy had partially pulled over her face. The long sleeves clung all the way down her thin arms.

"You're all dressed up," my brother said.

"I can't be accused of not dressing for a party," the girl said cheerfully to our faces. "You're looking mighty fine too, Morgan-Lee." I shrugged in response. For the party, I'd borrowed Dana's pink slacks and white T-shirt. I'd even allowed my sister to fix my hair. Sweety-Boy nodded to Ginx. "And how do you do, sir?"

"Just fine," Ginx responded, "and yourself?"

"Well, today is hot, but it's the most perfect yet. It's all perfect because it's Jacob's birthday, and everything's been arranged." Sweety-Boy cast her gaze out to Dead Man's Field as if she were responsible for having set it there just that morning, along with the large oak trees, the sun, the pale scar of moon, the few houses scattered along the border of the field—as if she had created the whole backdrop against which we would celebrate. "I will show you the Patch," she said. "Our Patch, where it's cool. This is our garden party."

"Perfect for a party in the Patch," I mumbled to my brother.

"Perfect for a party in the Patch provided Pete proclaims penance," Ginx added.

"Penance for what?" Sweety-Boy asked. We stopped.

"Nothing," Ginx said, after a pause during which he indicated himself and me with flicks of his thumb. "It's just something we do."

The girl did not inquire any further. She gathered up her wedding train and turned to walk around to the back of the house. "If my grandpa—if Mr. Winston comes out, just wave and say, 'How do you do, sir?' He doesn't know about the party. Mr. Winston loves parties, but he just don't have the energy for them anymore. They wear him out. If we don't act like it's a party, he won't suspect." We followed her around the corner and stood in the backyard, a tall circular fence overgrown with ivy before us. "Where's Dana?" Sweety-Boy asked.

"Dana doesn't like walking with me, especially if she's going to meet someone new," Ginx explained matter-of-factly, one hand fumbling in his pocket. "She'd rather walk alone."

"Naw," I said, because I thought we were telling this girl way too much, "that's not it. She was wrapping a present for Jacob." I looked at Ginx, hoping he wouldn't argue. "That's why she's late."

Sweety-Boy didn't even consider what I was saying. She narrowed her eyes at my brother and shook her head. "That's just rude, rude, rude behavior on Dana's part," the girl breathed. "Family should stick together, show up as a unit." She pushed at the flimsy green door to the Patch. We entered a small circular room with a flat dirt floor just as red and dusty as her yard. The walls were made of wood garden fencing and stood about six feet tall. The roof was made of the same fence material. The whole thing was all painted green, but you could hardly see this because it was covered inches thick in kudzu, which wound through the tiny diamonds of the fencing, intertwining with itself and offering forth rich green leaves that I just had to reach into for the coolness, which tickled all the way up my forearm.

"Our aunt rips this stuff out if she finds it growing in the garden," I said.

"Once that kudzu takes root, you just can't stop it—specially not in the summertime," Sweety-Boy informed me.

There was only a small table inside, and it was loaded with bags of chips and three six-packs of Pepsi; there were cartons stacked underneath. Sweety-Boy went to the table and put down her Pepsi can.

"Where's Jacob?" I asked.

"Oh," Sweety-Boy said, "he's giving Mr. Winston his dinner, then he'll have to help get him to bed." She paused for a minute. "Mr. Winston—my grandpa, like I said. My momma's daddy." She sighed. "Jacob loves taking care of people. He's good to us, real good."

"Who else is coming?" I asked, looking around the small fenced-in space and wondering how it was going to fit a whole party of people.

"Well now, just you, me, Ginx, Dana, and Jacob, of course," she replied, turning to shut the green door.

"Dana and Jacob are the only ones missing then," Ginx stated. "There will be five of us."

"That's enough," Sweety-Boy said, her veil puffing with each word. "Enough for me." Ginx nodded, and Sweety-Boy began to rock. I was relieved, but I wondered if it counted as a true party. I heard Ginx repeat "party" twice. A hard word, taut and wiry, much like the girl. My brother looked down at Sweety-Boy's feet, then up to the roof of the Patch. He stroked his chin and studied the kudzu leaves.

"Nice place you got here," Ginx then said, too loudly.

"It's humble," Sweety-Boy replied, discreet as a good housewife, "but it's ours, mine and Jacob's."

"The walls are nice," Ginx remarked, reaching out to touch one of the rich green kudzu leaves.

"I'll turn on the light," she offered, flipping a switch. A wire had been tangled all the way up the fence and over the roof, terminating in a naked hanging bulb.

I felt I should say something, so I said, "Great."

As the course of conversation faltered, I looked over to the table with the bags of food. "Please help yourself," Sweety-Boy offered. Ginx immediately took one large step toward the table, picked up a bag of Chee-tos, and pulled it open. "You wanted more guests, Morgan-Lee? You disappointed?" Sweety-Boy asked, reaching up to pick off a dry kudzu leaf. As she did, the top few buttons on the back of her dress came undone. When she turned back to me, the front of her dress had slipped forward, and I saw the slope where her breasts began, a tough valley where no flowers would ever grow. I scratched my earlobe. "This'll give us all a chance to get acquainted."

"Acquainted," Ginx repeated.

"No problem," I said. Sweety-Boy cast the dead leaf to the ground.

"Good," Ginx exclaimed, stepping back to us with the Chee-tos. "These are quite nice. Really. Where is Jacob?"

She lifted her veil. "He'll be along shortly."

"Please have some," Ginx said, offering the open bag to Sweety-Boy and then grabbing up a handful to stuff in his mouth. I reached in the bag and took some too. We crunched, the orange food a striking contrast to the white of Sweety-Boy's dress. "So you live with your grandpa?" Ginx asked, licking his lips.

"Yeah," Sweety-Boy said, her eyes roaming across the smooth surface of my brother's face. She took in his hair, his lips, and his chin.

"Ginx," I said firmly, interrupting her gaze, "I would like Chee-tos now too."

He looked at me. "Sure." He looked at the hand holding the bag. "Here," he offered quietly, extending the bag toward me. "Take as many as you like, *Pike.*"

The girl did not laugh at his behavior. We stood there a little longer just chewing. After a while, there was a knock on the door, and Sweety-Boy said, "That must be Dana."

There was a scrape and the hollow sound of knocking

against wood, and we turned to watch Dana step through the opened Patch door. "I heard y'all talking back here," she said. She was carrying a box wrapped in gold paper with a red bow.

She looked worried as she handed her gift to Sweety-Boy, who exclaimed, "Oh, a present, and just in time!"

Ginx moved toward me so Dana would not be forced to stand too close to him. He turned to the fence, separated the kudzu vines, and peered through one of the wooden dia-monds. Ginx and I had chipped in for Jacob's present, but Dana didn't mention this. "From me to Jacob," my sister said.

Sweety-Boy pulled back and studied my sister. "Y'all should be informed," she said, after a long pause, "that back in Asheville, Jacob lifted a tractor off a man." She spoke low and looked impatient, as if the message she was trying to transmit were vital, crucial to understanding why we had come, exactly who we were celebrating.

"He saved a man at Johnny Johnson's, too," Dana rejoined, excited. The girl sucked on her upper lip with increased irritation, but Dana repeated more loudly, as if she hadn't heard, "He saved a man at Johnny Johnson's too."

Sweety-Boy exhaled. "There was a neighbor of ours back in Asheville, a Mr. Keene, out working, and his tractor must've hit a rock or something. It turned over and trapped him underneath. Jacob saw it all happen and just ran into that field and lifted the side of the tractor up enough for Mr.

Keene to crawl clear from under it." Sweety-Boy gave a nod, and a slab of black hair fell over her shoulder.

"I've never heard of anyone able to do that," Dana offered, unaware that the girl's eyes were probing from her arms to her legs and hair. "Oh, Jacob is so strong!"

"Let him alone," Sweety-Boy warned.

"Well, guess your brother'll go to heaven," I said loudly, hoping to deflect Sweety-Boy's glare away from my sister.

The girl took a step back; then she turned from us and went to the table. She said, "Some people find out early what they are capable of. They know the kind of person they are. I mean, they really know whether they're good or bad. Some people are just lucky that way." She opened another bag of chips.

Dana and I stood, not looking at each other. I felt it was time for me to give my sister something, a piece of advice, a strong word or phrase that she could understand and cling to while navigating the murky seas of love. Our mother never thought about how to do this, and Aunt Lois would certainly lead her astray.

"Most people—" Ginx began, talking to Sweety-Boy.

As he spoke, I whispered to Dana, "Love is not a pie." That was the capsule of knowledge I managed to tell my sister while we stood there, avoiding each other's eyes. "Not a pie," I repeated as kindly as I possibly could. It was something I had heard once, a phrase to cherish.

"May I have chips?" Ginx asked, when he was finished

with what he had to say. So far, he had kept from humming. "Could I please have some of your chips?" he asked Sweety-Boy.

"Fatten you up," she said, laughing. "You're way too skinny."

"Yeah," my brother agreed, laughing as well. "I'm skinny, all right. I should eat more pie. Pumpkin pie and pretzels." Ginx looked at me. He nodded and even smiled. With both hands, he split his bangs across his forehead and said, "Thank you" to Sweety-Boy, who held open her bag. He took a handful of chips.

The Patch door scraped open once more, and a large boy hunched down and lumbered through. His hair was a grown-out crew cut, so his head looked to be covered in a spread of soft nettles. He was wearing an old blue T-shirt tucked into a pair of stone-washed jeans. "And together they licked the platter clean," Sweety-Boy sang out, as he came in and joined our semicircle.

"Surprise!" Dana yelped.

Without looking the least bit surprised, the large boy smiled and told us all hello. "This is Jacob," the girl announced. Dana's gaze traveled from his face to his feet. "This is my brother, Jacob," Sweety-Boy said, "and he got himself a Saturday off work."

"Surprise," Ginx sputtered, between crunches.

"Oh, well, look here. Thank y'all for coming." Jacob thumped into the middle of the small Patch. "Man, it's hot in here," he said, pushing up the sleeves of his T-shirt. Then he squashed a thick eyebrow under his thumb pad. Sweety-Boy bent backward, graceful as a willow. Ginx wiped his entire arm across his mouth.

"Hi, Jacob," my sister said. The boy's face and body were expanded versions of themselves. He was as big as Amos.

"Hello," Jacob said, looking at Dana as she half closed her eyes, a trick Aunt Lois had told us to use sparingly. "It works especially well," Aunt Lois had promised, "if you've dazzled the lids with Brun de Nuit."

I asked Dana, "What eye shadow are you wearing?"

"Brun de Nuit!" my sister answered loudly, enunciating the French so everyone could hear.

Jacob leaned back on his heels as Sweety-Boy introduced us. "This is Morgan-Lee, this is Ginx, and this is Dana." I smiled.

Jacob lifted a thick hand in greeting as each of our names was spoken. His face was pleasant, although each individual feature was poorly formed: his eyes were too close and small, pinning down a large nose. "Hey," Jacob said to Dana, hand running through his hair, "what'd you say just now?"

Dana's fingers wriggled into fists, which she pressed over her heart. "Oh! It was French." She sighed wistfully, thumping her growing chest and shaking her head so you could tell just by looking that her hair was smooth as water. Jacob's face was muscled and soft, lacking the dark, rough places in Sweety-Boy's face. In fact, the two of them looked nothing alike.

"You know our Aunt Lois. Lois Cook," I told him.

"Sure, Mrs. Cook. She's real sweet," the boy told us. "Comes to the garage all the time. She won that car of hers as a prize, right?"

"She didn't *win* it; that car was an award for hard work. It's not like winning a prize, you know, something for nothing," Dana explained. "Anyway, now she's in line for getting the Deena Fae Cadillac."

"Jacob," Ginx mumbled through a mouthful of chips. He swallowed. "Yeah. My sister has a crush on you."

"Shut up, Ginx!" Dana hissed.

Jacob pursed his lips and looked at me, so I quickly interceded. "Not me," I said, and pointed at Dana.

"The other one," Sweety-Boy shrilled. "The other one."

Dana blushed a deep red and sniffled. "Gawd!"

"Hi, Jacob," I loudly interjected, attempting to start from scratch. "Happy birthday. I guess you're sixteen now."

"That's right," Jacob confirmed, grateful to me for having provided a bridge over disaster. He said, "Glad you could be here. Thank y'all for showing up."

"It's a sad, sad occasion," Sweety-Boy interjected, suddenly serious, biting her lip as if trying to shove away tears. "Y'all don't know this, but Jacob got his driver's license today."

"People often get a license at sixteen," Ginx affirmed. "Often that happens."

"Aw," Jacob said, "now come on, Sweety."

"Yeah," Sweety-Boy agreed halfheartedly, "people do." Then she looked at my brother and added, "Jacob's itching to get out of here, and I don't know yet if I can go with him."

"Vegas is my dream," the large boy added; then he winked at Sweety-Boy. He was blunt. "I always wanted to go, but she knows I wouldn't go without her. I ain't going without my sister; she knows that. Vegas has always been a dream, though." Ginx cocked his head and stopped crunching, surprised that dreaming was even a possibility for such a large boy.

"Of course not. He's not going to leave you," Ginx reassured Sweety-Boy, as if he had known them both a long time. Jacob put his arm out and pulled his sister to him, crumpling her hard white polyester against his chest. Ginx's hand went to his ear, and I instinctively looked away from the scene. Sweety-Boy was not the kind of girl who should be touched; this is what I thought. But she leaned into Jacob nonetheless.

"Ginx knows what I'm talking about. A brother and a sister gotta stay together," she said. I kept my eyes averted, and suddenly Sister Lucca was there on the field below, drawing a wriggling black snake from her branch, placing it between her teeth, and biting it so hard the head snapped off. Jacob released Sweety-Boy and reached for a handful of Ginx's Chee-tos.

Ginx stood very straight, holding the bag from the bottom so as not to risk being touched. "What's your favorite kind of car?" he asked Jacob. Once Jacob's hand was out of the bag, Ginx blew all potential germs off his wrist in case it had been grazed without his having noticed.

"Probably the 1972 Mustang," Jacob said. "I got one now from a man said he was practically killed in it. But a guy brought in a little Pontiac the other day that near about brought me to tears."

"I got you something," Dana piped up, holding forth her golden box.

"We all chipped in for it," Ginx added.

"I picked it out, and I wrapped it!" Dana hastened to exclaim.

"For *me?*" Jacob said with a wink, taking the box.

"For the devil himself," Sweety-Boy muttered, brushing away the orange Chee-to crumbs that clung to the front of her wedding dress. She gave her skirts a rustle so my sister's gaze switched off Jacob and onto her.

"Why are you wearing that?" Dana asked.

"It's a wedding dress," Ginx answered promptly and so matter-of-factly that Dana grew more disconcerted.

"But this is a birthday party." My sister attempted to reason, trying to regain some ground. "And aren't you hot?"

"Aw," Jacob said, fussing with the fancy gold ribbon on his package, "that wedding dress belonged to my momma. That's half the reason Sweety wears it." He balled up the curly ribbon and stuffed it into the pocket of his jeans. "My momma and our daddy eloped, so it's kind of a memory of how we got to be brother and sister."

"Kind of." Sweety-Boy smiled. "Iris Orange—that's *my* momma—stole his heart, but then he left her too. She never stopped loving our daddy, I can tell you that."

"Eloped," Ginx repeated, the new sound bulging out, full and impregnable. No one, not even Dana, suggested that we move to stand nearer the table rather than huddling close to the door. My sister turned back to Jacob.

"Do you like my present?" she asked, as he pulled off the tape and carefully unwrapped the small box. Two leather workmen's gloves lay in a bed of golden tissue paper taken from Aunt Lois's gift-wrapping cabinet.

"Well," Jacob breathed, "these are just too nice for me." He stroked the leather.

"You work so much with your *hands,* I know," Dana cooed, "and you can wear them year-round." Sweety-Boy's eyes darted straight to my sister's fingers, which balled immediately into fists.

"He works in the junkyard too," Ginx added, smacking on more food. Jacob wrapped his gift back up in its tissue, thanked Dana again, and went over to set the box on the table.

"Well," Dana bubbled, "you are just so welcome."

Sweety-Boy spoke out. "Back in the mountains, Jacob and me had a Patch similar to this one. We used to have to meet there in secret so Iris Orange wouldn't find out. I don't think I ever told anyone this before." The four of us looked at her as she started up the story, her sentences drawn out, weighted down. "When Jacob and me were kids, we'd go back to our Patch and he'd let me weave honeysuckle into his hair."

"Aw, stop it now," Jacob protested. Ginx crumpled the bag he was holding. I saw him trying not to shrug or turn his head to the side, but he did both.

"He had this long hair, longer and blacker than any of the little boys around. I liked it. I'd sit back in the Patch with him for hours, just combing it and weaving in those flowers. I called him the Fairy God." The intimacy was too much. Ginx's bag spilled onto the ground as both hands shot to his ears.

"Enough, Sweety," Jacob stammered. "They're gonna get the wrong idea."

"Do you miss the mountains?" I asked, trying to change the subject. Ginx succeeded in dropping a greasy hand and shoving it into his pocket, imitating Jacob, who had a hand in his pocket.

Sweety-Boy stood straight and flatly asked Jacob, "Now, what would the wrong idea be?" When her brother just shook his head, she went on to say, "Hours. We'd sit there for hours. The sky would change colors, that's how long we'd sit there."

Back in the days of our business, I would have taken notes on a patch of red dust under a wild honeysuckle canopy. Of course I would have spent extra time on a letter like that, detailing the part about how love is actually simple. Even just sitting with a person to watch the changing shades of sky can be enough. I would have written how there's no real need for kissing, how touch is frivolous, frippery, flotsam, the extra that gets tacked on at the day's end, not the minute-by-minute day of one person next to another, of stillness together. I wished I could write a letter like that for Billy. He would love a letter like that.

My brother had gotten hold of a jar of Sweety-Boy's jam. Near the table, one of the cartons had been torn open. He popped the top, twisted it off, and began by sinking his forefinger into the jam as deeply as it would go.

"You can see one of the houses I service from here," Sweety-Boy told us, parting the kudzu vines and peering through. "There's a woman in that house with the caving-in roof—you can barely see it. She buys a good amount of jam, but she won't shut up about that damn roof. Every time I go over there, she's telling me that her roof just caved in the night before and she has to get it fixed immediately. She puts on airs, telling me the roof has to be fixed regardless of cost; she's a busy woman, don't you know." Sweety-Boy shook her head over the desperation. "So I just make up a name and number for someone she can call who will come right away. A little more expensive, but worth it. And every time I go there, she thanks me. She's looped her loop!"

"How much jam can you sell?" I asked.

"How do you think I afforded to build this?" Sweety-Boy was facing both Dana and me head-on, indicating the Patch with a sweep of her arm in a gesture eerily similar to Aunt

Lois's. "And you should see my bedroom, with a pink canopy bed and all!" Then she rubbed at her right knee. While keeping watch on her unpredictable frame, I stroked the base of my neck. "You know," she said, "I hate to set foot in poor people's houses—all of 'em smell. Fact is, I just won't do it."

Her announcement was startling. Our father had told me, "We are middle class. We will probably always be middle class." This sounded fine to me, and I couldn't remember ever really wanting to be rich, although Dana certainly did. I bit my lip and tried to think of what to say. Ginx chewed with his mouth open. Our father would categorize Sweety-Boy as lower class; Aunt Lois had called her white trash.

"You don't like poor people because they can't afford jams?" Dana asked, trying to be agreeable.

"What do you mean you don't like poor people?" I asked.

"Donor," Ginx said.

"I don't like the way they smell," she explained casually, leaning back so she could address all three of us at once. "Their houses smell like worn-out dresses, like fatback and ammonia." She paused, her lips cracking apart for those perfect teeth. Her speech turned slick. "Fact is, I shouldn't complain. I've made some good money off poor people in my time. They love jam. When my grandpa was young and working all day in the mill, he said he could lick a whole jar clean, and that was just for starters. I don't discriminate on the selling part; cash looks the same no matter whose hands are giving it out. It's just that there're some houses I won't go inside."

"You really should see her room," Jacob broke in. "Lives better than a queen." He cleared his throat.

"Well, our house sure don't smell of ammonia and fatback. Tell you that much. I make certain of it," Sweety-Boy announced, blinking fiercely. There was anger in her voice. "Having money is a choice like anything else. You don't gotta be poor, not in this country. There's a way out of everything; no reason to sit around the house in some sorry worn-out version of what you could be and just *take* it." Our father would say it was wrong to talk like that, that most people couldn't help what class they were in. But to me, her firm pronouncement soothed like balm. I had never before imagined the possibility of standing in front of shelves stacked with life's most unwieldy worries and blessings and simply choosing what to keep and what to discard—not to be poor, not to be afraid, not to be hurt, not to be misled.

"Hand me a Pepsi, Dana, please," Sweety-Boy requested, while pinching up a flimsy layer of her dress. "It's hard to move in this thing."

"Sure," Dana said. I leaned over to finger the cheap fabric of her dress.

"Can I feel, too?" Ginx asked, sending Sweety-Boy into a seesaw laugh.

"You must be a gentleman, sir, for asking so nice." She smiled. "Be my guest." She took the Pepsi can from Dana, popped it open, and handed it to Jacob. She asked for another, which Dana promptly got.

"Chicory." Ginx rubbed the scratchy fabric together between his fingers.

That was a beautiful word, and I didn't like his just handing such a word to her like that, so I quickly instructed, "A dress is a dress, Ginx. It doesn't mean a thing about the person wearing it." He let go and wiped his hands on his pants.

"True," he told me. "You have to be careful."

I noticed that Jacob was looking at the place on my upper arm, the collection of little bruises not covered by my T-shirt. I rarely wore such short sleeves. I pretended not to notice and allowed him to stare. Then, from somewhere in all her whiteness, Sweety-Boy produced a silver object. She opened her Pepsi can, took a long deep swig, then held the object in view long enough for me to see that it was an upscale version of the flask that the boys at school usually kept hidden in paper bags. Jacob drank down a few gulps of his Pepsi and averted his eyes. His sheepish smile surprised me. I hadn't suspected that a boy who'd lifted a tractor would ever feel sheepish. He held out his can so she could pour a good stream of thick brown liquid to fill it back up again.

"Bacardi," she said. "Only the best for my brother's birthday." Ginx began a hum attached to a distant buzzing. He hooked his pointer finger in order to dig at the jam, swiping dollop after dollop into his mouth.

"Enjoy yourself," Sweety-Boy told my brother.

"Ginx," I commanded in order to divert his attention from that girl. He stopped the hum.

Sweety-Boy chucked out a laugh. "Would y'all care to join us in this little *extravaganza*?" Dana sifted her fingers through her hair, again and again, as if she might eventually grab the answer from her scalp, but the hand kept coming out clean each time. I pressed down on the front of my pants the way Sweety-Boy had at Aunt Lois's house. Then I reached to take a dollop from my brother's jar. The jam was horrible: pure sugar with a chemical aftertaste; I nearly spit it out.

"Gimme something to rinse my mouth," I demanded.

"Don't take to my jams?" the girl asked. She laughed, and my brother bit his lip, watching her tenderly as I had never seen him watch anyone but me.

"We will join you, ma'am," Ginx offered in calm decision. He grabbed a Pepsi can for each of us and tore off the caps. I drank a few swigs of mine, while keeping my eyes fixed on the girl.

"Your dress is undone," Dana whispered to Sweety-Boy. Jacob touched his sister's back.

"It's okay," Jacob said, "it's hot."

Ginx took a few gulps of his Pepsi, then we stuck out our cans the way Jacob had done. Sweety-Boy held up the flask for each of us in turn, pouring from a greater height than she needed to, so we could all enjoy the refreshing sound of liquor catapulting into the Pepsi.

"Uncle Pete drinks this stuff sometimes," Dana informed us, trying to make the situation familiar. My brother blushed when the girl poured his liquor, his eyes full of good black earth, of warmth, of the present. Things were not at all familiar.

"Your uncle probably drinks more of this than he lets you know," Sweety-Boy said.

"Aw," Jacob guffawed, "nothing wrong with a nip now and then."

"And this," Sweety-Boy announced, closing and stashing the flask as quickly as it had appeared, then raising her Pepsi can in the air, "is a celebration!"

"Sure," I joined in, the first to clink my can with hers, a sound Ginx immediately tried to repeat by tapping at various places on his own can. But when he couldn't find the right sound he actually gave up and turned around to clink with Dana and then with Jacob. My brother looked Jacob straight in the eye, leaned back, and took a long, greedy swallow. Dana and I watched Ginx; then we drank too.

"Well, now," Sweety-Boy mocked, "don't beat us to it." Ginx pulled the can from his mouth with a clocking sound, his eyes not leaving Jacob's face. His breath drew in and out, laden with the sweet smell of liquor and soda: a man's breath.

"You're a lot nicer than I thought you might be," Ginx confessed to Jacob. He burped. "A lot."

Jacob brought his own can down, his smile so seemingly uninterrupted by any thought that I could not help but feel a bit lighter, a little more free. "Thank you, sir," Jacob said with another generous clink of his can. They both drank again.

"Just stings a little going down," Dana observed, not bothering to cover her mouth when she coughed. It did sting, and I didn't much like the taste, but I swigged again because my bones were loosening, and it seemed the world below might begin to float to the surface if I kept it up. The house on water. It would feel good, I thought, not to have a house weighing me down.

"About time the three of you grew up," Sweety-Boy said, winking at me. She finished her Pepsi first, then we were all done and on to seconds, except Dana, who was giggling just after her first.

"Jacob," she said. He turned toward her, but she had not yet formulated a question. "You like work?" she asked a few seconds too late. The boy just smiled. I took a long swallow from my second can.

Dana started on a second Pepsi and Bacardi and began her confession. "I saw you before, Jacob. I mean, before we met just now. Myra and me spied on you; her brother's Eric." Her eyes were mooning over Jacob's face.

"Yeah?" he asked. "That's all right. Eric's a good man. It's all right." The boy nodded at my sister. I believed him: Things were all right. Dana would be all right; we'd all be all right if he had any say in the matter. Jacob's eyes wandered back to my bruises. Dana rubbed freely at her chest.

"I wish you were our friends," Ginx observed. "Things

have been really good today. It's fun." He took another swig, and I imagined we lived a whole other life, one in which the three of us had friends in common and went to parties.

"Well," Sweety-Boy began, gripping her Pepsi can hard enough that it dented, "things should be good. God made them to be that way. Things were meant to be good." I stood squarely on both feet and wiped at my sweaty face.

"I don't believe in God," I said.

"Sure we can be friends," Jacob said. "What's all the fuss?"

"All things in time," Ginx answered. "We must work toward friendships." I recognized this last sentence as belonging to Mr. McIntyre, our school guidance counselor, whom Ginx visited once a week. My brother was crumpling borrowed lines together like someone balling up the nearest newspaper pages in order to stuff a hole.

Dana's mascara was smeared. I looked from her to Ginx, Sweety-Boy, and Jacob. We were children. We were just five children in a garden patch on a warm July afternoon. The Luccas were now floating. There was lightness within me. Perhaps we were safe. I looked at Sweety-Boy again and saw that she was staring at me. Her dress by now was hanging farther off her shoulders, so a light-green halter top was peeking through. Her black hair stuck to her cheeks and neck. "Time you grew up," she whispered. I stumbled sideways as the floodwaters suddenly rose, rushing the Luccas so far down the river I could no longer see them.

"Ginx, there's a flood," I tried to warn him. But he didn't hear me, or perhaps chose not to.

"Man," Jacob swore to my brother, "I can't believe this is your first time drinking hard liquor." Ginx's rhythmic drinking had matched Jacob's, draft for draft. I looked around the Patch, which was unclear in dimension but smelled much sweeter than I'd remembered upon first entering. The waters rushed on below. I grabbed at a vine of kudzu to steady myself.

Ginx nodded when his swallow was done. "All considered," he said, "this is my first time drinking any alcohol ever." He traced the rim of his can. "I tend to keep clear of bad things." *Tend.* A rivulet of sweat fell from Ginx's temple to his nose, over his mouth, and then on down his neck to where it was absorbed by the collar of the white shirt he was wearing. I wiped my forehead with the back of my hand and then drew my forearm across my cheek.

"May I offer you a handkerchief, ma'am?" Jacob asked, pulling a sturdy blue cloth from his back pocket. "Don't worry, it's clean."

"I wouldn't care if it was clean or not!" Dana blurted out.

"Well, now, that's love talking," Sweety-Boy said.

Jacob handed me the cloth, his entire face absorbed in a smile. I dabbed it against my forehead, and Dana asked Jacob if she could borrow one too.

"Well, now, let me go get one for each of you," Jacob said. "I got plenty. Be right back." Jacob left the Patch to get the cloths; as soon as the door shut behind him, Dana grabbed the jam jar. She lapped at the disgusting stuff with her tongue.

"You like my jam, not like your sister!" Sweety-Boy exclaimed, arms outstretched as if in preparation to receive the largest of blessings. "Isn't it just good?" she called up to the single raw light bulb.

"Yes," Ginx agreed, "yes, it is good." He had no idea that the Luccas were drowning, which struck me as simultaneously awful and hilarious. I hacked out a laugh. Sweety-Boy hit my back. "You don't go back to Asheville, then," Ginx said. "Your momma still lives there, though?"

"Iris Orange?" It must have been over 100 degrees in there, but Sweety-Boy was not sweating. "Yeah, she still lives there. I don't go back because we had a fight. She did me wrong. I'm not saying it's her fault, but what happened happened, and I don't forgive easy."

Ginx nodded. I wiped at my neck and forehead with Jacob's cloth. No one talked to Ginx the way this girl was talking. My brother stood there, his arms and legs too long for his torso, his handsome face moving against the tide of sounds that, in a perfect world, would have replaced all chatter. We might have been celebrating some romantic union, an elopement with Sweety-Boy as the bride.

"Here he is, the birthday boy!" the girl announced again as Jacob came through the door with four different colored cloths the size and shape of the one he'd given me.

"Here we are." Jacob handed Dana and Ginx cloths and then wiped his forehead with a red one. Ginx held his between two fingers and blew away all the germs. He then proceeded to stick it under his shirt and mop up the sweat on his chest.

"Oh," Dana exclaimed, dropping the jam jar onto the table. "Oh, I've never drunk hard liquor! This is the first time, just my first time ever," she told Jacob.

"Baptism by fire," Jacob said, a sentence that Ginx ingested, mouthing it over soundlessly to himself before again bringing his Pepsi can to his lips. That was when I noticed his other hand, rubbing up and down on his thigh and then in front in a continual search for his pants pocket. Ginx seemed to have lost all notion of where a pants pocket might be. I took another long, hard, burning swallow.

Sweety-Boy's veiled headpiece was on the ground. She stood close to me. "Unzip my dress the rest of the way, Morgan-Lee." With one deep breath, I took in the smell of decay, kudzu, and honeysuckle. "Go on, you can see I got clothes on underneath."

"My daddy used to beat me too, when I was little, Morgan-Lee," I heard Jacob confess behind me, low and determined, as if he'd been waiting for the right time to reveal this information. I immediately understood his mistake about my bruises.

I straightened a little. "Oh, my!" Dana exclaimed, taking a wobbly step toward him. "How awful." But he wasn't speaking to her, and I felt his stare remain on me. I blushed as I put my hand under Sweety-Boy's long black hair in search of the zipper. Her hair was damp and thick as compost. Ginx banged his Pepsi can down on the table.

"Not my *daddy*," I tried to tell Jacob, but the words scrambled into one. *"Marketpaddy."*

"Marketpaddy," Ginx repeated. I concentrated on finding Sweety-Boy's zipper and then tried pulling it down quickly, the way Aunt Lois had taught us to rip a Band-Aid from a sore, but my fingers were trembling, and the zipper stuck somewhere in the middle.

"If you get beaten, you gotta leave," Jacob was saying, speaking as if addressing an audience of boys and girls. *We are just five children,* I was repeating to myself, *on an afternoon in July.*

"Aw," Dana said to Jacob, "don't think about all that sadness now. You got away, and you're here. With me." She paused, pushed out her right hip, and said sweetly, "Now, I hear you lifted a tractor off a man. It must have weighed like thousands of pounds."

"Marketpaddy," Ginx repeated. *"Toolcaddy. Rolandnaddy."*

But Jacob was not taken in. "It didn't weigh thousands," he said, "but, yeah, I saved a guy a while back." He spoke firmly, letting us know that he was capable and willing to do it again if necessary. He mashed his left eyebrow with his thumb pad, and this time a rivulet of sweat ran down the side of his face. Jacob's cloth looked insufficient for the job of keeping him dry.

"My brother takes care of people. That's how he is. Can't help it," Sweety-Boy chimed in, then finished her Pepsi with a long swig. "Just his nature."

"Oh, we know, we know!" Dana exclaimed, tumbling back into the conversation. I was dizzy and stared at Jacob to steady myself. Sweety-Boy handed me her Pepsi and jerked at her zipper. When she finally unzipped the dress, she let it fall, then emerged in the opposite way of a butterfly—discarding her rare cocoon to reveal less interesting possibilities. I studied Jacob's arms and neck and understood why my sister would want to be close to this boy. But there was still so much she didn't know and needed to learn about love. Dana sighed and leaned too far forward, saving herself from falling by taking another step toward Jacob. There was no Momma Lucca watching, ready to help me, no B.J. spitting and swearing and loving his sister, no Sister howling naked over a field. They were gone. I was light and giddy and surprised to catch myself caring so deeply about the fact that Jacob had large arms and a great thick neck just like Amos's. Ginx was drinking and speaking to himself: *Generous. Billous. Toffee.* Billy would most certainly be jealous of Jacob.

"Don't dirty that dress," Dana warned loudly, clutching the jam jar.

"Dana, don't shout," I told her, but she just dolloped more jam onto her tongue, sucking her finger clean between each wail.

"Marriage is sacred," she spat at Sweety-Boy. We all looked

down at the dress lying in a puff at our feet, like a cloud shot down from the sky.

"Dana"—Ginx tried to comfort her—"a dress is a dress."

"Oh, God, how true that is!" I exclaimed, woozing in and out of dizziness, wishing my sister were happier and wondering how the man must have felt as Jacob lifted the tractor off him.

"You going to dirty it," Dana warned. "And red clay don't wash off," she insisted, her slur thick as syrup, her finger plunging again into the bright red jam. Sweety-Boy shook her head and clucked her tongue.

"You're not feeling too good, are you, girl?" Jacob touched my sister's elbow and Dana immediately dropped the jar and her Pepsi can. She forgot all about her sausage fingers, which she spread over her eyes in a useless attempt to hide her tears as she broke into sobs that had been retained far too long.

"Dana," I began. But she had come to this Patch as if to a stopping place, and a large kind boy was standing there, as though he'd been waiting for her all along. Dana's sobs sprang and receded, sprang and receded. She needed a piece of advice, a line to hold on to but all that I could hear in my head was *Marketpaddy, marketpaddy.* My brother hummed viscously, but I wasn't sure to what. I rubbed the front of my pants. Up, down. Up.

"It's a tired old dress, worn all wrong," Sweety-Boy sang. For no reason, joy sprouted down in me; a kernel of joy cracked open, and the girl seemed to know it. She was watching me as she sang, and I was trying to pick that kernel out from all the scrappy mud and river water, squeeze it between two fingers, and force it to grow faster.

"Oh, God," Dana said, "I just can't take it anymore." She collapsed, falling straight into Jacob's arms.

"Aw, now," he said, finally surprised, catching her and holding her straight again. That's when she did it. She declared in shrieks, "I love you, I love you, I love you!"

"God almighty!" Ginx swore, a phrase I'd never heard him use.

"Help that girl out of her misery," Sweety-Boy said, laughing. "Sweet Jesus, look at that! If she were a horse, they'd shoot her." Jacob's face filled with hardship and concern.

"Shut up!" I told the girl, then turned to my brother. "Ginx," I cried. Despite all the intimacy, he hadn't covered his ears. "Help us!" My brother looked away, so I repeated myself. "Help us." He folded his arms against his chest, forcing them to stay still; his hands were in fists, and he turned to Sweety-Boy.

"You have a wagon," Ginx accused. She nodded, flipping up a nickel-sized lighter and fishing a slim cigarette from under her halter top.

"Jacob, tell me you love me," Dana begged, her fingers now kneading his chest. "I can't take it anymore!"

"Come on, Dana," Jacob soothed, trying to keep her at arm's length. "You know you're too good for me." I thought of the saved man examining his crushed limbs. I pressed hard against one of my faded bruises. It hurt. I was angry with my sister for allowing herself to fall, but maybe even angrier that someone had been there to catch her. "I only like the simple kinds of girls," Jacob was trying to explain, as Dana searched his eyes, obviously misunderstanding every word, "the kind who don't expect much, not the ones all pretty and sweet like you, who could have anybody." At that, Dana's shoulders reared backward, snapping her head away from his chest for a second and then heaving forward, mouth open, spewing orange-flecked, raspberry-red vomit all over the large boy. She woozed sideways, smiling, as if this had been the real gift. Then she collapsed again into his arms, smack into her own mess. The boy's big jaw clamped shut, but that was the only reaction he allowed himself.

"God almighty!" I screamed. "Didn't Aunt Lois teach you anything?" I didn't even know what I was asking.

"Just the rum talking back now," Sweety-Boy assured us, blowing out a long, cool stream of smoke. "She'll be okay."

My brother stood straight. "Get the wagon now," he ordered, a powerful sergeant, his face white and clenched.

"Sir?" Sweety-Boy asked. Her upper lip curled from the rancid smell of vomit, exposing just the tips of her good teeth. "Smells worse than fried fatback in here."

"Dana, stand straight, for God's sake," I ordered. I wanted to yell that I had a whole separate world to monitor buried under years upon years of stillness that, long ago, would have wrecked a weaker heart, but no one saw *me* standing there throwing up and falling down, sputtering stupidly over the load I carried. I'd never ask anyone to catch *me*.

You were such a quiet baby, our father had always said of me. Once again, without even bothering to turn, Dana spit up. The mess blotched Jacob's left arm, splattering down to his hand.

Again, Jacob's jaw clenched and released. "You gonna be okay, baby," he assured, managing to hold my sister tighter against his vomit-filled chest and using his cloth to wipe her face clean. "It's better when you chuck it up."

"Get the wagon now," Ginx ordered again, unable to keep his arms folded. His hands began rubbing, his fingers tugging on each other. *Jeckinz. Tiddlywink. Cribbing.*

"Aw," Sweety-Boy said, winking at her brother, "she just needs a little tender care; that's all. No different than any of us."

"A little hugging goes a long way," I quoted, from one of Aunt Lois's books on relationships.

More agile without her dress, Sweety-Boy slipped past Dana and Jacob to open the Patch door.

"We'd better get back," I called after her. "We gotta go now before our momma catches us."

"Catches us," Sweety-Boy repeated, slipping out the door, letting it spring closed behind her, and chuckling to herself over whatever implications were multiplying in her head. "Catches us," I heard her say again, outside.

"Let's get out of here, Ginx," I begged. There was nothing below but river. Nothing but river. The Luccas were nowhere to be found.

Ginx looked at me and nodded. "We need to go."

Jacob seemed about to speak, but I was waiting for my brother. "You gotta take care of her, please, Ginx," I pleaded.

Ginx pursed his lips. "It's all right," he said, slipping a finger back and forth across his upper lip. "I will help us."

Sweety-Boy propped open the Patch door with the handle of her red wagon. While Jacob scooped Dana into his arms and gently laid her in it, Sweety-Boy said, "Listen, Morgan-Lee, you got what it takes. I want you to work with me." She slipped a piece of paper into my pants pocket. "That there is my phone number."

"I don't need work," I told the girl.

"Meet me on the corner of Margaret Lane and King Street on Sunday at three. Call if you need to."

"I don't need work," I repeated, but she didn't care. I almost told her about my letter business. "Really," I told Sweety-Boy, "what I need is a vacation."

Minutes later, I was trotting as straight as possible after Ginx, who continued in a committed narrow march back down Margaret Lane. Dusk was warm and gray, and Dana was sitting in the wagon clutching her ankles, her face burrowed between her knees. Ginx kept his eyes fixed on the road ahead, as if any deviation risked running us straight to ruin. He held one arm behind him as he pulled Sweety-Boy's jam wagon, loaded down with Dana, away from Dead Man's

Field. We left the Patch, the jams, Jacob's arms, the ruined wedding dress. Dragging Dana behind, we hustled away from the only party Ginx and I had ever attended in all our teenage years. As we passed Charley Morgan's house, my brother matched his hum to the rattling wagon wheels. We turned into the cul de sac and made it back home much faster than it had taken us to get to Sweety-Boy's. *Tone. Small. Collar.*

"I gotta make sure Momma and Daddy don't find out," I muttered, when we reached the front door of our house.

"Oh," Dana slurred from the wagon, "naw, don' let them in on it."

Ginx looked at me, his jaw still clenched. He was breathing through his nose. "We're here," he stated to Dana and me. I slid an arm around Dana and lifted her out of the wagon, then held her against me. She wiped the whole back of her hand across her face. She didn't ask to go to our aunt's house. Aunt Lois, of course, would know in a second that we were drunk, and Uncle Pete would have taken down Dana's pants, leaned her over his knee, and belted her—no question about it. So we'd have to shelter Dana; we'd have to get Momma to call Aunt Lois and tell her Dana would be sleeping in her old bed that night. "Be sure you tell Momma we're tired," my sister sputtered, her face wet and rancid. "Did I throw up on him?" she asked, then went on. "Tell Momma we're too tired for anything. We can't take it anymore!" I was dragging her, my arm tucked under hers, helping her walk foot after foot. "Did I spit up on him?" she asked again.

When I didn't answer, Ginx dropped the wagon handle

and meshed his fingers together. "No, Dana," he almost shouted. It was the first time he'd ever told a straight-out lie. I looked at him over Dana's shoulder, and he knitted his eyebrows and started to rock a little from side to side, but he managed to say it, this time in a complete sentence, the kind our mother spoke for Valeria. "No, Dana, you did not spit up on him." I nodded.

"Thank God. Oh, God," Dana breathed. "I thought maybe I'd upchucked all over him. *Mon amour.*"

Despite what I'd said, none of us took any precautions to make sure that our parents weren't around or wouldn't see us. Ginx opened the front door; I wrapped both arms around Dana and limped forward as she leaned her head on my shoulder.

Our mother was sitting on the couch. "Oh, children," she exclaimed upon our entrance. She was preparing a lesson. "Oh, you're back from your party," she said.

"Yes, ma'am," Ginx answered, scrambling through the door behind us.

"We're not chillren," Dana slurred in protest, so our mother looked at her, saw that my arm was around her, and realized something must be wrong.

"Is Dana sick?" our mother asked Ginx as she stood to face us.

"Yes," I said. The smell was overwhelming, and Dana looked awful but managed to stand straight.

My sister was gearing up. "Aren't you tired or something?

You should be in bed, on up in bed, now, shouldn't you?" Dana shouted.

"You *are* sick," our mother said. "Come here, Dana."

"Are you so tired you might as well just die?" my sister wondered, letting out a small, cruel laugh. Our mother was wearing a dark blue sundress, and her hair was back in a silver barrette. She was barefoot and crossed one ankle over the other, her hands on her hips, like a girl examining the front counter for exactly the right kind of candy.

"Come here, Dana," she said again.

"No," Ginx advised our mother, shaking his head as she examined my sister. "No," he said. But our mother did not heed his warning. Dana was regaining her balance, so I let my arm slip away. She was bending forward a little too much but managed to stand on her own, nonetheless.

"Oh," our mother said, looking at Dana's spoiled shirt, then down to her shoes. "Dana. Where did you get alcohol?" She looked at all of us. "Where did you kids get alcohol?" She pronounced the word the way the policeman had when he'd come to talk to our class about how teenagers get in trouble with the law. She took out the barrette and shook her hair loose.

Ginx considered the question. "There was alcohol at the party," he answered. Our mother's reading light shone behind her, all that dark hair so thick that her face looked no bigger than a thumbnail or one of those grains of rice that Aunt Lois would buy at the State Fair, the kind artists painted with a person's name or an entire miniature land-scape. People would pay good money for the depiction of such an intricate tiny face. She moved closer. Dana's head lolled sideways onto my shoulder, her eyes closed briefly. Ginx and I were still, letting the evening waft in through our big window to encircle the light.

Our mother addressed my sister in a whisper. "You don't live here anymore." Her meaning was perfectly clear. "You chose to live with Lois." Ginx began to hum. I thought of morning, the coming of a raw orange sun, the squawk of birds swooping down as if to catch and carry the light, unburdening the world of the weight of its new day. Perhaps there were people somewhere who woke up not thinking of everything from the previous day that had been left undone.

Our mother's gaze remained fixed on Dana, a reminder that for us there would not be any swooping or squawking; there was no unburdening. "You should go to Lois's and have *her* clean you up," our mother said. A strand of hair slipped close to her mouth, so she tucked it behind her ear. "I raised you," she insisted, "and you throw me away like old trash. You don't want to be in this family, so *get out.*"

"Want," Ginx repeated.

Our mother bit her lip and looked at him. She was breathing hard through her nostrils. "Listen up," she told us. "Do you-all know that your father is planning a family ther-apy appointment with Dr. Sampson? Do you-all know he's intent upon that?" she asked.

"Please stop. We're drunk," I cried, bold and awkward as daylight. But she looked back at Dana. My sister gasped, stinking and startled.

"Dr. Sampson. Sampson," Ginx said, laughing now. "Likeable and lickable as a lollipop."

Our mother lowered her voice and spoke to my sister. "You left me. I'm not the best mother, but I loved you, and you left me." Her words floated into the room and paused in order to launch their meaning, which twirled through the air like a dangerous unmanned weapon. "Be careful about wanting something too much," I'd instructed my sister once, "or you just might get it." Dana grabbed my hand, but I could not return her grasp. There were some things she needed to learn on her own.

"That's not true!" my sister shouted, in general protest. Ginx looked at our mother, and then he looked at Dana. *We are children,* I pleaded within myself. The word echoed over the floodwaters below: *children.* Ginx pressed his lips in utter effort; then he stepped forward. I let go of my sister as Ginx clumsily encircled her in his arms and pulled her to his chest, copying Jacob as best he could. "Stop it," he pleaded with our mother. The room hushed as our mother and I watched. Dana hadn't even had time to move.

"Oh, my," our mother wheezed. We had never seen Ginx hug before.

"Oh," Dana exclaimed, stiffening but not pushing him away.

"You've been cruel, Momma," Ginx spoke near Dana's ear. I was proud.

"Cruel," I repeated, the sound soft and cool as the petals of my bruises.

"Oh," our mother pleaded. "You don't know. You can't know what it is like to be a mother." She touched her forehead, then her neck. "Please, Dana," she said. "Sleep here in your old bed tonight." Ginx released Dana and stepped back, not even allowing himself the ritual of blowing his hands and arms clean of her germs.

"Mmmm," was all Dana could reply; tears had done away with her makeup, and her clothes were ruined. "Oh, my God."

"Let's go upstairs," Ginx suggested. The three of us turned. The perfect triad, the lovely lot.

Our mother followed us to the base of the stairs. "It is not and has never been the case that I don't love you," she called after us, as we climbed. "All of you," she added more enthusiastically, as if addressing an entire marching army. "Your father will be home shortly, but you're tired. Go on to bed. To bed!" she ordered, continuing to speak even as we reached the top of the stairs. "He is meeting with the school administration about next fall. Plans for the fall." She coughed. "Maybe we need therapy. Maybe your father is right and we'll go and try to figure things out in public."

"We are going to our rooms now," I called down.

"Yes, go on to bed," she commanded.

I ushered Dana into her bedroom; then I went to the bathroom and wet a towel. I helped her get her clothes off and wiped away what I could of the vomit and then helped her change into pajamas. "As you make your bed, so you shall lie," was the last lesson I whispered to my sister that evening. "Good night, Dana," I told her more quietly, because she looked as though she was already asleep.

But as I headed out the door, she said, "Come back, Morgan-Lee, I want to tell you something." She reached out, but then let her hand drop as she looked at the ceiling. With her other hand, she smoothed back her hair. She was starting to cry, so I concentrated on her earlobe and tried to be as gentle as possible.

"Let's talk tomorrow," I suggested, looking out the window. I could see part of the side of Old Mrs. Dean's house and thought of Billy. I wondered what he was doing, what it was like not having a brother or a sister and having to learn everything alone. Billy had told me that after his father's death he would still talk to his father, talk out loud. But once his mother had heard him, and it made her cry so hard that he swore to himself he'd never to do it again, even if he was sure no one was around. One day, I'd seen him by the river all alone talking, and I had thought he was talking to his father. But he had been talking to me. To me!

Dana said something. I could have reached down and helped her brush the hair from her forehead, but I didn't. "What?" I asked, locking my hands together instead.

"I've never kissed anyone," she told me. "And I'm almost thirteen. Myra's already kissed two boys." She pulled her white sheet all the way up to her chin, even though it was so hot in her room that my armpits were sweating. "No offense, Morgan-Lee," she said, looking at me, "but I don't want to end up like you."

"No offense taken," I said, quickly adding, "You're not like me at all. No danger of that."

"Really," she told me, "no offense." She turned to look at me. "I mean, to tell you the truth, I don't care if I kiss Jacob Little or someone else for the first time. I'd just like it to be someone big and strong like him. And he's kind, too. I want to kiss a boy like that, but it doesn't really have to be him."

"Anyway," I continued, aggravated, "how do you know I haven't kissed anyone? Just exactly how do you know that, Dana?"

My sister blinked twice, and I realized that she really wasn't meaning to offend me. "Who would kiss you?" she asked. The question was quiet and sincere, and the sound of the word *kiss* immediately sliced through the long grass in the empty field below, stopped to sun itself on a rock, twitched once, then once again, and eventually slithered off toward some other place. Sister was definitely gone. Otherwise, she would have bitten the head off this word. But there it went, wriggling through me, and it hurt.

"Whatever." I shrugged again.

"I mean," Dana said, "you could almost be pretty if you

just cleaned yourself up and paid a little more attention." She scratched at her neck beneath the sheet. "I mean, just try a little harder," she said, more as a plea. "Myra says she's never seen anyone who tries so little." Dana breathed out, her eyes still on me. "I told Myra to shut up. I told her you could kiss someone if you wanted to. And you know what she said?" Now Dana propped her head up so she could turn toward me. "I wasn't gonna tell you this, but since we're on the subject now I'm gonna tell you, even though I wasn't gonna."

I took a step back, sure that what she was about to say required its own breathing space.

"Myra said the only boy who would ever kiss you would have to be a little desperate. She said it doesn't help that you smell, which isn't true most of the time, Morgan-Lee. It's just when she was over here last time you did maybe smell a little." Dana looked down for a second, but then her face lit up. "But I told her to shut up anyway. I told her none of it was true, that she was just jealous. And she said, 'Jealous of what? That I don't have a crazy brother and a smelly sister? By the time you get to high school no one's gonna want to be your friend.'" Dana took in a breath and let it out—the thought had obviously been worrying her for some time. "Then," she began again, but it was more of a whisper, "Myra said you didn't like boys, that kids in your class say you'd rather kiss a girl." I was still. I did not move. "Anyway, that's what Myra said." Dana stopped there and rolled back onto her pillow, as though she had carried this news too long and now that it was delivered, she could finally rest.

I waited a few seconds. "Doesn't matter to me what Myra says," I told Dana, who screwed her mouth to the right.

"Can I just tell her you've kissed a boy?" my sister asked. "We can make up the name, but can I just tell her? Thing is, she'll ask you for confirmation, so we have to agree on the name."

"Tell her what you want," I said. "What Myra thinks doesn't matter." But if it really hadn't mattered, I would have forced myself to bend down next to Dana and touch her and whisper that everything would be okay, that it was time to sleep. Instead, I just turned and left.

"Let me just say that you kissed Billy," Dana called after me. "That's at least believable." Without saying good night, I went out of her room, pulling the door shut a little harder than necessary, not caring if it sounded like a slam.

When I was safely in my bedroom, I took out my journal. It was just past seven o'clock. The river within me had subsided, leaving in its wake a residue of junk. I proceeded to scan the banks below to assess what the floods had left and what they had taken. The field was there, but at its edge lay slimy milk cartons and tiny bird bones, plastic chair sets, and individual, yellowed animal teeth. There was no trace of the Luccas. The place had been completely transformed by destruction. They were not coming back. I lay there, bathed in a mixture of fright and comfort.

Outside my window, billions and billions of microscopic hands quietly descended, each slipping to cup a particle of light, displaying it on the palm only a few seconds and then closing to fists, one by one, gently shutting the dusk away into darkness.

FOOD

～

IN THE MORNING, we went downstairs. Since we hadn't eaten any dinner the day before, our mother set out plates full of eggs, bacon, and toast. It had been a long while since our mother had prepared an actual meal. Dana took one look at the food and pushed it away. I, on the other hand, began eating immediately, my hunger deepening with every swallow. Our mother wore an apron that Aunt Lois had given her after a trip to Louisiana. *New Orleans* was written in green cursive on the front. She put her hands on her hips. Her dark hair was combed back into a neat ponytail, which is what I concentrated on in order to avoid looking at her tiny, surprised cheekbones when she smiled.

"Who would like more?" she asked, picking up Ginx's plate and slipping her hand onto his neck, so that we were all taken aback, including Ginx, who managed the moment by holding his breath till she had turned from us and walked into the kitchen.

"Hello, everyone." Our father came down the stairs. He was dressed in jeans and a red polo shirt. "Look, we need to talk as a family."

My brother immediately informed us that the birds this month were particularly brown. He said that the cardinal especially, the North Carolina state bird, had come to us brown rather than red, that there were indications of a disappearance of redness in general—not just among birds—the way volcanic red disappears once it has spilled out and cooled. There are ways, even, to measure the cardinal's wingspan, but no assurance that its red will be with us forever. Really, none at all. A cooling of lava, maybe.

Dana nibbled at her butterless toast. She stared at her glass of orange juice as Ginx spoke what was to her the unpleasant background music of mornings and evenings, the atonal humdrum that could ruin a meal. Perhaps she was thinking about Jacob, but from her face I didn't think so. "My head hurts," she complained. Our father sat, and she studied his right wrist while Ginx's fingers tapped out an electric beat against the edge of the table.

"Here we go, Carl," our mother said, coming out of the kitchen, "this is for you." She slipped an egg from her spatula onto our father's plate.

"Your mother told me about yesterday, and so today I will

make an appointment for our family to see Dr. Sampson," our father said, touching the prongs of his fork. "It is time for us to see somebody and straighten things out. Time," he said, but I did not hear the rest. My heart beat as quickly as a bird's heart; the steps I had taken so far in life were small. I thought about Sweety-Boy. Maybe I'd work with her after all.

"The kids don't want to," our mother announced, standing in front of me so I read *New Orleans* as many times as I could while she spoke. "The kids refuse to go," she said. "We will work things out at home, Carl. Work things out here."

"Marion." Our father stopped touching the fork prongs and held the rim of his plate with both hands. "Marion, I thought we were in agreement," he pleaded. "We spoke about this."

"I changed my mind," she said, smiling again.

Ginx put down his utensils and started scratching inside his nose with his pinkie.

"Gross!" Dana exclaimed, dropping the remainder of her toast into her uneaten egg. He looked at her but kept on, his finger digging deeper. "Ick!" she shouted at our mother. "Can't you make him stop?"

Our mother squinted as if the picture of the model mother she'd been imitating had suddenly gone blurry, leaving her with no clue as to how to proceed.

"Momma," Dana squawked. I, too, was annoyed. Our mother let Ginx speak of the disappearance of red and pick his nose without interruption. If he went on to say that the stars were scattered each night from a shaker of salt, our mother would have considered this with the same involved interest. She did nothing to stop him.

"We don't need a therapist," I told our father.

"I know how you feel, Morgan-Lee," he said, "but—"

"Momma!" Dana complained again, interrupting him, but by then Ginx had stopped on his own and returned to his breakfast. Since Dana had succeeded in getting our mother's attention, she went on, "I wish we could sometimes have waffles for breakfast. You can buy them in a box and just heat them in the toaster; they're less work than eggs and a lot better."

"Dana," our father told her, "you have a perfectly good breakfast you haven't even touched."

"Touched," Ginx muttered.

"What do you mean by 'a lot better'?" our mother demanded to know. She put the spatula on the table and sat down next to our father. "It's all work. Cleaning up is work; setting the table is work. If you put together all the time of making a meal and eating it, already a good chunk of your day is gone, and what are the results? Well, your family is a little fatter, or at least not starving, and that is supposed to justify another day of doing and undoing. There's not a lot of trick to routine, Dana, except finding ways to ignore it."

"The ultimate routine is death," our father pointed out, putting a healthy forkful of egg into his mouth.

I needed to intercede at this juncture. "So make routines around what you love," I said.

"If I had children, I would love making them breakfast,

and I would make them exactly what they wanted," Dana cried. "Not like her." Our mother's hands folded, her fingers weaving together like lace. Ginx quickly said that the breakfast was great; nonetheless, our mother began to cry.

"You don't even live here anymore," she said. "You have no right."

"Oh, now, Marion," our father said, rubbing her back with the palm of his hand. "Now, this is what I mean." He looked at us, his dark eyes level and patient. Our father was kind, and he wanted the best for us. Of course. "This is why we need help."

"Ginx," our mother ordered, sniffling twice, "come switch chairs with Morgan-Lee." My brother nodded. I got up, and he slid into my chair. Dana watched these proceedings. Whatever was happening, my sister must have felt it was a trick being played against her that would eventually come around to harm her.

"Dana," I said, "forgive and forget."

"Not a bad motto," our father told me, as he finished off his breakfast. It was not a motto to live by; my sister knew this as well as I did. It was a plug, a bridge perhaps, a line for pulling yourself out of an emergency situation, a temporary solution. Our mother slipped her hand onto Ginx's neck as she had before. This time, however, she kept it there. My brother avoided looking at me. He was staring into the plate of half-eaten food that I had left, studying it as if the curiosity were spelled out in my cold eggs and nibbled toast.

"Ginx loves his mother," our mother bragged. She tossed her head so her dark hair swished against her white skin. My brother still did not pull away.

Dana shoved her chair back from the table and stood up. "Sit down," our father demanded, "we haven't finished talking."

"We're clearing the plates," I told him, pushing my chair back and standing up as well.

"Sultry. Pallor. Bulk," Ginx provided, pushing the pad of his pointer finger against the holes in the top of the salt shaker. Our mother dropped her hand.

"Enough," she said, taking off her apron. "Ginx and Carl will come outside with me and help spread the mulch while you girls do the dishes. No more talking for now."

"All right," our father said, getting up. My brother got up as well. He looked at me. "This is not the end of the conversation," our father reminded us, "just an intermission."

"Of course," our mother said, heading for the door.

Dana and I collected as many dishes as we could and walked into the kitchen, where she bumped against my arm on purpose so the silverware went clattering into the sink.

"You owe me a favor," she whispered, angry. "You owe me."

"What for?" I asked her, picking up the plates and scraping off the leftovers. "Why do I owe you?"

"I always have to pay! I always have to be embarrassed, and now to top it off we have to go to Dr. Sampson. Are you kidding?" she asked. "Did you hear what Poppa said? That's because of you and Ginx, and now what am I gonna do?" Dana pushed a knife into the sink. "You owe me big-time."

I stared at my sister. I just looked at her and felt the distance between us, the gap that kept pulling us farther and farther apart.

"Dana," I said, tilting my head back and sounding like our mother, "whether or not you like it, you are in this family." I turned on the sink. "That's just how it is." My sister slammed her hand on the counter so the fork and spoon lying there jumped and the plates clattered.

"What's with you?"

"Aunt Lois," my sister breathed out. "Aunt Lois says"— she was speaking low and direct, pronouncing each word as if what she was telling me had a life span of only a few seconds before it would vanish, unrepeatable—"she says that you're in love with Ginx."

I snapped off the water, grabbed the plate I was holding, and turned, flinging it. The plate grazed her knee, smashed against the lower cabinets, and then shattered, fragmenting over the kitchen tiles. "Get out!" I spat at her.

She yelped once and ran. I heard her go upstairs, come down again, and then leave. All the while, I stood there, contemplating the broken plate, remembering how, when I was little, our father had bought me a kaleidoscope. I loved looking through the hole and turning it; no matter how the colors broke apart they always found a pattern. They changed form but re-collected in beautiful geometrical shapes, creating something new.

I grabbed a broom, swept up the plate, and finished cleaning the kitchen. Nothing in me was startled now. I was calm. Washing, drying, stacking—the movements were quiet and fluid, and the kitchen was thoroughly clean by the time I left it. Gazing at the sparkling tiles, I wished I were trapped under a car or a tractor, something that a boy as big as Jacob could lift and add to his list of triumphs. "I'll call him," I determined out of nowhere, then went upstairs and found the slip of paper in my pants pocket where Sweety-Boy had stuck it. I went to the phone in Dana's room and dialed the number the girl had written there.

He picked up after two rings. "Hello?"

"Hi, Jacob," I said, then waited. My calm disappeared. I considered hanging up.

"Who's calling, please?"

"It's Morgan-Lee," I confessed. "Hey," I said.

"Well, now, Morgan-Lee, did you want Sweety-Boy? You called up here and you weren't even gonna say hey to me? It was real nice having you all come to my birthday party. Tell your sister I'll wear those gloves she gave me and try to keep them as clean as I can, but it won't be easy working in a garage."

"Hey, Jacob," was all I could manage.

He cleared his throat. "Hey again."

"Listen, now," I said. "I actually need to talk to you, but at a time when it won't disturb. You know?"

"Well, go ahead. Something I can help you with?"

"Could I stop by sometime?" I blurted.

"Sure," he said. "Listen, why don't you come round this evening? Sweety is out tonight, and Mr. Winston's already told me he's not gonna eat the dinner I got prepared. In other words, I'm alone for dinner. How about you come over here around five-thirty or so and have a little something to eat just to keep me company."

"Are you really going to go to Las Vegas?" I asked, because I knew I couldn't just accept a dinner invitation right off the bat, and this was the only question that came to mind.

"Well, I'll tell you all about that over some ham and greens. You want me to come pick you up? I can drive legally now."

"No," I said. "No, my aunt will drive me." I realized I'd accepted his offer through driving arrangements.

"All right, then, I'll see you at five-thirty." I could picture his big jaw and hulking calm. I told myself that this date with Jacob might teach me what other girls and boys my age wanted, and I could go back to Billy with letters he could sell. As soon as I hung up the receiver, I picked it up again and called Aunt Lois.

Our aunt was so excited about my dinner invitation that she could afford no more than a whisper. "Is it really true?" she asked. "Little Morgan-Lee who I never thought would even look at a boy, let alone go to dinner with one!" I could hear her smack her lips together as if trying to hold back tears.

"It's not that big a deal, Aunt Lois. Now I wish I hadn't agreed to go. Just tell me whether you'll take me."

"Let me fix your hair and makeup," our aunt breathed. "I'll fix you up and drive you over," she promised.

"Look," I said. "Don't say a word to Dana."

"Dana stopped by here, all breathless, saying she was through with your family and was going to Myra's to spend the night. So it'll be our little secret," Aunt Lois said.

"Okay. All right. You can make me up just this once."

"That's all it takes!" she promised and hung up.

I showered quickly and dressed in clothes that Dana would have approved. I was headed to Aunt Lois's when I stopped to look over at the stretch of yard on the other side of the cul de sac: mid-July afternoon, warm, Ginx shoveling at the ground. Ever since my birthday, he worked at digging every day. Perhaps it was in deference to our mother that he had recently stopped asking me for stories, or maybe all his energy was being spent on digging. Whatever the reason, I had been spared having to tell him about the Luccas' absence and the horrible desert wind that was all that was left below.

My brother rested against the tree and stared into his pit as he prepared our possible future. He had said he would bring a clock and begin time wherever we chose to begin it; there would be, he reminded me, no sunlight to guide us then, so we could actually choose an hour at which to start. I pointed out that there would be no need for a clock if there were just two of us. Time would be arbitrary. But Ginx had just stared at me. "That's not the arrangement," he'd pointed out sternly. I let it go.

Ginx crouched, and that is when I saw the suitcase beside him. It was our mother's suitcase, a large blue one she'd bought once for a trip she never took. Ginx proceeded to unzip it. His lean body bent as he opened the front flap and stared inside for a long while. I did not move. I practiced my expertise from a distance, offering Ginx my stillness even though he'd never know. I wanted to be generous, even when my brother reached into the suitcase and pulled out my favorite T-shirt, held it to his face, reached back in and grabbed a pair of my socks, reached back in and took out my jeans. Even as he crouched there, rocking and arranging my clothes—shirt, pants, socks, so that the ghost of me was lying before him, accompanying him as he dug—I kept my stillness intact for him, for the background of this endeavor on my behalf. I owed him at least that. His digging was rhythmic, constant. I bit my lip.

Enough, I mouthed, a word that, for all its seeming plumpness, is a lie. It is, in fact, the stingiest, most meager of all words, incapable of offering the nourishment promised by the sound. I could not love Ginx enough, no matter what I gave him, no matter that I had carried Momma Lucca and Sister and B.J. inside me for whenever he had needed them. Stories were not enough; my stillness would never be enough. "*Trowl*," I said softly, letting the sound surround me and, hopefully, embrace him as well.

I turned and trudged toward our aunt's house.

As soon as I shut the door to our aunt's living room, a

light rain started, a good, small, summer rain. The clothing Ginx had arranged would smell more richly of me. Maybe my brother would stretch out on the ground as if beside me, the way we used to do when we were little, when we were each other's best friends.

I walked to the table and sat in the chair that Aunt Lois indicated. I knew exactly what was about to be given and what was about to be taken; I would not be fooled. "Just this once," I repeated. "This is the first and last time. Ever."

"Free of charge," Aunt Lois pointed out, clapping her hands together and then adjusting the tiny pink kit. "There we are now." The voice of progress and success. Aunt Lois locked my chin in her hand and quickly brushed on some Bleu de Soir eye shadow, which she'd always said was my color. She used a matching liner. Then she softly dropped her fingers down the side of my face and over my lips, fingers cool and fragrant as if they'd pierced through a flower, mulled around in the stamen, and then plunged a level deeper to uproot it from the inside. I kept my eyes closed.

"Open now."

The thick, curly brush tickled as she stroked mascara onto my lashes, expertly alternating the small brush with a cotton pad so I could blink away any extra. Then she clenched my lashes with a metal tool till they were curved, dark, and luscious. "Soon we'll be getting in the waterproof mascara so there will be no more worries about crying or perspiring," our aunt remarked, breathing out fragrance, her lips near my face. Two quivering half-moons had been traced with lip liner on her upper lip, enhancing the heart shape, heightening the peaks of her mouth as it pulsated, pumped, contracted, and bloomed all at once. "Sweet Jesus!" she exclaimed, smiling. "You're gonna be a beauty now, Morgan-Lee. A real beauty. A woman now." Aunt Lois stood before me, dazzled. "He'll be stunned." I could not help but think that I should have begun my makeovers long ago, and that a well-covered face may have averted certain difficulties.

"Perhaps more blush," she suggested, her fingers mercifully back on my face. Billy had once given me a few detailed notes from a girl about a kiss. I imagined writing about the fleshy, primal feel of another human being's lips. As I closed my eyes, I discovered that there is no need for kissing—that want can be quenched so much less rudely and less obtrusively. My face drank in the touch of our aunt's fingertips, which gave freely, asking nothing in return.

"All right now, sweetheart," Aunt Lois whispered, her hands leaving my face to pick up her thick oval-shaped mirror. "Tell me just what you think now." I saw my cheeks lit up in Cerises d'Été and my lips defined by Pourquoi Pas Rouge? My eyelids carried the blue of the evening just as the package promised. In fact, there was so much evening weighing down my lids that my eyes were two sunken planets. "If your boy can't appreciate you now, then you know he's wrong."

I grabbed hold of the mirror myself. "I know," I agreed,

"you're right." I was someone new, ecstatic, unrecognizable. Before I realized it, Aunt Lois had a comb and was teasing my hair with her fingers, humming over the possibilities for the limp pieces clinging to the sides of my face. From deep inside the bureau a pair of scissors was produced.

"Just let's snip, snip around here some, Morgan-Lee." She tugged at the front, not waiting for me to agree before cutting off at least three inches.

"Jesus!" I exclaimed.

"Not a time to call on the Lord, sweetheart. Your aunt's got it under control." My face started to itch, but with all the makeup I had to suppress the urge to scratch. Aunt Lois was holding up the ends of my hair between two fingers and angling down the sides to make those ridiculous feathers she had been forever wanting me to wear, and I was letting her do it. "Oh, yes," she urged softly, fluffing out bangs and then reaching into the bureau to whip out a large white can of hair spray. She shielded my face and sprayed hard. It seemed that she had been prepared for this haircut a long time. With the teasing and spraying, my hair became crisp and twice as thick, shut against my head like a protective helmet. The perfect feathers angled their way down either side of my face. She finished it all by spraying me with Printemps. "There we go," our aunt rejoiced, taking the mirror from me and then kissing my forehead so swiftly I didn't even have time to pull away before I was on my feet again, someone new.

Her sigh mixed with the scent of aerosol spray. "This is the way God intended you to look, Morgan-Lee. The best of your potential. There's no sense denying yourself what you are capable of achieving." She adjusted the collar of my shirt and tugged at the pink cuffs. "Now I will drive you."

"All right." Words tasted different to my new mouth. "Thank you." From Aunt Lois's closet I grabbed a white leather purse, which she had given me a while back. It was scratched, though I'd never used it.

"Wait, wait, I've got something else," Aunt Lois exclaimed, turning to flash her trump card. "This." Aunt Lois flung out a red chiffon scarf, which I caught like a weapon.

"What's this?" I hissed, slipping the scarf over one arm.

"This is to be worn in the evening hours," she said. Aunt Lois pulled out a similar scarf in white for herself. "Like a cloud," she laughed out. "A scrape of cloud." Her summer gloves were crocheted by hand—a new pair every year.

I followed her to the garage, where we got into her Pontiac. "A few more points," she said, as the garage door slid open, "and I'll have that Cadillac. I'm well on my way."

"How many more?" I asked as we pulled out.

"That gorgeous pink Deena Fae Caddy! Uncle Pete won't know what to do with his self when he sees me driving around in that thing," she exclaimed, caressing her steering wheel. We got onto Margaret Lane. "His car's in the shop. He brags about that Lincoln, but it's always in the shop," she said. "Now, I myself request Jacob Little when I go to Johnny

Johnson's with my automobile, but Pete never liked that boy. Says he doesn't know anything about cars, that he's a brute. Eric's the one who works on his Lincoln."

She waited a minute to see if I'd defend Jacob. I didn't.

"Oh," she exclaimed, pointing, "the Methodists are having a potluck!" I saw our pharmacist, Jay Bridgett, standing in the front yard of the church. The food was spread on long banquet tables, and people were milling around it; a large man in a suit was pointing to the sky. I looked up briefly but saw nothing. Other people gathered around the man, squinting against the sun, watching with interest.

"Well," Aunt Lois said, "Sally Nathon's selling for me now. I get two more girls to do it, and that'll be enough points for the Cadillac. Deena Fae's next convention's coming up in January, so I got five and a half months."

"Great," I said. She turned to me; her hands couldn't help but follow her gaze, edging the car a little off the road.

"Now, listen here, Morgan-Lee." I did not need to look at our aunt to know her expression. "If Jacob wants you to stay over, you go ahead and do it. Just no funny stuff. I'll cover for you. I'll tell your daddy that you're over at my house since Dana's spending the night with Myra. Don't you worry." She touched the fine crackling ends of my new hair. "Dana had her eyes on that boy, but I have higher hopes for her." I turned back to the Methodists with their eyes bolted to heaven. "I mean, we will tell her everything in due time, but right now it's important—crucial—that she knows nothing. You just slip him out from under her," she said. "Just no funny stuff now, you hear?" Her right hand glided off the wheel and drew a line over my chest, right above the nipples.

"Ow!"

"I don't want him going anywhere below there! You hear? Take control."

"It's just dinner," I insisted. "That's all it is. Dinner!"

Our aunt looked at the road and set the car back on course. She raised her ferocious chin. "You're old enough now," she told me, "you should be able to lie in the arms of a boy. But I'm not advocating that you do any more than that; we're clear on it, right?"

"Did you do it before you married?" I asked, tensing my hand against the velveteen armrest.

"Yes. Yes, I did. I gave my virginity to your Uncle Pete."

"And how has Uncle Pete thanked you for that?" I spat out. "What about him and Sally Nathon, Aunt Lois? Or Tracy Pink? Or what about him asking my momma to date him after he'd already started flirting with you?" My fingers fluttered against the armrest the way Ginx's might have.

"Look at me," she demanded, glaring. "You look at me if you're gonna ask those kinds of questions." She glanced back at the road and screwed up her lips as if to send a bitter kiss to the world outside her car. Then our aunt sped up the hill and swerved gracefully off the road, shoring the car on the very edge of Dead Man's Field, where she slammed on the breaks, coming to a halt so abruptly that we both jerked forward. "Get out now, Morgan-Lee. I don't want that piece of white trash to see my car in case she's home. Go on." I opened the door, but she yanked me back in, sheathing my wrist in cool lace. "You got lots to learn," she said, so close to my face I could see the small wrinkles beneath the makeup around her mouth and eyes. "You may be the smart one of the bunch," she breathed, "but there's a lot you still gotta learn. Don't underestimate me." I was taken aback. I'd never seen her face so full of purpose, and I had no idea she considered me smart.

She put up a finger, her lips quivering to deliver their message, her fingers digging into my wrist for emphasis. "The good Lord knows that enough women have been wronged by some myth of weakness handed down through the centuries. You understand me, girl? The good Lord made heaven and earth thinking of you and of me." I looked outside. It was around five-thirty in the evening, but the sun was beating down, so Aunt Lois's car was an air-conditioned bubble in which we were floating, buoyed up by her wisdom. "He did not take any rib from Adam in order to create Eve. No. Eve was already there when Adam was made: a whole, laughing woman, done and perfected by the time Adam came along. Our sweet Lord took that rib right out of His new man and slipped it into the hands of Eve. *Handed* the rib to her so Adam would always feel incomplete, wanting, lacking. Now"—here our aunt leaned toward me with such conviction that I had to look away; Ebenezer Baptist Church sitting at the edge of Dead Man's Field was what I fixed on—"the price we pay for that is a lifetime connection to one man, and one man alone no matter how he cheats or does us wrong. We're sworn to love him 'cause we only get one man's rib per lifetime. Lots of women mess up, thinking they can leave one husband and get another. But it don't work that way. And if you follow the rules and read your Bible right, you can't go telling me that women're wedded to sadness. You got to remember that his rib is yours, girl. You're holding it in the hot pink palm of your hand. No woman can take it from you unless you hand it to her. And if you ever need to use it, if you ever gotta wield it in the air to remind him what he would be without you, then you do what you gotta do and don't ever doubt that the blessing of our sweet Jesus Christ is right there with you." She patted my arm. "Go on, now, and take care, you hear?"

"It's just dinner," I pleaded, but my voice was small as a little girl's.

She touched my cheek with expertise, with no risk of smearing my base and powder, then picked up my scarf and pulled it around my neck like a tongue of flame. I opened the car door and slipped from her, wishing that love were simpler, that it did not have to include all the bone wielding and betrayal. "You're fourteen now," she reminded me. "Time you kissed a boy."

As soon as I shut the car door, our aunt's Pontiac squealed

off the side of the Dead Man's Field and was back on the road, where it quickly disappeared from sight. I marched across the street and through the small yard of orange dirt, reaching the porch stairs just as Jacob opened the door. "Saw your aunt's car. You're a little early," he said. I raised my chin and stood straight as a warrior. He smiled big, his eyebrows knit so close they melded into one. "No, no," he added, "it's okay. It's good you're early. I'm glad for the company." His smile disappeared when he noticed the scarf, his stare becoming so raw and intimate that, on any other day, I would have turned away. But I did not turn. "And you look real pretty, Morgan-Lee. All dressed up. You look real nice." I thought of the rib bone, of how difficult it would have been when the Luccas were around for Sister to resist taking out the hammer to pound and hang such a bone on one of her money trees. I missed the jangle of those trees; I missed the shack, the field, and the family. Eve, I thought, would have to take good care of Adam's bone at surprising moments, pulling it from her sheath, caressing and polishing it till the surface shone.

Without a word, I pushed past Jacob and on into the house, untying the scarf and dropping it over the arm of a nearby chair.

"Want a Pepsi?" I heard him offer as he closed the door behind me, "or a Mellow Yellow?"

"Iced tea," I said, adding "please" as an afterthought. I immediately pulled my blouse straight and tried to picture how a girl would act and what she would say in such a situation. "This is so nice," I exclaimed. Billy would have winced at such a stupid sentence. The room was dark and L-shaped, part dining room and part living room. From the single living room window hung a set of pink flowered curtains. The kitchen began where a slender board divided wood floor from linoleum. A large oak table, awkwardly placed in the center of the dining room, was set with two white plates and tall plastic glasses. Jacob stood across the table from me. I blinked my Bleu de Soir eyes and then remembered to gaze at his well-combed hair. "I'd like to meet Mr. Winston," I told him.

"He's *asleep*," the big boy informed me, a word so familiar and difficult that I quickly concentrated on puckering my lips and drawing in my cheeks so the bones—though not nearly as high and fine as they should have been—were as pronounced as possible. I wanted to be the kind of girl for whom a boy would commission a letter, so I returned to fluttering my eyelids, because Bleu du Soir had been created for fluttering eyelids, making the eyes more distant, more sorrowful and European. I touched my cheek, forgetting that a girl should keep her hands off her face, especially in the summer. Besides smearing the makeup, oil from fingertips causes pimples and blackheads. By the time I remembered and withdrew my fingers, Jacob had already disappeared into the kitchen to bring out our meal. When he returned holding a tray of sliced ham and a bowl of collard greens, I shook my head a little to give the impression that a slight personal breeze was amusing itself with the lifting and caressing of my feathered hair.

"I made us ham and greens, and there's fries as well—if we want." He cleared his throat. "I really like the way you got your hair done, Morgan-Lee. It looks real pretty like that." There'd been letters and letters I'd written for the business; I'd invented all the breezes and night skies needed for bringing boys and girls together. For two years I had considered myself the supplier of words to match the small smiles and inadvertent nods across Cresset Christian's gym or cafeteria. But suddenly here I was, armed and helmeted myself, invoking romantic breezes and skies that no one would record.

I blinked twice, perfect lashes on perfect skin, and voiced a note of concern. "Is Mr. Winston sick?" I asked.

"He's just gotta get his rest," Jacob answered, studying me for a few seconds before pulling out a chair for me and then one for himself. "You're okay?" he asked.

"Wonderful," I said. "Couldn't be better."

"Okay," he said. "How about we eat?"

I sat down and noticed that beside each plate stood large white napkins in the shape of sailor's caps. He saw me examining my napkin, reddened a little, and explained. "That's the only shape I know how to make besides an airplane, and I didn't think that'd be right." He laughed. "It's my momma's doing. She loved a table full of sailor's hats."

"Yeah?" I stretched my fingers to caress the rim of the

dinner plate, an extra touch that would have pleased our aunt. "Sailor's caps are perfect." Finally, the years of listening to our aunt's advice were paying off.

"Well, now," he continued, serving me first. He told me straight out, "I was going to call you, you know. We do got things to talk about. Sweety's getting back late this evening." He paused. "Me and her are in an argument right now."

"People fight," I exclaimed, the way I might have spoken to Dana. I thought of Amos, of how a large face can absorb so much, even the awful fact of jealousy or betrayal. I missed Billy's angular face, with its questions darting out from all directions.

Jacob cut his ham into tiny pieces, a habit he said he'd gotten from all his practice in feeding Mr. Winston. He ate two forkfuls in a row. "Morgan-Lee," he said, "you don't gotta dress up special like that for me, or anything, you know." He offered this information so frankly I had the urge to cover my ear with a hand but managed to resist. I stood my ground, a woman with a mission.

"Yes, I do," I told him frankly. He looked confused, so to avoid any questions, I quickly said, "This is delicious," even though I hadn't yet tasted the food. Luckily, I was right. The ham was juicy, and the greens tasted rich and earthy. It had been a long time since I'd had fresh greens, and I told him so. Without responding, he got up from the table, went to the kitchen, and returned holding two open cans of Budweiser.

"I forgot your iced tea," he said with a wink, clunking the

can before me. I shrugged and took a thick sip, trying to get it down fast so the woolly taste wouldn't linger.

"Thanks," I said. "So, where is Sweety-Boy this evening, anyway?"

Jacob licked his lips and answered with unusual coldness. "Working, I s'pose." He took brief, familiar swallows from his own beer can. "Let's just forget about her right now, okay?"

"Well, all right," I agreed, friendly-like, even though no other topics of conversation were coming to mind. Conversing with anyone but Ginx or Billy was hard enough for me, but talking to this boy seemed close to impossible. I resorted to cutting off a huge slab of margarine and smacking it onto my greens.

"I'm not one to get mad easily," he explained, more gently. I billowed the sailor's cap beside me into a full napkin and wiped my mouth, hoping he would not tell me what they were fighting about. "We're not doing so good right now, is all." The *we* resounded: Sweety-Boy's presence was everywhere in that house, inextricable. A tingle began just to the left of my right eye. He smiled. "I like you," he went on. "None of the fancies or frills that most girls got."

I wasn't sure I'd understood him, and the tingle was becoming a full-fledged itch, so I chewed more vigorously in an attempt to calm it.

"So, we need to talk," I said, sounding so much like our father that I had to stop myself.

"We gotta talk," Jacob agreed. "But first let's eat." My

skin was inaccessible, far beneath the surface of my makeup. Jacob looked at his food. "Well," he went on, "Sweety-Boy's momma, Iris Orange, is plannin' to be up here next week." The itch crept down my face a quarter inch, but I was not about to smudge that base and powder; I kept my hands still, silently complimenting myself on my restraint, which, of course, was wasted on Jacob.

Jacob finished his ham in quick forkfuls and started on the greens. I took another sip of beer. I wanted my breath to smell of alcohol, my neck to smell of Printemps, and the blouse I'd selected to emit a pink sheen that could compete with the lavishness of any sunset. My letter for Billy might begin with the blouse and then slip into a description of the sky before the reader noticed the one merging with the other. It would, of course, include the word *usher*.

I had learned enough to raise a single eyebrow right before swallowing. The purpose was to smoothly bridge the gap in conversation during those seconds that food was being swallowed. We were not speaking, but I did it anyway. Then he looked up at the ceiling. "What's that?" he asked. "Did you hear something?"

"Not a thing." I took my beer and drank down as many drafts as I could stand. "It's Mr. Winston," Jacob said, shoving back his chair, getting up, and tossing his napkin onto the table. "I think he's calling me." With two strides, Jacob was at the stairs. I stood also, dropping my fork, my body warm and tingling from the beer. A made-up face is useless with no one keeping watch over it, a truth that lent me a purpose and a courage I would not otherwise have had. I resolved to stay near Jacob at all costs and followed him up the stairs. "Oh, you're here with me!" he exclaimed in the upstairs hallway.

"I am here," I promised, a woman prepared for any war.

I thought of Sweety-Boy. Half sister or not, it seemed to me that she carried this boy's rib bone. I imagined a duel between two Eves confronting each other with their separate rib bones, both from the same boy. There could be a fight, or one Eve might lay down her bone and simply walk away. Briefly, and without Jacob's noticing it, I reached up and touched the back of his T-shirt.

"Okay, now," he said as we stood in that tiny box of a hallway. "Let me see how he's doing." Jacob pushed Mr. Winston's door open a few inches to the long moan of intaken breath and the whistle of exhale. He closed the door just as gently as he'd opened it. "He's okay," Jacob affirmed. Then his eyes alighted on me. "Well, now," he said as I shifted my weight to stand evenly on both feet. "Long as we're up here, I could show you around."

"Guess so," I said, only then realizing that I'd forgotten to narrow my eyes and had missed the perfect chance for doing so.

"My bedroom's right here," Jacob told me, pushing the door and propping it open, so, like a girl with nothing to lose, I entered boldly, walking without looking back, as if I knew exactly how to step over a boy's threshold and into his room. *The lady cometh,* I would write somewhere, but in small letters, so that even if Billy judged it absurd it would not disrupt the letter's flow.

Jacob shut the door, and for a few seconds I contemplated the severance of my soul from the world I was leaving behind. The silence between us seemed intimately tied to the evening. "It's nice having you here," he said, moving to stand near me. He did not step backward or sideways or try in any other way to maneuver around my body, which would have been the natural thing for a person standing so close to do. "I saw those bruises," he whispered. "You can't let anyone hit you. People gotta take care of you, that's what. That's what you deserve." Jacob lifted a thick hand and stroked my cheek, his eyes studying my face, so again I sucked in my cheeks even more, puckering my Pourquoi Pas Rouge? mouth.

I am a fourteen-year-old girl, I told myself, repeating it in my head as he leaned slightly to the side and then came closer, his face inching toward the brink of explosion, the eyes pressing together, the nose enlarging, the chin supporting it all. I inhaled his thick breaths of musk and aftershave. I narrowed my eyes just in time; there was something thrilling in this accurate procedure of events, the way he leaned in, his soft mouth on mine, his scratchy chin, his lips too thin for his face, a detail I ceased to know as his hand slipped from my cheek to my neck. The base and powder could now legitimately be mangled; they were made for such moments. Jacob snaked his other arm around my waist. I had imagined kissing to be wispier, cool and sloppy, the sinews of a boy's neck too obvious. His tongue blindly prodded against my teeth and then my tongue. I closed my eyes, and it was like a dream in which I was charged to house a small, warm fish. Not unpleasant, just a little confusing. When Jacob pulled back, I remembered to shake my head for the breeze-through-hair effect, but my entire feathered helmet brushed his arm as he folded me against his huge crucial chest, his mouth slipping to my neck. I knew it was time to tell him, and so I whispered, "My sister is the one in love with you." Billy would crumple up a description of this scene—he would hold it to the candlelight and let it burn— but Jacob's skin and arms really did feel *nice,* smooth and simple as water.

"Let's not talk about love," Jacob mumbled against my skin, so I managed a delicate giggle that was round and roller-coastery enough to convince him to slip his right arm under my legs, pick me up, and carry me to his bed. I wished then that I had asked Aunt Lois to pile my hair into a bun, because I wanted to cast back my head and allow it to unravel lock by lock over his shoulder and then spread like silk on the pillow, as he stretched over me with the weight of a dead beast.

"Stop," I said, when I suddenly realized I was lying on a boy's bed and he was on top of me. "Dana has a crush on you."

He covered my forehead with a single hand. "You told me," he said.

"Well," I continued. What I was about to say almost buckled back into my throat and would have merely come out as a moan if I'd allowed it. But this boy deserved the truth. "I don't have a crush on you."

Jacob kissed my forehead. "I'm not looking to fall in love," he softly confessed now, pushing a wisp of hair behind my ear. "I just want to take care of you for a little while," he said. "You need it." His eyebrows must have been a half-inch thick. "And I sure need it too," he told me. "Anyway," he added, "I'm already in love."

"With whom?" I asked, as properly as though I were speaking to Valeria.

"I'll tell you one day."

"Jacob," I said, trying not to close my eyes as his large fingertips played with my earlobe. I cleared my throat. "My sister really does have a crush on you."

"I appreciate it, Morgan-Lee," he told me. "Tell her that she will do better one day. The both of you deserve to be treated good, the best possible," he said. "Right now, you and me'll just forget other people for a while, okay?" He kissed me again. "Just a little caretaking, that's all," he repeated, tugging at my shirt. "Now, how d'you get this thing off?"

"Here," I said, sitting up enough to slide my shirt off. It was the first time I had kissed a boy, much less taken any clothing off in front of one, but in front of this boy I pulled off my shirt as if I'd done it a million times before. My torso was bare except for my bra, my bruises suddenly displayed.

"Jesus Christ," he whispered, as I lay before him like one of Uncle Pete's newly gutted fish. "Who's doing this to you, Morgan-Lee?" He gently touched a bruise just above my right breast.

"What?" I asked, bending my neck to look, as though I did not understand what he was asking. "Oh," I said and lay down again, letting him scan my field of wild violets. "They match my eyelids," I joked.

But I almost did love him as he softly touched another bruise, circling it with his fingertip. "I'd kill a man for doing this to you, daddy or not," he confided. "You're getting out of that house."

"Oh," I began, forced to choke back the truth. "It's not my poppa," I said. "It's Uncle Pete."

"I should have guessed it. He's the asshole," he whispered, as I reached up to touch Jacob's hair. "No one's got a right to—" I was suddenly brave and pulled his face down, kissing him hard, pushing my own tongue against his. I wasn't used to touching anyone's hair, but his was extraordinarily soft. The words *soft, nice,* and *sweet* floated down, covering the rough territory below like a good thick blanket.

My hair crisped and crackled against the pillow. I lay there, hugging him as he began to move, heavy and light. The button on my jeans dug into the flesh of my stomach, and the sounds we were making were the strange, muffled sounds of people learning to communicate underwater. His lips were on my neck again, the warmth of his hand sliding under me. I caressed his head as his mouth moved onto the nipple of my left breast, where it throbbed away warmly like a tiny continuous sun till frozen things inside me started to melt and I just wanted him closer, wanted to be crushed under his weight. I could have been any girl except myself.

"This is nice," Jacob said. He snapped up, took off his shirt, and tossed it to the ground. He lay down again but more carefully this time, his tongue slipping back to prod softly at an old bruise while my hands went from his head to his neck and then to the smooth skin of his back with its ripple of spine. I caressed down to the waistline of his jeans, his large silver buckle riding against my belly. I was sure this boy could set the world straight again even if the walls of that room caved in and the earth, unplugged of every tree, began its slow crumble. I thought of Ginx, who held his frogs as though each time he'd found a warm and loving hand. If the walls came crashing down now, I told myself, Jacob would shelter me.

"This is nice," I repeated.

He caressed and kissed me, his naked chest a larger, fleshier version of his lips. It wasn't until he buried his head, resting it in the crook of my neck that I thought of Sweety-Boy: honeysuckle and kudzu, sweet and strangling. I thought of Jacob and Sweety-Boy as children just in from the Patch where she had spent hours grooming him to be her Fairy

God. Just for her. I tightened my embrace, wanting to own in a matter of seconds what it had taken that girl a whole childhood to acquire.

"When are you moving to Vegas?" I asked.

Jacob pulled back. "Morgan-Lee," he said, lying on his side, "don't talk about that."

I looked at his large jaw. "Just tell me," I said.

He played with my earlobe again while he spoke. "I'm leaving next week. Since Iris Orange is coming up to take care of Mr. Winston, there's no real reason for me to stay."

"Is Sweety-Boy going too?"

He caressed my face. "Remains to be seen," he said. In a love letter the boy would certainly tell the girl that he had decided not to leave but to stay as close to her as possible.

Mr. Winston snorted loudly from his room, startling us both. We laughed. I decided to test Jacob's capacity for still-ness by staring at his chest, but he propped himself up to hear better, decided Mr. Winston was okay, and quickly scrambled back on top of me. No one in the world, I thought, could bear as much stillness as Ginx and I. No one; not even Billy.

"Don't you worry," he whispered, hot into my ear; now I felt his hardness beneath his jeans, the stuff Aunt Lois's romance novels talked about. "You're gonna be okay." I gripped the bed with one hand.

"Okay," I agreed, relieved at finally being able to freely scratch my face whenever it itched.

I smiled as his kisses hastened; I kept whispering, "You've

got a back as big as the ocean." His body gave a sudden jerk, his moan seeming merely a deeper version of Mr. Winston's. I listened as the moan layered down, down, down into a hum. The boy didn't move for an entire minute, not till I was struggling for breath beneath him. That was it, I thought, that was the miniaturized version of it anyway, essentially what all those books were about—those few breathless seconds. I was amazed.

"Oh, Morgan-Lee," Jacob said, finally moving off me and wiping at his jeans with a corner of the sheet. "That really was sweet." He smiled.

"'Course," I answered, losing some of my delicacy as I pulled the sheet up to cover myself. I hadn't felt much except a deepening desire to tell Jacob that I was happy to be submerged in the ocean for a while. But I knew that would only confuse him. Anyway, Billy would have immediately torn up a letter with a sentence like that, his good eye glaring at me through the candlelight. "Don't make the girl sound so helpless," he'd say. I'd have to agree; only a weak person would want to be fully submerged, waiting to surrender, complete with smiles and winks and squeals.

Jacob lay down and held me close again so my face rested against his bare chest. This was better, and I breathed him in, shutting my eyes over his wiry, dark chest hairs. He tucked the sheet around me, then tried to stroke my hair, but it was too sticky with hair spray.

"Sweety-Boy's not gonna mind when she finds out?" I whispered.

"Shh," he said, smiling. "This is nice. Let's just lie here and be still; maybe sleep a bit." He moved to stroke my cheek and whispered, "Lord have mercy!"

Jacob's arm was around me. I pulled the sheet up as much as possible, but it did nothing to hide the fact that his bare arm was crossing my bare chest. His eyes were closed and he was breathing gently; I had become a girl who had kissed a boy. He pulled me just a notch closer, promising, "Your Uncle Pete will pay for his deeds, I swear it to you." I smiled against his skin, heard Mr. Winston moan once again from the other room, and then everything was quiet until Jacob began a light snore. My back ached from being in the same position for so long, but I managed to fall asleep nonetheless. When the door downstairs slammed a few hours later, I shot awake and listened as Sweety-Boy moved around, banging pots, growling over the dirty plates we'd left. The kitchen faucet went on. The refrigerator door popped open and closed, something metal hit the counter, the oven door thronged shut. Jacob must have been used to late night noise; he kept snoring, uninterrupted. I could smell frying: hot dogs or bacon, meat of some kind. The solid comfort of frying meat intertwined with the warm rise and fall of Jacob's body. After a while, the sounds of cooking a meal lulled me into a deep sleep, which was disturbed at some point during the night, but so briefly that it is hard to say even now whether or not I actually saw what I remember having seen.

I remember seeing Sweety-Boy standing at the foot of the bed watching Jacob sleep. The girl's smile flashed so perfectly, the crevices of her face more apparent and deeper in the moonlight. Then she rose, hovering above Jacob and me, unsupported, her long loose braid hanging down, caressing Jacob's face. I immediately thought of the morning after Sweety-Boy's visit when Uncle Pete ran downstairs and into the dining room where we were eating, declaring that he'd seen Jesus during the night. Aunt Lois had calmly looked up from her breakfast and asked for more details. She soon confirmed the accuracy of Uncle Pete's description of our Lord. In tears, she'd kissed Uncle Pete on the forehead and wept over his blessed vision. No one dared argue. For two days, Aunt Lois scanned our faces as she reached into the air just above Uncle Pete's head as though to touch the halo there. She looked gravely from Dana to me to Ginx to be sure we understood the mystery involved, but when none of us followed suit, she eventually gave up. I'd forgotten about Uncle Pete's Jesus until those few seconds at twilight when I could have sworn Sweety-Boy was hovering there, looking furiously down at Jacob and me.

When I awoke fully, it was six in the morning. I was startled by the sight of my bra and the sleek blouse I'd borrowed from Dana hanging on the bedpost. Jacob was still sleeping, so I quickly leaned over, grabbed my shirt, and put it on. Then I slipped off the bed, pulled on my socks and shoes, stuffed my bra into the pocket of my jeans, and stood for a few seconds in the semi-dark trying to remember where I'd left the scarf. Of course, I thought, I left it downstairs. Swiping my shoes from the floor, I accidentally caught a glimpse of my face in a lopsided oval mirror that Jacob had nailed above his bureau. Even in the dim light I could see that the Bleu de Soir had bled out till my eyes were big as saucers, and the Pourquoi Pas Rouge? of my lips had dropped its question mark of red and lay smeared around the corners of my mouth.

I slipped out of Jacob's room. Once in the tiny hallway, I looked over at Sweety-Boy's shut door and then tiptoed down those dusky steps that led to the living room. On top of the TV was a box of Saltine crackers. My scarf was stretched out over the dining table, and my purse was beside it. I grabbed both things. My crackling hair was sticking out in all directions, so I licked my hand a couple of times and tried mashing it down. I went to the kitchen for some water, which is when I found the slip of paper addressed to me.

> *Morgan-Lee. Met me next Sunday, a week from today, and we'll do bizniss so you can earn your money. See you on the corner of margarit lane and Queen Street. Sweety-Boy. PS: Three o'clock pm. Dont be late.*

When I shuffled out of that house and into the new morning, I closed the door behind me, telling myself I would never go back. Pausing on that rickety porch, I breathed in the smell of summer grass from Dead Man's

Field and felt shame over having kissed a boy I did not love, over having been a girl like any other girl, over losing the Luccas, over finding myself in cahoots with Aunt Lois, and over not understanding where things had gone so wrong.

I stood on that porch and closed my eyes, trying to get to the Luccas. "God," I even begged, *please.* But there was still nothing more than steady wind and blank desert, which left me so empty that I wanted to walk back up to Jacob's room and hide myself in his arms again. I probably would have done just that had Sweety-Boy not been home. So I started down those porch steps, finally understanding why it was that girls returned to boys again and again, even when they swore the relationship was over, the love gone. Another's hands, arms, chest are indispensable when the imagination falters. The prison of solitude that so often kept people together, no matter how unhappily, was constructed out of pure, empty yearning. Nonetheless, I walked away bravely, passing Dead Man's Field; my arms were folded tight, my red scarf securely balled in one fist.

Although I remember heading for Aunt Lois's house and climbing her porch stairs, and I remember washing my face and even going to the Baby's Room to sleep, the arch of that night still seems as exaggerated and fictitious as Uncle Pete's Jesus. I crept into Dana's bed in the Baby's Room, where I slept for two hours before Aunt Lois came in to wake me. "Don't you worry, honey," she said, leaning over me, raw and bright as the morning sun. I rubbed my eyes, and she went on. "I did just like I promised and told them all you were spending the night with me. Your daddy said fine; Ginx did his usual stuff. I said I was taking you with me to help out at Sunday school over the next four Sundays. Oh, and I brought you over some clothes so you have a fresh change." She spoke more secretively. "Dana won't be home from Myra's till after church." Our aunt laid the clothes out on the chair by the small dresser. "You did good to stay with him, Morgan-Lee. Tell you the truth, I never thought you'd have a boyfriend. I don't have worries about Dana in that depart-ment, but now my mind is at ease for you both. Come down to breakfast, and then we can go to church. Just be sure not to call him. Let him be the one that calls." She clapped her hands together and said, "I got two clients coming this after-noon, so we gotta get ready now."

Aunt Lois was walking out the door when I realized I'd been roped into going to church for the next month.

"You mean you set it up so I have to go to church for the next four Sundays to help you out?" I demanded to know.

"You owe me a *little* something, sweetheart, don't you agree?" she asked. "I mean, after all, look at how much effort this has all been for me." She paused before exiting. "I just want you to be happy," she reassured me. "Are you happy?" I looked from her face down to her wiry bosom, clothed in its green silk blouse. Sitting upright in bed, I nodded slowly, blankly. "Good," she whispered. "This's how things are sup-posed to go; this is how they'll go from now on if you get smart and figure out how to keep your boy." I nodded again. With a graceful flick of her wrist, she opened the bedroom door, and in one fluid movement she was gone. I flung back my sheet and got out of bed to dress for the second time that morning.

I scurried to the bathroom and showered in less than a minute, hopped out, and didn't even bother to dry my hair, which dampened the shirt I pulled on. I could hear Aunt Lois preparing the breakfast; grits and ham were her usual. I was hungry. On the dresser in the Baby's Room lay Deena Fae eye pencils arranged in order from light to dark.

I raised my eyes and looked in the mirror. My makeup was all washed away, and with it the feel of his scratchy face against my chest and the dullness of his prodding tongue. All of it was gone, as if the layer of someone I could have become had been stripped away and I had been left with only a vague impression of a life I might have led. I realized then that I was really looking at myself in the mirror for the first time in a long while. I left the bathroom and returned to the Baby's Room.

A good letter meant forming words into a smooth golden chin rest upon which the reader might repose while trying to follow the crazy paths of love branching through the world, the veins and arteries of a complete, unified body that it is not our privilege to know, unless we get to heaven one day and God in all His bounty drops the veil and offers us a glimpse. Unless God in all His bounty says, "This is why you suffered. You see? Yours was a tiny portion of the collective love that created this one glorious being that will endure forever and ever, Amen. You were always part of a greater whole. You were never, in truth, alone."

But I had no idea how to begin such a letter, so I grabbed an eye pencil from the little dressing table and wrote on the mirror, *Lord have mercy.*

I put the eye pencil back where it belonged but left the words, figuring that Aunt Lois would be ecstatic over possible evidence of my conversion, which seemed a fair gift in exchange for all her concern.

FEAR

⌒

A FEW DAYS LATER, I awoke at 3 A.M. to screaming. It hadn't happened for years, but it was as terrible as it had always been, hollow and long. I used to go right back to sleep, but this time I got out of bed. Not bothering to be in a hurry, I followed a strange routine that wasn't mine: I put on my slippers, plucked the summer robe I'd never worn off my rack, and shuffled down the hall like an old lady accustomed to disaster.

"Oooohlaa, oohla!" Ginx was screaming when I arrived at the door to his room. He was crying, sitting up in bed, pounding his fist against the wall and wailing as our mother stroked his shoulders. Our father was standing at the foot of his bed.

"This cannot go on," our father announced.

"Please," our mother begged. "Oh, Ginx." She was studying the rhythmic pounding of his fists. I put my hand on the doorframe to his bedroom. I was an old lady in bedclothes, a tired woman who had awoken one thousand times to screams in the early morning. I stood straight, wonderfully prim amid the mess of Ginx's carrying on. "Ooohla, ooohala!" He rocked forward and our mother caught him, holding him fast against her chest as if all her days of resting had resulted, finally, in this enormous strength. As if, all along, there had been a purpose behind the sleep she'd required.

Our father stood at the foot of Ginx's bed. "What's wrong, son?" he wanted to know. The room rearranged itself, the furniture in the dark accommodating my brother's hollow, protracted howl. Our mother held Ginx and stroked the tears from his face, as he resisted her pull, his breath rattling in and out like an angry box of jacks. My brother's hands were seeking, desperately trying to arrange the sheet so that the hem was straight across the cover, but our mother's hugs made this work impossible. No one realized I was there, not even my brother, who was so wholly unaware of the fact that our mother was using all her strength to hold him, that the sum of her quiet days, the times I'd been yelled at for waking her up, the continuous hush in our house—all of it—was being spent on him alone, and he didn't care. I cleared my throat.

"There are no more Luccas," I announced above all the noise, coldly, sternly, playing my old-lady role. Our mother turned, so I told her directly. "They left us, just like you wanted."

Our father, one hand on the bedpost, said, "Go back to bed, young lady, now! Go. You're not helping." Ginx was heaving; he was wheezing and heaving, but he knew I'd spoken the truth and shook his head. He pounded the wall once, then let his hand splat flatly against it and studied that hand a second or two.

My brother did not look at me. He folded his arms across his chest and rocked back and forth—the gentle rhythm that, in the past, would have floated us away together to some place where other people were merely faces breaking our dark at random but nothing permanent, nothing to fear.

"*Sodden. Mull. Redolent. Flush. Clumsy.*" My brother spoke in a monotone.

Our mother bent so I could barely see her. "Morgan-Lee, go away. Why do you do this to me?" she cried, one hand covering her eyes. "Why are you children doing this to me?" Her question seemed simple at the time: Why were we doing this to her? It felt absurd to have no answer.

"That's enough, Marion," our father said. "Morgan-Lee is going back to bed, and Ginx is going to calm down. That's enough."

"*Plop. Huff. Tron.*" Ginx had plucked apart *enough* to reveal these sounds.

Our mother sniffled, then placed her hands on my brother's upper arms, trying to hug him. There were choices: I could have slumped against the doorframe, I could have bawled tears of my own, I could have told them I was fourteen years old and was trying to grow up normal. I merely backed away.

"Morgan-Lee, Morgan-Lee," Ginx called, not caring that repeating my name would anger our mother. "Morgan-Lee," he begged again.

"Momma's got you now, Ginx," I told him generously. A good person. Perhaps I would become a good person, forgiving and kind. I turned to walk away from that ocean of our mother's love and our father's constancy.

"Go on to bed now, Morgan-Lee," our father prompted.

"Here, honey, here," I heard our mother soothing Ginx as the hem of my cotton robe swished against the floor of the hallway like a lovely blue evening gown. Once in my room, I went to the window and sat.

I put my elbow on the windowsill, leaned my head against my hand, and fell asleep for a while, awaking when Billy passed through our yard. I'd seen him there before when I was up early enough. He walked the two blocks from his new house and came to our yard at 5:30 A.M., precise as clockwork. I pressed my head on the windowpane, catching the glints of new sun and watched him pause, bend down, and pick something up. He held the object in his hand to examine it, then dug a hole with the toe of his shoe and dropped it in. He is alone, I thought; no one knows his rituals.

Billy looked at our house, but he did not look up to my window. He stared for a long while and then turned the other way, as though it were his duty to guard us.

FAITH

〜

A FEW DAYS LATER, it was Sunday again. I decided I'd meet Sweety-Boy at her scheduled time and place after church. I got up, threw on a dress, and went to the bathroom. It was time for a new business, I told myself, time to start making money again. The comb went easily through my hair, leaving streak marks near the part. The feathers Aunt Lois had cut hung in limp angles down the sides of my face. I had some lilac eau de toilette that our mother had once given me, and I dabbed this behind each ear.

As I walked down the last stair, I looked up and stumbled at the sight of Ginx sitting at the dining room table, hands rigid against its edge. "Morgan-Lee," he said calmly, fingers around the base of our large wooden fruit bowl. His face brought back that night he'd spent rocking and crying. I drew in a breath. He tensed. "Why are you scared?" he asked.

"I'm not scared; I was surprised," I told him. In the days since his breakdown, he had become quieter. I went out twice with him to the pit and watched him dig, pushing the shovel into the ground. All his shoveling was building muscles, which rose and fell under the sleeves of his T-shirt as he worked. I sat there the whole time, but we didn't say much.

"You were scared of me just now," he insisted. This truth sank like a rock, all the way to the bottom of my stomach, and refused to rise again. It was a rock that would stay till grass grew up the sides and the sun moved, so that when the Luccas returned, Sister's branch would cast a shadow over it: Seeing my brother had startled me.

"Upon this rock, I will build my church" was the heading of one of the chapters in Aunt Lois's Relationship book. "Find a center, a strong point, call it God, call it Love," the author advised, "and let that be your place of worship."

"Why are you here?" I asked.

"Waiting," he answered, as he looked toward the wall and then at the TV stand under which his Emergency Kit was hidden. His knuckles were scratched raw, and his forehead was damp with sweat. He caressed the wooden fruit bowl.

"Have you been waiting long?" I asked, regaining composure. He smiled, because this was the right question. Anyone else would have asked him what he was waiting for. "Have you been waiting long?" I repeated.

"For all the time I've waited" was his lovely response, which sounded like a piece of ancient wisdom but was in fact merely the mimicking in language of the struggle between anxiety and patience. He released the bowl and began rubbing at his knuckles. "There is a strange sound," Ginx said, shaking his head as if to hear it better. "Can you hear it?"

"Oh, that's the sound of a rusty hinge," I rejoined. "It is a cat. And the dripping sound is dew falling from the trees onto the tracks."

"The empty tracks now. The tracks with nowhere to go." I thought my brother was going to reprimand me for losing the Luccas, but instead he made room for a gift I could not have expected. *"Must,"* he said loudly. He repeated it for me, *"Must. Must. Must."* His brilliant lips shaped around the contours of my favorite little word, popping it out again and again till I realized how much I missed looking in a mirror, repeating *must* until it lost all meaning.

"Morgan-Lee!" I heard Dana calling from outside. The front door opened and she bounced into the house.

"It's time for church," I told Ginx, as I took a banana from his bowl. "I promised Aunt Lois."

"Good for you," he said, sitting beautifully straight, a little man with measured praise.

"I'm here!" I shouted to my sister and turned toward her. I'd hardly seen her since our fight, but I was sure neither of us would mention it.

Dana stopped short and studied me from head to toe.

"You can't wear that," she said, pointing to my light pink cotton dress, which had been red once upon a time. I peeled the banana and took a bite, head-on.

"Why not?" I wanted to know

She looked at my hair, my face, and the old brown sandals I was wearing. "You look awful, Morgan-Lee," my sister gasped. "Really awful. How can you help with Sunday school looking like that?"

"Okay, Dana," I agreed, chewing. "All right, okay, I'll change."

Dana shook her head, walked past me, and wrinkled her nose at the bowl of bananas. She didn't say a thing to Ginx.

"I'll wait for you in the car," she told me, as she walked toward the door. "Just hurry! Aunt Lois and Uncle Pete are right outside."

I went back upstairs, took off my shoes, grabbed a big pair of scissors from my desk and cut my toenails. Then I went to the closet and slipped an inoffensive blue polyester dress off the hanger. It was over a year old, but I'd never worn it. After pulling it on, I put on a headband so my hair wouldn't hang in my face and ran back downstairs.

"Good-bye, Ginx," I said, then opened the door and waited a few seconds before closing it, but he said nothing. "Good-bye," I said again, closing the door, feeling that there was something I'd forgotten, some fairy tale I should have known by heart and delivered in exchange for his generosity.

Aunt Lois, Uncle Pete, and Dana were sitting in the car

with the air-conditioning turned up as high as it would go. I climbed in.

"Wonderful to have Morgan-Lee and Uncle Pete along, isn't it, Dana?" Aunt Lois asked, watching in the rearview mirror as I slid into the backseat and closed the door. "The Lord God welcomes to the fold even those who stray."

"Especially those who stray," Dana pointed out. Aunt Lois sat there in the car about as happy as I'd ever seen her. She touched Uncle Pete's hair carefully and gave him little kisses as though his halo had returned. "The Good Lord has visited," she whispered.

"All right," Uncle Pete said, "are we ready?" I grasped the velvety-blue handle and closed the door, noticing that our uncle's summer suit was regrettably similar in color to my dress.

"Believe we are!" Aunt Lois sang, as she patted her curls and clicked the sunshade down so she could look in the small mirror at its center.

"After church I'm going to Johnny Johnson's to pick up my car. I can't take driving this lady-car another day!" Uncle Pete muttered.

"Why, Pete, Johnny Johnson's is not open on Sunday!" Aunt Lois said.

Uncle Pete cleared his throat. "The boys are working in the back today, and Eric said he'd have the car ready for me. I paid for it all last Friday."

It was so cold in that car I had to fold my arms to keep myself warm.

"You just wait till I get my Caddy. You won't be complaining then!" Aunt Lois told him.

"Oh, Lois, I ain't complaining!"

"You look pretty, Morgan-Lee," Dana whispered to me. Of course it was a lie, but I thanked her anyway and glanced at her shining hair. I wondered if we'd become the kind of sisters who kept their distance, who made chicken soup when one or the other was sick, who gave compliments weighted with complaint, who promptly wrote thank-you notes for gifts.

"Look, Pete," Aunt Lois said, "there're Jim and Ellen. We're going to have to have them to dinner either this weekend or next." She gave a twist to her earrings. "Reciprocate," she said.

"Right." Uncle Pete drove with one hand and slipped the other around the back of Aunt Lois's shoulders. She wiped a speck of shaving cream off his jaw with her thumb. He said, "How about we all go watch the Bulls play and get hot dogs? How about it, Lois? It's been a while since we went to a good game."

Aunt Lois smiled. I watched her face in the sunshade mirror. She smiled and tilted her head back a little so if you were looking as closely as I was you would have seen a sparkle of sunshine on her lower lip.

She'd once told me she was careful to dress well every day, even on days at home without appointments, because she didn't want to die and have a whole bunch of strangers find her sprawled on the floor in ratty old clothes. And God forbid if it were a heart attack and they had to rip open her shirt, exposing to the world some saggy, off-color brassiere!

"Well, now, a ball game would be nice." Our aunt touched the breast pocket of Uncle Pete's blazer with her fingertips. "That would be just the thing. I will call them as soon as we're home."

Uncle Pete grinned. It was as if he'd won a small prize. Not a large stuffed dog or anything; it was more like he'd guessed the number of candy corns in a jarful and could now tuck the jar under an arm and take it home. "Well, now, instead of getting hot dogs at the ballpark, we'll come home after the game and I'll light the grill and cook some T-bone steaks. I'll throw some vegetables on that grill, too. You make a potato salad, and we'll have ourselves a picnic out on the terrace, if you want."

Aunt Lois didn't need to answer. That was exactly what she wanted. She flashed a smile as she checked her mirror to make sure I was paying attention and learning how things were done.

SEARCHING

AFTER CHURCH, DANA decided to go with Uncle Pete to pick his car up at the shop. "You come too, Morgan-Lee, if you want," she whispered, while Uncle Pete and Aunt Lois were talking to the Lattas.

"No, Dana," I answered. "I told Sweety-Boy I'd meet up with her."

"You're gonna do that jam business?" she asked.

I shrugged. "Dana," I said, "you got to forget Jacob. He's in love with somebody else."

My sister frowned. "How do you know?" she asked.

"Sweety-Boy told me," I lied. "Look, just forget him."

"Sweety-Boy doesn't know anything about who he likes or doesn't like," Dana told me. I said nothing. I barely remembered what kissing him had felt like.

Aunt Lois let Dana and our uncle off at Johnny Johnson's shop. As soon as they were out of the car, Aunt Lois lowered her window and reiterated my advice. "Dana." My sister turned around. Aunt Lois pushed her sunglasses up over her hair so Dana could see her eyes. "You best just forget that boy. You've got better things in store."

My sister nodded. "I know. I'm just keeping Uncle Pete company is all." Uncle Pete placed one hand right above Aunt Lois's window and leaned in so he was only inches away from her face. He smiled.

"That's right," Uncle Pete told Aunt Lois. "Dana won't get involved with that redneck piece of trash. I'd break him in half before I'd let that happen." Then he leaned all the way in and kissed our aunt, holding that kiss for a good ten seconds so by the time she pulled away she had forgotten all about Dana, just zipped the window shut and screeched us out of that lot as though running from a fire.

"See there," she said to me, when we were on the road home, patting my hand before I could yank it away, "that there's the kind of medicine your momma needs a little more of."

⌒

At three o'clock, I headed toward the corner of Margaret Lane and Queen Street.

"Sweety-Boy?" I called. She was standing there, as promised.

"You're four minutes late," she complained, when I was only a few feet away.

"You're lucky I'm here at all," I told her, preparing to turn around, irritated that she'd actually been expecting me.

"Yeah," she affirmed. The girl was wearing the same pink tank top and black stretch pants she'd worn the day she'd come to Aunt Lois's. The pants looked too hot for a July afternoon, and she was sweating. "You're here. That's what counts." She pulled out the wagon, offering me the black handle like a nursery school teacher handing over the best-loved crayon. "You pull this for now, and I'll make the sales. All right?" She swiped a red rag out from the waist of her stretch pants and wiped her forehead. "God, it's hot," she commented. "I'm just getting too old to do all the work on my own." She dropped the rag on the street. "I never reuse those things," she told me. "Brings bad luck."

I grunted. "I'm not promising to make a career out of selling jam."

"That's right," she affirmed again, her eyes already set on the beyond, the breeze just a hot breath of emptiness behind us. I shrugged and took the handle. We began to walk. Sweety-Boy sighed and lurched forward, glad to be moving again. I followed her, letting my arm go straight as I pulled. The boxes were heavy, and Sweety-Boy was walking fast.

"So," I said, as she scratched her head and reached a hand under her tank top. "Where are we going?"

She pulled a piece of paper from the waistband of her pants. "First on the list," she announced. "The Mulvahills."

"Oh, yeah?" I exclaimed, recalling the mother and daughter who'd come to Aunt Lois's house back in late June. "I met them before, I think. They were—"

"No." She cut me off. "Scratch that. We're going to the Carringtons' house first." I had no idea who the Carringtons were, but I told her she could save her breath; it didn't matter to me where we were going. "Oh, it matters," she corrected. "Just up thataway," she said, waving in the general direction. The paper and even a pen were tucked into her waistband so her hands could be free, her long arms swinging at her sides.

"Slow down," I ordered, tugging at the wagon. "You might not have anything to pull, but some of us do." When her stride shortened and her arms stopped swinging, Sweety-Boy's walk grew crooked and deliberate—a leggy staccato. We went on together that way, not talking.

After a while, she said, "Glad you decided to come with me. Sometimes it can get lonely out here."

"Thanks," I said, giving the wagon an extra tug. I swallowed hard. I was afraid she might bring up Jacob, but as the girl allowed her stride to lengthen back to normal, I realized that something inside me had been put to rest, and I appreciated the July afternoon in which there were houses, a road, a destination.

"That's it right there," Sweety-Boy said suddenly, pointing to one of the uninteresting brick houses in the no-man's-land between East and West Hillsborough. I followed her onto the walkway. The girl winked at me as she rang the doorbell. Then she smiled, exposing those teeth. "Thank you for helping out," she whispered again.

"As long as you pay me," I said, mistrusting her gratitude. I dug a fingernail into the cuticle of my left thumb. "Maybe the people aren't home."

"Naw, just slow at answering the door. When she gets here, just peek inside and you'll see stacks and stacks of catalogs," she explained. "Can't help herself from buying loads of crap. She buys so much jam from me that now I just let her pay by the month." The door opened, and the prospect of earning money threaded my chest with excitement. I looked at the cartons in the wagon and thought of the luminous jars stacked inside them: cherry, strawberry, banana, grape.

"Well, hello." A thin woman in a purple dress was standing before us. She couldn't have been much older than thirty-five, but she spoke slowly, as though saddled for life to pull each word up by its root. "Hey there, Sweety-Boy," she said. "I felt sure you'd be comin' round today, but I don't know why. I guess it's 'cause my husband's not here. You know how he hates for me to buy."

"How's your little boy?" Sweety-Boy asked, expertly redirecting the conversation.

"Well, now, he's okay. Every day's about like the next."

The woman's face was vacant, void of purpose, the kind of face Aunt Lois loved to work on. A "blank canvas," she would say. "Under professional hands, it can be anything."

"Just about like the next," the woman repeated, lowering her arm. Her blue eyes were pale and restless. They searched, stopping to suckle in vain at various places on Sweety-Boy's wiry figure or to nestle in the long braid of her hair. "Won't you come in, Sweety?" this woman asked. "You never come in. Sammy's napping; you could sit down and have a Pepsi or something. We could talk some."

"Naw, ma'am, we're in a rush, I'm afraid." The woman looked at me for the first time.

"You got a friend there, honey?"

"Hello," I said. "I'm Morgan-Lee." I shifted the wagon handle to my left hand so I could extend my right, the way I was supposed to do with adults. But it was fruitless; the woman's hand remained by her side.

"Won't y'all come in out of that heat?" she asked. While talking about the weather, Sweety-Boy snaked her fingers beneath her tank top and under her waistband, popped out the folded order form, then shook it open.

"If you'll sign right here, we'll leave you two cartons of jam." The woman blinked and turned back to Sweety-Boy. I wondered what she was going to do with two cartons of that stuff, but she signed the paper, and Sweety-Boy stacked the cartons on her stoop. We both smiled, thanked her, and turned with efficient steps from that brick box of a house.

"She'd buy sand in the desert," Sweety-Boy told me, once we were back on the road. "And she's right: I always do come to sell when the husband's not around. He'd throw a fit."

"I figured," I said, then asked, "How much do you charge for those things, anyway, I mean per jar?"

"Oh, ho, ho." Sweety-Boy laughed. "The price varies."

I kicked at a loose piece of asphalt in the road. "Well, just as long as I get a good five dollars by the end of this afternoon."

"You could get more than a good five," Sweety-Boy said. "We'll see how you do." The girl had not yet mentioned the night I'd spent with Jacob at her house. I wondered if she'd just decided to drop it.

I switched the wagon handle to my other hand. The clouds crowded in as the muggy afternoon drew on. My hand pulling the wagon was slippery with sweat. We were nearing the south side of Dead Man's Field, near where Ginx and I had discovered the Luccas all those years ago.

"So," I said, after a few minutes of silence, "how did you end up living with your grandpa—with Mr. Winston?" At the sound of the old man's name, Sweety-Boy kissed the back of her hand and then pressed the kiss to her heart.

"God, I will miss him if I go," she said quietly, then cleared her throat. "Mr. Winston," she explained with childish reverence, "is the best man in the whole wide world." Her eyes slid sideways toward me, and I saw the tendons of her neck tighten. "He needed caretaking, and I needed to get away from my momma. He's my momma's daddy, so he'd never seen or even heard about Jacob till I asked him if Jacob could come live with us. Mr. Winston took Jacob in like he was his own. Fact is, he saw how sad and lonely I was without my brother. Half brother. 'Sweety,' he told me, 'call him up and tell him there's room for him to live here too.'" She sighed. "What Jacob said before, about getting beaten by his daddy—our daddy—you know, it's true. Jacob lived with our daddy awhile. Not like me."

"Oh," I said. "Your momma's still up in Asheville?"

"Yeah," she replied, "but she says she's coming here next week. She says she wants to take care of Mr. Winston, but the truth is she's probably run out of money. I don't want to be around when she comes."

"So you ran away from home to come here?" I asked. "And you're gonna run away again?" The girl scowled; a shudder ran through her long hair.

"You have to be so unpleasant?" she asked, lengthening her stride even more, so I was struggling to keep up with her.

"I didn't mean it unpleasant-like," I said.

She began to laugh, a hooting laugh I wouldn't have minded joining. "The truth," she said, "is that my grandpa would split his only coat in half if someone so much as asked him to. That's just how he is." The left side of her face snarled, and Sweety-Boy let a hand slap against her thigh. "Him and Jacob both. They'd do the world for anyone. Gets them in trouble, though." She breathed deeply. "Anyway, I haven't made up my mind yet whether or not I'll go to Vegas with Jacob. We're in an argument right now." She spat a hunk of white foamy spit onto the asphalt. "I don't care to talk about it no more," she said, and pointed. "This's the house right here. Now, just let me do all the talking."

"Fine," I agreed, with an irritated tug at the wagon.

"All right then," she said. Her lips pursed. Her skin was so transparent, I could see the veins in her neck, crossing and tangling like blue wires beneath her skin. "Listen," she added, "if we don't treat each other like ladies, we won't be able to work together."

"Maybe I don't want to work," I told her, but she obviously didn't believe me. I looked away. I was thinking of Billy, of wood, flame, letters, and stillness. We'd had our system, ordered and secretive, the woven-in sentences, his smile. I missed him.

"Here we are, now; stop that humming," Sweety-Boy ordered.

"I wasn't humming!" I countered. She merely shook her head.

The house we'd come to was large, and it stood at the top of a small hill. It was a red brick house with dark green shutters, and it was by far the nicest of any that we'd passed en route. Sweety-Boy lifted the real brass knocker and let it drop three times. *Thrice* was the word that came to mind, a waterfall of a word: *thrice*.

A stubby man opened the door just enough to expose his torso. "Oh, my," he whimpered, foolishly fingering his shirt. "Hey, Sweety-Boy." He was at least half an inch shorter than she was, with deep black eyes and gelled brown hair, a nose that hooked in a perfect curve all the way down to the nostrils. "I—" he began, then paused, looking at the wagon full of cartons. "I don't have all your jam money today, just half." The sound of his voice came out squelched, as if originating somewhere far down in his belly, only to short circuit in his throat, unable to arrive completely into the outer world.

"It's quite all right, sir," Sweety-Boy said, with an accent I'd never heard before. "Not to worry," she assured him. "You pay me half today, and I'll deliver half the jams today. I'll come back tomorrow with the rest."

"But, I thought you'd *deliver* everything today," the man complained. He stared at me and said irrelevantly, "I'm the only one home." He paused, "I just didn't go to the bank Friday, that's all." I looked at Sweety-Boy, who laughed out loud at the absurdity of this man's desire for her jams.

She arched her eyebrows in a clear loss of patience. "As I said, I will give you half the jams today and come back with the rest just as soon as you can pay full fare."

He stomped with irritation, like an angry mule; then he looked from her to me, his eyes turning enthusiastic. "Wait now, you both?" he asked. "You both working together now? Is that the deal?"

"Me," Sweety-Boy insisted harshly, her real accent slipping back on that word. "I said *I* would come back. Morgan-Lee here works only on Sundays."

"That's right," I affirmed. There seemed no better way to confront the situation than stating the facts in good clear English. "I work only on Sundays."

The man dug into his pocket, his bottom lip tucked under his front teeth, and pulled out his money. It was crumpled and hard, not at all like Billy's smooth bills. Sweety-Boy took one look at his fist of cash. "Don't give me that mess. Straighten those out," she demanded, nudging me with an elbow so I'd pay attention to how she did her business. The man nodded. He tugged each bill straight, counting them one by one into her hand. The girl kept one bill out, then folded the rest, and tucked them into her waistband. "You come back tomorrow at one P.M.," he said. "Right?"

Without answering, we turned away. When we were back on the road, she slid me the unfolded bill, which turned out to be ten dollars. "Two more houses," she said. I stared at the money, then immediately slipped it into my pocket in case she tried to take it back.

"Thanks," I said, doing the best I could to hide my surprise.

The next house was not spectacular, but the lawn was well kept and the shutters were generously proportioned and newly painted. It was a light-yellow wooden house with a signpost outside that read, Nash House, 1863. We turned onto the narrow brick walkway. "Nash House," Sweety-Boy announced like a tour guide, "1863." She hopped up the few steps and knocked, again three times.

"Just a second!" a woman's voice shrilled from inside.

"Shit," Sweety-Boy muttered under her breath, nonetheless managing to produce a smile to display her lovely teeth as soon as the woman opened the door and asked how she

could help us. "Jam delivery," Sweety-Boy announced, right
into the woman's face, using that accent she reserved for the
wealthy. "Smoky Mountain Secrets, fresh from the hills,
straight from my place to yours, Mrs. Freedman."

"Oh!" the woman gasped, backing up a step from the
girl. She was around forty and wore her hair in a bun. Gold-
rimmed glasses perched on her nose, making her face prissy
and discreet. She looked at me. "We don't want jams," she
said defensively, as if having been accused of desires that
were never hers. "We didn't order them; you must be mistaken." The woman was closing the door, which was inches
away from being shut when Sweety-Boy rasped out, "Your
husband. *Mr.* Freedman is the one. He ordered my jams.
Ask him." I watched Sweety-Boy's profile, her rough skin,
her dark hair, her way of getting what she wanted, and I
couldn't help liking her. Jacob, who was used to taking care
of people, wouldn't have had to do much for this girl, it
seemed.

A flustered, overweight man immediately came up behind
his wife and slid a hand onto her shoulder. His helpless eyes
settled on Sweety-Boy. The way she stood, squarely confronting that couple, reminded me of our mother back in
my childhood. I believed that our mother had once had a
special brand of magic, a power that had dissipated over the
years. Sweety-Boy's hand went up, her fingers spread, the
mess of thick blue veins knotted even more tightly beneath
her skin. I felt that I could follow this girl for a very long

time. "Oh!" the husband exclaimed. "Yes, dear. Yes, I ordered jams. Doesn't seem we ever have enough of them, and it's a good cause."

"Jam?" the wife asked, looking at her husband and pushing the glasses back up on her nose. "What cause?"

"Yes, jams," Sweety-Boy brightly chimed in as she turned, plunging down into the wagon and lifting out a carton. "Cherries ripened on the cherry tree. Abraham Lincoln couldn't have gotten fresher cherries himself." I covered my mouth to stifle a laugh.

"George Washington, you mean," the wife sharply corrected, not noticing her blushing husband, who pushed a twenty into the girl's open palm as he accepted the carton.

"My mistake, ma'am." Sweety-Boy smiled, giving something between a nod and a bow. "You're right, ma'am. George Washington it was." The girl expertly folded the bill with two quick fingers and turned on one heel, and I followed her back down the steps. Twenty dollars for the awful stuff! We walked away, Sweety-Boy singing, "Smoky Mountain Secrets. The secret in sweet, the sweetness of the mountain!" The wagon rattled hard down that brick path; then Sweety-Boy's arm slipped around my shoulders, and she pulled me against her. I didn't mind. Together, we walked like two girls who could afford to toss away joy by the fistfuls, who were stocked to the gills with happiness.

As soon as we were on the road again and heading east, I heard the low growl of thunder. She must have heard it too, but neither one of us said anything. She whistled, and I tugged. The sky could take it no more and let go a few large drops. The girl's face darkened. She spoke flatly, without looking at me. "You should not have come to my house the other night," she admonished. "You should not have come to see Jacob. You know that, right?" Her tone was low, echoing the thunder. Then the skies swirled apart, and the rain pounded arrow-straight to the ground. I did not look at her; I did not answer. The rain quickly soaked through my clothes. My church dress slid against my skin, the wet polyester sleek as spit. "Let's speed it up," Sweety-Boy called, starting to run. I tried to keep up, but it was impossible. My hair clung to the sides of my face and the remaining two cartons slid and rattled in the wagon, sending it off course.

"Wait," I called.

"No!" Sweety-Boy shouted. "Hurry up! It's just down Churton Street, girl." Finally, she slowed. I pointed to the cartons, which were already dark and mushy.

The girl stopped in front of the house toward which we'd been running. She spread her arms. "This," she said, "is wealth. This is the kind of house that I—"

Sweety-Boy continued, but the last part of her sentence was unclear. I was breathing hard and eyeing the steps, which led up to a large wraparound porch. I bent down to pick up the wagon so I could carry it up the stairs, my body dripping a mixture of sweat and rain. Sweety-Boy took the steps two by two. As I struggled up the stairs, she leaned on the creamy railing of the porch, overlooking a large rose garden, and clucked her tongue like a contented plantation owner. "My, my, my," she said, in the clipped accent she adopted for the rich. "My, my."

"Go on and knock," I told her, wet and irritated. I placed the little red wagon on the porch. The house was not appealing to me. "A house is a house," I said, trying to interrupt the dazed smile that had overcome her face. "Just knock."

"Time, my dear girl, time," Sweety-Boy advised, relishing each second. There was a long pause, during which I almost decided to leave her. I could run, get away, and never see her or her half brother again, is how I comforted myself, looking back out at the rain, thinking that I could run very hard and fast. I would never have to witness her magic or the way men put money into her hands, the pitted landscape of her face. As if she'd suddenly guessed my thoughts, I heard her say, "Time will tell, Morgan-Lee. Time will tell." She turned swiftly and lifted the big brass knocker as if she were picking up a handful of gold. "Mr. Crumb lives alone, thank God," she informed me quietly, with one hard blink of her narrow eyes. She knocked twice. "We're gonna make us some real money now." I stared at that large well-painted door. She threw back her hair. "Sound rich and be lovely," she instructed. I was going to say I didn't know how to do either, but then it occurred to me that I was no longer in control of what was happening and that loveliness might be much easier to achieve than I'd thought. Perhaps it was possible for me after all. The playing of her game was different from any other. All I had to do was follow.

"*Plume, glorious, harrow,*" I whispered, soft words that came naturally. Her smile this time was like our mother's, more the idea of a smile.

The door opened with a reluctant pop. "Well, you're finally here," said a chinless man with large blue eyes. The cool from inside his house wafted over us, and I could see to a corner of his living room, where the floor was covered in a rich blue carpet. "You are here now," he repeated softly, looking with some desperation at Sweety-Boy, who took a step backward in order to keep her gaze focused just above his head.

"*We* are here," she said. I remembered that our father had once told me that most of the rich people in town were Episcopalians. I wondered if this man went to church. He stared uncomprehendingly at Sweety-Boy for another few seconds; then he noticed me and quickly pursed his lips.

"Hello," I said. He did not answer. Those blue eyes would have been considered beautiful in a baby or a little boy, but they looked all wrong in a grown man. I repeated, "Hello."

"You," he accused, his finger rising only slightly to point at me. He looked down at the wagon on his porch as if the soggy cartons contained an explanation. Sweety-Boy took over.

"Morgan-Lee," she introduced, her wealthy-people accent dressing up my name so it was fit for such a house. Then her tone proceeded to harden, becoming more matter-of-fact. "Austin, we are wet and want to come in."

"Well, now, I thought you were going to—" the man began, but Sweety-Boy walked straight past him and into his house without giving him time to finish. I gripped the wagon handle more tightly; the man was left looking only at me. He spoke without smiling.

"Austin's my name," he said. It was the first time a grown-up had ever introduced himself to me using only his first name.

"I'm Morgan-Lee, in case you didn't hear before." While I spoke my own version of the wealthy-people's accent, I noticed his eyes drop to my arms and chest, but they didn't linger there long.

"Very good," he said, seriously enough to convince me that he believed I naturally spoke in that ridiculous manner. "It's raining out there, Morgan-Lee," he observed.

"We came to deliver your jams." I plodded on, unsure of how to proceed.

"Ask her to come in," Sweety-Boy instructed from inside. Without waiting for the man to invite me, I stepped over the threshold just as Sweety-Boy had done and with as much pomp as I could manage. Austin quickly shut the door, so the three of us were all together inside that comfortable kitchen, which smelled of cinnamon.

"Well, here we are." Sweety-Boy exhaled, having moved so deeply into the room it almost seemed she'd been waiting there a long time for my arrival. "Here we are, and it's pouring out." Sweety-Boy lifted a fat clay jar from the counter, carried it to the kitchen table, and thunked it down. As she sat, she sank her hand in the jar and pulled out a cookie. "Cozy in here," she continued, more to herself, the accent momentarily forgotten, then remembered. "The rain's cooled things down out there now." I had to bite my lip to keep from laughing. I was leaning against the kitchen counter in the house of a rich man with a dangerously innocent face, watching a girl whose one desire to possess became clear as she scanned that room, seizing upon certain objects and rejecting others.

Sweety-Boy nibbled vigorously at her cookie. The man didn't seem to care that the jam cartons we'd come to deliver had been left on his porch. Sweety-Boy saw me shiver and said, "Could you get us a towel or something?"

"Of course, of course I can," the man hastened to say, his eyes on anything but Sweety-Boy. "I can do better than that," he offered. The kitchen was homey, though it was a bigger kitchen than any one person would need, with real tile floors and a wet bar in the back, the kind of bar Uncle Pete had talked about building for himself, with whole shelves full of liquor and even a place for an ice bucket. "Whoo-ee!" Sweety-Boy breathed out to me as Austin left to get our towels.

"You know him well?" I asked, not yet ready to seat myself in this house.

"I've been delivering a long, long time now. Ever since I arrived." Sweety-Boy yawned.

"But you just moved here," I countered.

"You forget, I don't go to school much during the year. I have time to get acquainted with the community." She smiled and smoothed her hand over the ridge of the table. *Acquainted.* "Jesus, Morgan-Lee," she said. "I'm sorry to be so frank with you, but you sure do stink."

"I'm wet," I snapped, "and you've been making me pull that wagon the whole afternoon. It's no wonder."

"Here we go with two towels," the man offered, moving to stand before us, a bright white towel on each arm. "How about two glasses of Bacardi and Pepsi, now?"

Sweety-Boy winked at me, fished another cookie from the jar, crumbled it with one hand, and funneled it into her mouth. "Just Bacardi. Forget the Pepsi," she ordered, chewing. "No ice."

Austin tiptoed to the liquor cabinet, where he poured two glasses of straight rum. "One for the new girl," he said, smiling as he walked toward me, holding forth a glass of the dark gold liquor. "And one for the old," he said more quietly, turning toward Sweety-Boy but not facing her. The man had a peculiar manner, a practiced kind of grace. Uncle Pete would have hated him.

"That's just fine," Sweety-Boy said, and tacked on a quick "Thank you."

"I don't drink myself," he explained apologetically, both hands sliding into the pockets of his khakis. "No," he told us again, looking at the kitchen tiles, "I don't drink myself." His fingers were moving inside his pockets, and I thought of

Ginx's fingers, which were never still, always in the act of grabbing or rubbing or avoiding. I took a sip, then coughed over the burn of the rum.

"Before messing up those nice towels you got there, Austin, how about offering my friend here a good long shower?" Sweety-Boy pinned down his face with her eyes, the way I remembered her having done with our aunt. She pulled off her shoes, only to fling her left foot with its sopping wet sock onto the kitchen table. Then she crossed it with the other foot. "Meanwhile, we can throw these wet clothes into the dryer." Sweety-Boy went back to sipping. I put my glass on the counter.

"Of course," the man said, his blue eyes brightening and then clouding over as he stared at the girl's feet on his spotless table. This man was as easily pleased as he was confused.

"A shower," I repeated softly. Sweety-Boy looked at me, and I knew she had raised the stakes as high as they would go. I felt tired and just wanted to follow, foot over foot. It was time to go home. "Morgan-Lee will shower first," Sweety-Boy announced.

"Of course," Austin answered. His small hand was shaking a little; when he saw me watching, he quickly reached out to take my glass, though it was still full. "Whatever you want," he said. I wondered what our mother would think if I never returned home again. If she would pace the house or go looking for me all over town. I wondered how long it would take before she gave up. Despite the air-conditioning, my palms were sweating; I rubbed them against my wet dress.

"You may have your shower now," Sweety-Boy said to me, as if bestowing a favor. She slid her feet off the table, reached back into the cookie jar, pulled it toward herself, and informed us that she had not eaten all day. "I got me a new diet plan." She laughed, the accent completely vanished. She laid another cookie on the table and smashed it with one fist as if cracking a nut. Again, she funneled the crumbs directly down her throat as Austin draped one of his large white towels around her shoulders. "I'm lookin' like some sorta white widow now. Man!" the girl sang out, clutching the towel. I fell into the first deep-throated genuine laugh that I'd let out in a long while. She winked. "Sure no cookies?"

"No, thank you," I said, "I'm really not hungry."

"Then Austin may show us to the shower," she announced, as she stood.

"Yes, yes indeed," he offered, scurrying across the floor. I followed right behind Sweety-Boy.

On our way to the staircase, we walked through a large living room.

"And I'll get everything ready while you shower," the man said, prim as a housewife.

"Lovely."

I allowed the girl's word to travel once around the room, bouncing off the floors and the walls. Then I said, "Fine."

The floors were varnished, and paintings hung on the walls. They weren't actually even paintings, just canvases with dots of colors randomly crammed together with big blank spaces in between. "Someone you know make these?" I asked Austin.

"My ex-wife painted all that stuff," he said, smiling, then quickly reprimanding his mouth with two smacks.

"They call it Modern Art," Sweety-Boy informed me.

There was a fireplace in that large living room, and a bay window that let on to a gently sloping hill. We followed Austin up the stairs, which, like the living room, were carpeted the color of his eyes. Upstairs was just a long narrow hallway with rooms on the left side. A large Chinese vase had been placed on a stand against the wall, and there were more paintings, some with stripes of color and no dots.

"Here we go," Austin said, pointing. "Here we are," he whispered, halting in the middle of the hallway so that, once again, Sweety-Boy had to push past him. "I'll wait for you downstairs, Sweety," he said. She didn't answer. It took her only four strides to reach the bathroom door. With one royal flush of her arm, she pushed the door open for me.

"Here we are," Sweety-Boy breathed out as I brushed by her and into the bathroom. The first thing I noticed was a large ivory tub blooming in the middle. It had brass lion's paws for feet and stood on a marble platform. A matching golden showerhead bent gracefully, and there was a long blue shower curtain so ample it could have been pulled twice around that tub. An oversized window dressed with white linen curtains took up a good portion of one wall. The towel rack was brass, and beside the large initialed towel stood a small table, its top made of the same blue tile as the walls, royal as the evening sky and struck against a floor crisp and white as those curtains. There was no toilet or sink, just the mushrooming ivory tub in the middle of the bathroom.

"See there? There's just a bathtub," Sweety-Boy said in quiet reverence, as she closed the door. "He's got a whole separate room for the toilet and sink." Hanging my towel next to the initialed one, I thought about how Aunt Lois would have done just about anything for a bathroom like this. "You go ahead and undress," Sweety-Boy said, "and I'll take those clothes and put them in the dryer."

I leveled my eyes at her. I was not about to undress in front of this girl. "You leave, and I'll throw my clothes out to you," I suggested instead.

The girl rolled her eyes and muttered Uncle Pete's old phrase: "Piece of work." But she did leave the bathroom as I had asked. When finally alone, I slipped the dress over my head. My fingers were stiff, so I fumbled with the buttons much longer than it should have taken. I badly wanted to get into that tub. Maybe I was even half hoping that, during my shower, Sweety-Boy would somehow chase Austin out— get rid of him. He would be gone, I thought, and then she and I could stay in that house, where she would be happy and I would be hidden. Ginx could go on living, unhindered by me, the way our mother intended. Perhaps Billy would reread all my old letters and miss me. Perhaps he'd come find us and live here too, and we would start a whole new grown-up life in that large house with its cinnamon kitchen and evening-blue bathroom. Sweety-Boy and I would learn to get along.

"Here you go, Sweety-Boy," I called, opening the door just enough to throw out all my clothes, then quickly shutting it again.

"I'll take care of business," was her muffled promise from the other side. "You just go ahead and enjoy yourself in there. Don't even worry about saving hot water for me; in this house, there's enough of everything." *Enough.*

I do not know how long that shower lasted, but I had never taken a shower like it before. The warm water coursed over me from its golden faucet head, running down my body in thick rivers. Outside, the light was beginning to fade. I hopped out of the tub only to close the curtains, then hopped back in again. The darkness turned the water sleeker and more magical. I spread my fingers, lifting them against the warm spray, the inevitable downpour. I felt nothing below—no wind, no loss—I could feel nothing but the water pelting my skin, and I closed my eyes, tilting my head so the water coursed through my hair and down my back, smooth as Sweety-Boy's single braid. The forgetting was easy and could have gone on and on. It rinsed through all the layers, the mornings, evenings, afternoons, the times the Luccas had appeared for me alone and I had not been sure of what to tell Ginx or had worried over how to begin the story.

It seemed that hours had passed when Sweety-Boy reached a hand through to shut off the faucets. She yanked open the shower curtain so suddenly that I clutched my naked body in surprise. I thought I'd locked the door.

Her face was hard as I'd never seen before, her lips carrying nothing of their usual joke. I saw that she was standing just as naked as I was. Her dark eyes sparkled, and her face was sly as though she had stolen something or was in the process of stealing.

"Sweety-Boy?" I asked, trying to rattle her out of the fixed stare. She took two steps backward in my large bathroom. "Sweety?"

"You best come on out of there," she warned flatly.

"What is it?" I asked, covering myself with my arms as I stepped out of the tub.

"It's your turn," she informed me. "I only fuck the rich," she added, leaning to open the curtains so the evening light could come through. She was standing close enough that I could scan the onion-yellow skin of her breasts, small and lumpy, their nipples hard as scar tissue. Around her nipples grew sporadic black hairs, wiry as a man's. The rest of her body was long and just as yellow as her breasts, with tough outcroppings of hair sprouting angrily from between her legs. Her fists were pressed against her hips.

Austin started calling from somewhere downstairs. "Come to me, Morgan-T. Come to me, my Sara-Lee!"

"Actually, that's a lie," she mused, clutching my right arm, which hung at my side. She slid her fingers down to my hand and lifted it to her chest, placing it on the tender juncture just under her throat so I could feel her pulse. My heart was beating twice as fast as hers. "I fuck the ones that'll pay what I want." Her speech vibrated through her skin and slender bones. She was the one person I'd met who seemed to know what she wanted, which is perhaps why I continued standing there listening to her rather than escaping. Sweety-Boy must have seen my small bruises, but she made no comment. "You know," she went on, "Jacob's the only boy I can ever be in love with." I squinted my eyes and focused as she went on to explain, "We've been fighting lately. That's all."

"I'm not blind," I said. "You think I didn't get what was going on between you?" She had just crossed into my territory, where I knew the landscape, could hear love squawking over the barren hills, seizing and dropping, locking its claws into beating hearts, dragging them up and into the sky. "Doesn't matter that he's your brother, right?"

She smiled. "Fact is," she said, "I think you understand better than anyone I know."

"I've done some research into love, if that's what you mean."

Her mouth pushed sideways so the teeth were hidden, allowing her face to indulge in a rare chaos. "That's not what

I mean," she said. "What if I told you that Jacob and me ain't related?" We were standing in that bathroom, naked, talking like we had nothing to lose, but I let her expand on the lie. "We told Mr. Winston that Jacob was my half brother just so he could come up and we could live together. Didn't he tell you that? I'm surprised," she said. "But, see, we got into a fight when Jacob found out about what it is I do to make a living, to make it be that we won't ever have to scrounge like poor people." She stood straighter and breathed. "The work I do to be sure he'll never suffer, you know?"

"Yeah," I said. "You're a whore." It was Ginx's word, accomplished in a single breath, an open-ended sound that could attach itself almost anywhere. Her jaw clenched.

"It's payback time for what you did to me, so go on down to Austin, girl." She went on as if in explanation. "You owe me. You shouldn't of ever come to my house. You coulda seen that Jacob was to be left alone. I know you coulda seen it."

I watched her bare feet with their sprawling toes. "You thought Jacob wouldn't mind you doing this business?" I asked.

"Look," she said, "I tried to explain it to him, that it's a whole separate thing from love, but he wouldn't hear none of it. He said I either quit the job or quit him." She reared back, and I heard the man calling my name again, amusing himself with the various combinations.

"He's your brother," I said, just to make it clear that I knew the truth, "and I don't care."

She looked down at my knees and spoke more quietly. "Half," she corrected. "He's my half brother."

"Whatever," I said. "Not a problem." She dropped her hand so we were no longer touching. I looked at her arms.

"We gotta get out of here," I told her.

But she went on. "Love don't got a thing to do with my business. It's him I love, but I gotta do what I gotta do, and he's asking too much. You can't ask a person to stop *being* something." The girl paused. Her voice was pleading. "You can't change your life for someone else, or you'll always feel vengeful. I know that much," she insisted. From downstairs, Austin called out to ask if I was playing hide-and-seek.

"I'm outa here," I yelped, but the girl still did not move.

"You and me could set up shop together," she said. "The business is clean, I make sure of that, and the money's good." She pushed back her hair and smiled like she was trying to charm me. "We'd be real good working together," she promised, flashing her teeth and then speaking more quietly, "provided I don't give it all up and go to Vegas and marry him like he wants." Her body was there, demanding, her eyes waiting for instructions that would be straightforward enough to save us both, to slip us out the window and ride us far from the mess we were standing in. I heard Austin on the stairs.

With one yank, I split open the white curtains and pushed at the oversized window and the screen, both of which glided up with surprising ease. The windowsill was large and so white it practically shone. Aunt Lois would have ruined all that blankness with trinkets and knickknacks. I pulled myself up, closing my eyes in order to feel exactly where to place my feet. "What're you doing? Go on to him, girl!" Sweety-Boy heckled. "He's waiting just for you." She gathered her clothes. "Not much going on upstairs with poor Austin"—she laughed—"but down there he's bigger than his looks promise."

She was standing right behind me, and without another word she took her ball of clothes and threw it out the window. Then she lifted herself up so she could crouch next to me. I was as still as humanly possible.

"Mine're still in the wash, right?" I said when we were beside each other, her body brushing warmly against mine. "You didn't bring them like you said you would, did you?"

She peered down without answering and gazed at the slope below us. "It's not as high as I'd have thought." She shook her head as if disappointed at not jumping from more impressive heights. Of course, together we probably could have shoved Austin aside and escaped from that house through the front door just as easily as we got in, but neither of us mentioned this.

Instead, I told her, "Since there's clothes just enough for one person, I'm taking them."

She nodded. "You got more to hide," she stated matter-of-factly.

Austin was thudding to the top of the carpeted stairs.

"Don't keep me waiting now. Let's not play hide-and-seek!" he cried.

"Jesus Christ," I breathed into the grim air, where the rain had lessened to a drizzle.

"Amen," Sweety-Boy added in her tough way, not looking at me; then there was this long, shining moment when we were side by side, together in the wet dark, our bodies outstretched and clear of the world.

HIDING

~~~

AS SOON AS I reached our cul de sac, I went straight into Old Mrs. Dean's yard and down to the tree house. I climbed the ladder and even landed on my knees as carefully as though he were there. Of course, the little house was empty. Billy kept my box of letters behind a stack of books on a bookshelf in his old room. You'd never suspect it wasn't just a regular bookshelf. No one entering would see my letters or the picture of him and his father sitting on a Ferris wheel. To see the picture, you'd have to open an old red Bible to the New Testament, where he'd cut a thick square through the pages and pressed to the bottom a piece of velvet, on top of which the picture lay.

The rain outside had lessened to a sputter on the roof of the tree house and the leaves. I looked down at the clothes I was wearing: Sweety-Boy's tank top and black stretch pants. We hadn't even said good-bye. When we landed, I stumbled and fell on my right side. She landed on her feet and sprang away, naked, toward West Hillsborough. I hadn't even watched her run; I was staring at the ground as though I were being paid to examine the grass blade by blade. The boys at school would stretch a blade of grass between two thumbs and blow, making a hollow, whistling kind of noise. I wondered if Austin would come outside looking for me and Sweety-Boy. Of course, he'd just find me in her clothes, but it didn't matter anymore. If he came looking outside, I'd push myself up, stand facing him, and explain that there was no Sweety-Boy; it was just me pretending to be two people all along. He was so dumb, he'd probably believe me. Then I'd walk right past him, not even bothering to keep an eye out because no one would dare touch the two of us girls together without our permission. No one.

I'd explain to Dana one day and make her understand that if you live too long believing yourself capable of only certain things, the world will eventually have to shift, moving atoms and molecules—the building blocks of the universe—so that the other self can step forth as a whole new person and take command. Ginx would have supplied *render,* because that must be the sound for realizing that it is possible to split apart and eventually come back together again. As our father often instructed, "You won't be lonely if you just learn how to be alone."

I smoothed one hand over the plywood floor, picked up the spent candle, and put it down. I wanted to tell Billy about that evening, but not in such stupid words; I wanted to kiss him. I wanted Billy to climb the ladder and land behind me, wrapping his arms around my chest in the dark of the tree house under the rain, bringing with him the memory of fireflies and ashes, and the accident that took his father and twisted his eye, and my old, old need of his jealousy and his love.

VIOLENCE

⌒

THERE SHOULD HAVE been months or even years that passed between the moment I left Sweety-Boy and my arrival home. Summer after summer should have ended, and each season in between should have drifted to an uneventful close. But instead it was later that very same evening that Dana told me about Uncle Pete and how Jacob Little had taken him down in the junkyard behind Johnny Johnson's shop. "Momma and Poppa are still over there helping Aunt Lois tend to his jaw," Dana explained. "He wouldn't go to the doctor."

"How did it happen?" I asked, glancing at Ginx. He was sitting at the dining room table and hadn't even looked up when I'd entered.

Dana glared at my right shoulder and licked her lips;

then she took in a breath and said, "Uncle Pete swore he wasn't going to the hospital on account of Jacob. He said it's Jacob that's gonna be the one ending up in the hospital." My sister looked me over, not even remarking on the fact that I was muddy and wet and wearing Sweety-Boy's clothing. Her eyes narrowed a little, and she folded her arms like she was getting ready to criticize. "Jacob socked him because of you," she said, point-blank. "He thinks Uncle Pete beats you."

I thought of Jacob slugging Uncle Pete on my account, of our uncle's gilded hair on the ground—maybe a bit of blood—all sprawled out there behind Johnny Johnson's.

"Because of me?" I looked again at my brother, but he would not look at me.

Dana lowered her folded arms so she could cap a hand around each elbow. "How come Jacob thinks Uncle Pete hits you?" she wanted to know.

"Ginx," I snapped, trying to break his focus. "Did you hear what happened?" He was holding a straightened paper clip, tracing it over his knuckles, finishing one hand, going over the other, and then back again.

"Why're you in Sweety-Boy's clothes?" Dana finally asked.

"Just tell me what happened," I said.

My sister bit her lip and shook her head before jumping back into her story. "Me and Myra hid in one of the cars out back to spy on Jacob. So Uncle Pete didn't know it, but we

watched the whole thing, and they talked about you.
Jacob—he talked about you. He accused Uncle Pete of hitting you." In a single gesture, Dana swept all her hair back.
She stepped closer to me, as if we were the kind of sisters
who shared secrets. "Morgan-Lee," she confessed in a whisper, as if Ginx couldn't hear, "I stayed put; I didn't tell anybody any different about it's being Ginx who hits you. Plus,
it was Uncle Pete who started the fight."

"That's okay," I told her. "You did okay."

"See, Uncle Pete was looking for Eric, and he saw Jacob
working on another car. He saw him. No one else was
around besides Eric and Jacob, seeing as how it was Sunday
and all. So Uncle Pete yells out to Eric real loud, you know,
so Jacob can hear it. He says, 'Glad to have my automobile
fixed by a real mechanic 'stead of a sister-fucker like him.'"
Dana clapped a hand on her cheek and looked briefly at the
door. "That's what he said," she pleaded.

"Dana," I began.

"Uncle Pete just yells out that Jacob and Sweety-Boy are
going to Vegas to get married 'cause that's where a brother
and sister can marry without anybody caring." She sucked in
her bottom lip and then told me, "So then he goes, 'That sister of yours does fuck good; we can agree on that at least.'"

I looked back at Ginx, who just kept up with that spooky
tracing of the paper clip over his knuckles. This conversation
should have sent his hands immediately over his ears; ordi-
narily he would have been humming a blanket of sound to

keep it all out. But my brother, his head leaning too far to the right, examining the slow weave of the paper clip over his knuckle, did nothing. I stood there as though I were someone else, a saleslady who had entered the home of a pretty girl and her idiot brother. Poor girl, the lady would have thought, poor girl talking and talking to keep me from noticing that boy sitting there tracing his knuckles.

"So Jacob, he wipes off his hands," Dana says. "Oh, he wipes off his hands all slow, and he goes, 'For the record, sir, *you're* the fucker.'" Dana took in a breath. "I mean, Morgan-Lee, he was all gentleman-like. Even when he said that, he was a gentleman. He goes, 'I seen the bruises you left on your niece.' Well, at first Uncle Pete said my name, but then Jacob told him, 'Not on Dana. Morgan-Lee.'" My sister fanned her face with her hand. "So of course I wasn't gonna jump out and interrupt anyone right then." Her eyes grew serious in a way I'd never seen. "Besides that, Uncle Pete deserved it," she said. "He deserved to get hit."

I studied her face. It hadn't ever occurred to me that she would think this. Ginx continued his tracing, staring as if the pattern might reveal the answer he'd been waiting for.

"Jacob punched him. I'm telling you, he socked him once in the jaw, then let him be." Now she waited. "Morgan-Lee, it can't be true about Jacob and Sweety-Boy, can it?"

I nodded. "Yeah, Dana. It's true." And because I didn't want to go into adulthood without coming clean, I said, "I kissed Jacob the other night and he pretty much told me." I didn't look at my sister. I was looking at Ginx. "I kissed Jacob. That's how come he knew about my bruises. I told him Uncle Pete did it. He saw my chest when I took my shirt off."

"Jesus Christ!" Dana gasped. "You kissed him? You took your shirt off?" She looked at me and grabbed at the tiny gold cross on her neck. "You kissed a boy that's in love with his sister?"

"Half. Sweety-Boy's his half sister," I corrected, still staring at Ginx, making sure he heard. But my brother said nothing. He went back to tracing. It was harder and faster, but it was the same trace again and again. "And there's Billy," I added, hoping to break the simple pattern riding over and around Ginx's knuckles, trying to recall him to the mess of the world where one thing happens, another doesn't, and sounds are more often than not split from their meanings so it is an entire lifetime's work to patch even a few of them back together. "I have a crush on Billy," I said.

Ginx dropped the paper clip but kept his eyes fixed on it as he stood. He turned, watching his feet and muttering numbers, and walked right past Dana and me to kneel in front of the television stand. He bent forward, slipping his arm underneath, and pulled out the Emergency Kit he'd packed in case of nuclear war, in case of insufficient warning. He fastened his fingers around the slender leather handles, held it against his chest, and simply returned to the place at the table where he'd been sitting. He was still for a little bit; then he laid the kit in front of him. By that point I was crying. The tears were running, and I could not even stifle my sobs.

My brother's hum fluctuated, a difficult sound trying to organize itself. He was shifting to catch the exact tone of the lamp buzzing on the table.

"Ginx," I pleaded, but when he caught the right note, he would not stop for me.

Dana, still standing there, had watched the scene without comment. She studied my face, so I looked away and wiped my eyes against my wrist. "You have a crush on Billy?" she asked. My sister turned from me and flopped into the over-stuffed living room chair as though exhausted. "How come you kissed Jacob if you have a crush on Billy?"

I continued to watch my brother.

Ginx finally spoke. "You were gone a very long time. I was waiting for you all day. It's dark out now."

"Thank God," I said, moving toward the dining room table in order to stand near him. But his look did not change except for the terrible smile that played across his lips.

"Tell me a story," he dared, dropping his paper clip so it lay beside the knuckle it had been tracing. I only moved closer, squeezing the edge of the table with my hands, averting my eyes in order to avoid being lost in Ginx's vacant stare, as well as to escape the extreme beauty of his face, strangely emptied of need, sorrow, longing.

"I'm outa here," Dana yelled at us, as she got up from where she was sitting. "Out! Y'all hear? I'm telling."

"Aduage," I whispered, repeating it because so little else had been left us. The word had basic, primal softness. He allowed a whole minute to pass while I tried to push downward.

I fought noise and thoughts and the world's flat surface, but even for this the Luccas did not return. No one came to save us by recalling the night to its proper place. My brother and I waited. *Must, must, must,* I repeated, trying to beat away the sudden wind of the desert, which rose in one harsh burst, scorching our eyes with sand as we stared straight into the pale, unblinking sun, refusing to relinquish hope. *"Adu-age,"* I moaned, but my mouth was dry, and I could not see a thing. Ginx winced, but he could not help matching his words to the rolling desert wind.

"Redolent. Once. Pollution. Parrot. Acquainted."

"Thank God!" I rasped again, mistaking his list for wholesome chatter.

"Drop. Somber. Pickax. Clock. Squash," my brother continued, which is when I knew something was wrong. Hard and soft words were mixed together; sounds Ginx had kept separate his whole life were stacked senselessly against each other: a junkyard of sounds.

"Many. Bolster. Magic. Weep. Pucker. Roll. Tuck. Plush. Pony. Peek. Caramel. Enough. Enough. Enough. Rocker. Porch. Fat. Out-In. Delicious. Tinker-Tanker. Plump. Ridden. Sodden. Cardinal. Hammer. Cricket. Prawn. Birch Branch. Pose. Creak. Crack. Enough. Enough. Horse. Bedpost. Horror. Disaster. Cookie. Echolalia. Mollify. Run. Open. Knickknacks. Hungry. Duckling. Elope."

My brother and I were alone now. I leaned toward him, my face so close to his that I could feel the warm sputter of his breath. Close up, a mirror will distort a face—nose too large, cheeks too thin, eyes too muddy a green. Ginx must have been frightened I would touch him because he winced, shrugging his shoulders while his long fingers curled into a fist that I didn't see but which he drew back and struck directly into my stomach, pummeling the breath out of me. With his other hand, he cracked at my left jaw, so my mouth stunned to a smile. I jerked my head back. Cold, sharp streaks of pain ran from my jaw to my feet. A few seconds later, when I actually screamed, my brother smashed an open hand flat against my mouth, slitting my upper lip so it bled onto my teeth. His high-noted hum penetrated the house as my scream plummeted to aching, raw sobs so deep they canceled out an entire childhood of restraint and stillness. Ginx carried on:

"*Porridge. Carousel. Muck. Pillage. Sorrow. Raft. Puck. Crook. or By. Not. Willow. Pulse. Nuance. Follow. Rat. Kickerkacker. Mellow. Fuck. Chortle. Gap. Ponderous. Fickle.*"

Then he looked up, reveling in the sparks and ash raining down from the fireworks display whizzing and exploding above us. "Gone, now. All gone," Ginx said, folding his arms and turning to stare at our front door. "Let's just wait," he instructed, smiling. I touched my face, but the pain was gone. We watched the door; both of us were still. After a few minutes, our mother and Dana came bursting in, our father behind them.

"Oh, my God, Morgan-Lee!" our mother cried, when she

saw my face. Her fingers fluttered with ecstatic energy to her forehead, then over her hair and down to her chest. Our mother went straight to the staircase and held to the banister. She looked at my brother, then exhaled in one deep whoop.

Dana covered her mouth, repeating through her fingers, "Oh, Jesus, oh, Jesus."

"That's it!" our father shouted, slamming a hand against the doorframe. He leaned on his arm, his face a thin red layer of anger blanketing the deep folds of exhaustion, layers of tiredness upon tiredness. He deserved to hear someone say, You try very hard, you really try so hard, and we appreciate all your effort on our behalf. Our father inhaled, waited a few seconds, and then said, "You promised you'd control yourself, Ginx. We had a deal."

My brother stood up. "We are going to the hospital now," he announced, all the while staring straight ahead. "Poppa will take me to see Dr. Sampson now."

"Ginx, I can help," our mother pleaded. But she did not move from where she stood near the staircase. She did not reach out to touch or stop him. My brother clutched the handle of his Emergency Kit and listened till she said something that I could not make out. It had a sound that dove and struggled, rolling over its consonants as though they were mountains, airy and distant with syllables that came from faraway places, parts of the world where summer and winter were reversed. Ginx gave a little bow, and then he smiled, locking the sound within him where he could elicit it again and again and never lose the music.

"*Now*, Ginx!" our father commanded, still standing on the stoop. "Let's go."

"Down, now," Ginx said. "Down to Dr. Sampson." He turned to me and repeated, "Dr. Sampson," as if I needed repetition in order to understand the small, lickable spot in this name—as though I were already too far gone to ever hear it again.

"*Dwill. Norous. Ronlo,*" Ginx said. "*Tomorrow,*" he added.

"Stay here," I tried, but it was flat and wrong, an imitation. My brother only shrugged enough to cover his left ear as he hurried toward our father. He stepped onto the porch and then allowed our father to slip an arm over his shoulder and guide him to the car.

Dana was crying. She was motioning through what seemed to me to be a room full of fog. "But what happened?" she sobbed, clutching her T-shirt.

What could I tell her? The story spanned my entire life-time; there was nowhere to begin. To begin where I was, with a clean desert and an occasional wind, would make no sense at all. It would be like pointing to a skull to explain how a face had once been.

"Nothing," I said.

"Come here, Dana," our mother called. "Come here." Dana sniffled, her sobs subsiding.

"What?" she asked.

"Come here, baby," our mother urged, and Dana went to her. Our mother put her hand on my sister's cheek and explained, "Poppa's going to be gone awhile because he'll need to help your brother. Ginx will be staying at the hospital for a good spell. You sleep with me tonight, okay?"

Before Dana could answer, the front door swung open so hard it hit the wall. Aunt Lois stepped in, breathing loud through her nostrils. She looked at me.

"I saw them leaving. What the goddamn hell is going on over here?" she demanded to know, the satin of her dressing robe swishing against her legs, too red not to be signifying some sort of end. "Look at you, Morgan-Lee!" she cried, which is when I felt my jaw throb and swell, drinking the purple and black straight out of that warm evening. Dana snaked both her arms around our mother's waist.

"They've gone crazy!" Aunt Lois shouted at my sister, whose grasp on our mother only tightened. "The whole lot of them."

"No," I insisted, "that's not what's happened."

"That's not what's happened," Dana repeated.

"We'll be okay, Lois," our mother told our aunt, as if she knew exactly how to proceed.

"Get away from her, baby," Aunt Lois ordered my sister, planting herself in the doorframe with a ferocity that would allow no soul to slip by. She swallowed, then exhaled.

"No," Dana protested.

"We need to dress that cut," our mother said to me.

Aunt Lois raised her finger at me and advised, "Take off those clothes and pull yourself together. Tomorrow's a new day."

"I'm going," I said. "I am going to my room."

I stared hard at the corner of Aunt Lois's red robe and realized then that we are allotted at least two lives, that one breaks apart to usher in the next, and that we assume the second life with no fewer shrieks and cries than we began the first. Of course, there is silence afterward; of course, there is eventually peace.

I passed Dana and our mother and started up the stairs. "I am going to my room now," I repeated. Dana was pressing her face against our mother's shoulder while our mother stroked her hair. "Good night," I called out, hoping Aunt Lois understood that Dana was coming back home again. But when I turned to look, our aunt was gone.

So I slunk up the stairs and toward my room. Then I sat at my desk and listened to the air conditioner hum—a sound Ginx always caught so perfectly.

He is that good. Really.

Enough, now, Billy.

Summer will soon be over, and tomorrow I will bring you this, the longest love letter of my life, written in the only way that I know how.

ACKNOWLEDGMENTS

A BOOK NEVER comes into the world without several attendants, and this one is no different. I am, of course, indebted to Bill Clegg, who was there from the first word and, no matter what, did not turn away. Not once. My gratitude is deep. I thank Frances Coady for her optimism, insightful editing, and for clearing the way to make it all actually happen. I thank the Ragdale Foundation, and I thank the Yaddo Foundation for many times providing peace, tranquility, and a place to write. The Thomas J. Watson Foundation lent its generous support with a grant that provided time to write as well as travel to Italy to meet with other writers. I thank my professor Blanche Boyd at Connecticut College for her encouragement. Many thanks to John Barth, who taught me in class at Johns Hopkins as well as through his own writing. To E. L. Doctorow, heaps of gratitude for all his insight and guidance, and for reading various drafts of this novel. I thank my fourth-grade and twelfth-grade teachers, Mrs. Wilkerson and Mr. Viglirolo, wherever in the world they might be. I am also grateful to the students I taught at Sacred Heart High School. Thanks to my colleague and friend Amy Rosenfeld and to the Working Playground, my wonderful partner teachers, Pankti and Kiran, and to the students in my poetry workshops at East Side Community High School, who reminded me of the fundamental importance of writing fiction. To Joe Caldwell, my literary godfather and light in such dark places, I owe a great deal. Debt upon debt to Key Kidder for her friendship, wisdom, and the logic that she brought to the readings of multiple drafts of this book. Thanks to my dear and clear-sighted Isabella. Thanks to Virginia and Sarah Freedman for their dedication and continuously thoughtful critique. Thank you Craig Offman for making the initial connection and for your constant encouragement. My gratitude to the Santalucia family, Alberto, Tom, Greg, Craig T., Alice, Claire, Daria, Charlotte, Marie, Mary, Martha, and all the friends whose steadfastness has helped battle doubt and frustration.

I thank my grandmother and grandfather, whose memories I cherish, Uncle Tom, Aunt Martha, Uncle Wayne, Aunt Gladys, Uncle Jim, and my cousins, Jennifer, Alison, Jay, Jeff, and Jamie, who have provided so much love and support over the years. To my mother and father, whose dedication to their own writing continues to be an inspiration, and who have been audience to every poem and story I have written since childhood, I owe all the happiness that books have brought. From my sister, Daria, and brother, Eric, who cross so effortlessly into the world of the imagination, I learned to want to return there again and again. Finally, my deep love and gratitude to Remo, who truly knows how to stand near, and to our young son, Giovanni, who has so wonderfully changed our lives. They are home to me.

ABOUT THE AUTHOR

MARTHA WITT grew up in Hillsborough, North Carolina. She received her MA in creative writing at Johns Hopkins University and an MFA in fiction writing at New York University, where she was a New York Times Fellow. She has been published in the Italian feminist journal *Leggere Donna,* and two of her short-story translations will appear in an anthology of Italian women writers to be published in 2004. Martha Witt's short stories have been published in various literary journals, including *Boulevard Magazine* and the anthology *The Literature of Tomorrow* (Holt, Rinehart and Winston). She has been awarded several residencies for fiction writing at the Yaddo Artists' Colony and one at the Ragdale Artists' Colony. Currently, she lives in New York City. *Broken as Things Are* is her first novel.